DEMON'S KISS

EVE SILVER

FOREVER

NEW YORK   BOSTON

Copyright © 2007 by Eve Silver
Excerpt from *Demon's Hunger* copyright © 2007 by Eve Silver
All rights reserved. Except as permitted under the U.S. Copyright Act of 1976, no part of this publication may be reproduced, distributed, or transmitted in any form or by any means, or stored in a database or retrieval system, without the prior written permission of the publisher.

Forever is an imprint of Grand Central Publishing

The Forever name and logo is a trademark of Hachette Book Group USA, Inc.

Art direction by Claire Brown
Cover art by Craig White
Typography by David Gatti
Book design by Giorgetta Bell McRee

Forever
Hachette Book Group USA
237 Park Avenue
New York, NY 10017
Visit our Web site at www.HachetteBookGroupUSA.com

Printed in the United States of America

First Printing: October 2007

10 9 8 7 6 5 4 3 2 1

Acknowledgments

A very special thank you:

To my wonderful editor, Michele Bidelspach, and to my incomparable agent, Sha-Shana Crichton, who planted the seed. With nurturing and care, and a little conjuring, out sprang sorcerers and demons.

To Nancy Frost and Brenda Hammond, who always work their magic.

And to Dylan, my light; Sheridan, my joy; and Henning, my forever love.

DEMON'S KISS

Prologue

DEATH. HE SMELLED IT. DEATH AND DARKNESS AND the stink of brimstone.

Ciarran D'Arbois spun a slow circle, taking in the stillness of the night, the thick copse of trees some hundred yards away, the long stretch of unlit road, primitive, unpaved, isolated.

Half-on, half-off the road was a car, crushed nearly flat, one side ripped open as though the metal were mere paper, the edges curled and blackened by fire. Embers yet cast their glow to the night sky, though the hours had dulled the flames, leaving them weak and small. Of a second vehicle there was no sign, and the rumpled metal remains of the station wagon were too far from any tree for one to have served as the source of impact.

But the sorcerer knew what had done the damage: something not of this world. His lip curled in disgust, and his gaze raked the shadows.

Fear. Horror. These emotions he sensed, so primal

and raw they congealed in the air, a glutinous mass leaking from the two dead mortals who lay in the road. Pale and bloody, the woman sprawled on the ground, her long limbs set at unnatural angles. The man was torn in half, his blood a glistening pool that stained the fine gravel.

The air shimmered about the bodies as their souls floated aimlessly, hovering, confused, torn from their vessels before the proper time. They looked at Ciarran, hopefully, desperately, and he turned away, though his gut twisted at his inability to heal them. For a millennium he had lived, acting as guardian of the wall between dimensions, the wall between the world of man and the demon realm, and in that time he had yet to master his empathy.

Ridiculous, really. After all he had seen, century after century of suffering and death, he should have found a way to stop caring. His compatriots in the Compact of Sorcerers—a brotherhood of magical beings who maintained the balance between the supernatural and the natural—would have called him a fool had they known of his weakness. What were two dead mortals?

Still, a part of him wanted to push the humans' souls back into their bodies, heal them with the power of his magic, give them a chance for the life that had been ripped away so brutally.

But to heal them would mean breaking the *Pact,* the eternal agreement that governed the actions of all those with magical bent, an agreement so old it predated all human measure of time.

So he turned away, moved quickly to the wall that

held back the demon horde, a wall invisible to human sight but so very clear to him. The barrier was damaged, breached by a great, gaping hole. Sending forth fine glittering strands from his fingertips, he brushed them lightly over the frayed edges of the void. Even now the fissure belched curling tendrils of smoke and the stink of brimstone and sulfur. He lifted what information he could, sensing the distinct trail of the demon, a fetid rot.

Ciarran was aware that one had come through from beyond, an ancient terror, antediluvian and strong, a terrible dark thing unleashed on the world of man. He felt the awful strength and, woven through that, the weak scent of minor demons, far down in the hierarchy. *They* had failed to come through. A small solace.

He made short work of closing the breach. This was his task, his highest duty. To hold back the demons. To protect mankind, for all they were, for all they might someday become. The wall shifted, bent to his will and the great magic of his hands.

His work sealed the hole. There was a small sound, a gasp, and only then did he become aware of the child.

Ten paces, and he found her sprawled in a ditch, her breathing ragged and shallow. She was slashed open, her intestines spilling out of her to lie in curled loops on her bloody belly and on the grass. Her left arm was shattered, her leg nearly completely severed. A slick puddle of blood surrounded her small body. He wondered that she yet lived, then he thought perhaps it was by strength of will alone. Such tragic waste.

A quick assessment of what little remained of her life force told the tale. Too much blood lost. Too much damage. The child would die. There was nothing human medicine could do for her now.

"Mommy," she whispered. "S-s-s-o-o-o-o dark."

His gut wrenched.

"Mommy," she said again, the words barely audible. "Tummy . . . hurts."

Healing her, and thereby interfering in the thread of mortal life, was forbidden by the *Pact,* but he could offer her some palliative comfort, ease her misery. Ciarran called his power, wrapped the child in magic, offered her what he could. He took her pain, wanting only to let her find the hereafter without the agony she suffered.

She blinked, turned her head, and he had only a second to understand that she *saw* him, *saw* his aura and his power, his magic, though such should not have been possible for he had chosen to refract light and veil himself from human sight.

With an overwhelming incredulity, he froze as the child's fingers twitched. She caught a strand of the undulating current of his power in her fist, pulled the glowing ribbon close, and rested it across her belly. Jerking back, he reined in his magic, but she held fast, leaching away his power, healing herself, a human child marked for death.

Impossible.

Her actions broke all laws of the *Pact,* but there was nothing he could do to stop her. *She pulled his magic. She healed.*

This human girl was an anomaly he had never before encountered, and for an instant he focused wholly on her.

Suddenly, Ciarran stiffened. He knew he was too slow

as he spun, calling the vast stores of his magic. Sly, furtive, a demon coming at his back.

It was too late.

And then there was only pain.

Chapter 1

CIARRAN D'ARBOIS WOULD HAVE LIKED IT TO BE colder. Just a few degrees. Enough to take the sleet that was beating down on him and turn it into nice fluffy flakes of snow. He was immortal, not impervious. Getting drenched was as unpleasant for him as it was for the next man.

The difference was, with a mere thought, Ciarran could be dry, could stop the downpour, could walk in a halo of sunshine though it be midnight. Instead, he chose to slog through the frigid sheet of rain. Though there was no law against it, he was reluctant to summon magic for mundane purposes.

Or maybe he just had a strong inclination to suffer, to atone for his immeasurable sins.

Turning up the collar of his leather jacket, he strode along the street, a couple of paces behind two women who huddled together under a large umbrella. They cast frequent glances at him over their shoulders and, at one point, the shorter woman called a bold invitation for him to step under the umbrella right along with them.

The taller one, a blonde, had a hip-swaying walk that grabbed a man's attention and held it, even if the man wasn't interested in the invitation. No, not quite accurate. He was interested but wise enough to turn her down.

She wanted to take a man home to her bed. But he doubted she wanted to wake up next to a monster.

With a shake of his head and a smile that promised sin, he slowed his pace and let them walk on. The blonde cast him one last look over her shoulder. Foolish.

Just up ahead was his destination, a run-down bar with a reputation. It was the kind of place Darqun favored. Ciarran's lip curled in foul humor. It was the kind of place *he* preferred to avoid.

A *snick* of sound caught his attention, and in the same instant the current of energy that formed the *continuum* shimmered with the faintest spark, a wrongness in the weave of dimensions. Again. More and more of late, the line of magical force had wavered, had carried darkness and a warning. There was a hint of brimstone, a whisper of malice. Pausing, he turned to face the alley on his right.

In the shadows, four bulky figures huddled around a supine form, a human male, battered and bruised from a beating. *Hybrids.* Half-human, half-demon minions of the Solitary. A malevolent demon of immeasurable power and equal malice, the Solitary was the greatest threat to the wall between dimensions. Trapped beyond the wall, the Solitary waited and plotted his escape.

Unless summoned, demons could not walk in the world of man, and once called, they were bound to the summoner, a situation they found both irksome and abhorrent. Hence, the advent of *hybrids,* foolish mortals faced with death who had chosen to allow demon will to overtake their souls.

Hybrids were able to walk the earth, doing the bidding of their masters. But the demons rarely made full disclosure. They never warned that, while *hybrids* could live a long, long while, their existence would be consumed by pain. Endless, daily pain, relieved only by death. Ciarran had found more than one such creature grateful for release. But therein lay the dark lure, the horrible enticement to release them all and to find enjoyment in it.

Sensing Ciarran's presence, they turned their heads, eyes glinting in the darkness, lips peeled back from long, sharp teeth. They meant to feed on the flesh of the man at their feet, after they beat him bloody. They had a predilection for tenderized meat.

Rage built inside him. They were in *his* territory, stalking a mortal under *his* protection.

Ciarran focused on the steady drum of the rain, the splash of tires on the wet road at his back, the panting breath of the *hybrids*. Seeking his center, he tethered his fury and waited until he was certain they knew what he was, until they turned fully toward him.

With a groan, their prey rolled to his side and lurched to his feet. The man stumbled, righted himself, then weaved unsteadily forward, one hand dragging along the graffiti-stained brick wall for support. The pungent scents of alcohol and old sweat stained the air as he shuffled past. The *hybrids* let him go, intent now on bigger game.

Ciarran smiled. Four to one. He liked the odds.

Stepping into the alley, Ciarran flexed his left hand, feeling the deep ache of torn sinew and mangled bone, healed some two decades past into a semblance of normal. Normal if one didn't look too closely, didn't peel back the leather glove to reveal a warded and bespelled alloy prison designed to contain the rot that threatened to spread and steal all that he was.

The shadows shifted and moved, and the four *hybrids* circled him warily. One of them held a long knife with a serrated blade. Another carried a wooden club. Mortal weapons, of paltry value in a battle against a sorcerer.

Ciarran shifted to one side, giving them a chance, though every cell in his body screamed for the fight. He offered them the opportunity to flee, to find a hole to tunnel into and hide. He had accomplished his goal, saved the human. His scruples, the fact that he did not simply slaughter the *hybrids* despite the hard pounding of his rage and bloodlust, marked the difference between sorcerer and demon.

The ache in his gloved hand intensified, reminding him that there were days when he wondered how much longer he would recognize that distinction.

"Go," he said, making a sweeping gesture to emphasize his offer of reprieve.

The *hybrid* with the club grunted, smacking the wood against his open palm as he stepped closer. There was a shimmer of movement. The creature's gaze flicked to Ciarran's left, and he snarled at one of his companions. "All at once, idiot."

Idiot, indeed. Ciarran didn't even bother to turn, sensing the assault, tasting his attacker's bloodlust. He uncurled the fingers of his right hand and sent razor-sharp shards of light spinning from his fingertips to dance across the wet pavement. His magic, nourished by the *continuum,* the dragon current, the eternal river of elemental energy that sustained all mortal and immortal realms. Light and dark in perfect balance.

Ciarran sidestepped the attack, but the *hybrid* spun and lunged again. A flare of light, and the *hybrid*'s knife clattered to the ground still clutched in a freshly severed fist. The creature screamed, a high, sharp sound of pain and rage.

"Go," Ciarran said again, and the *hybrid* with the club took the offer, lumbering from the alley, leaving the others to the fate they chose.

They lunged as one, a tactic they should have employed in the first place. With a defined twist of his wrist, Ciarran cast another lethal filament, wove it tight about the nearest *hybrid*'s neck. Its head followed its hand, tumbling end over end through the air before landing on the wet ground with a dull *thwack.* A gray mist rose; then the remains disintegrated in a hissing, bubbling mass.

A set of high beams shone through the grimy front window of the Blue Bay Motel, scattering light across the faded walls. Clea Masters jerked in surprise. She'd figured the night was a washout. Well, it looked like she'd been wrong. Looked like the Blue Bay would have a paying guest tonight.

Balling up the tissue in her hand, she tossed it in the waste bin beneath the reception desk. With a small sniff, she checked her face in the mirror that hung on the side wall. Her dark eyes looked bruised and forlorn, the hint of smudged mascara adding to the sad effect. Swiping her finger along the moisture that dotted her lower lashes, she blinked against the gritty sting. Tears never changed anything. They just made your skin blotchy and your eyes red.

They definitely wouldn't raise the dead.

She combed her fingers through her shoulder-length brown hair, tugged it into a parody of neatness. Not great, but at least she wouldn't scare anyone away.

A car door slammed. Clea rose, watching through the glass as a dark-haired man took three strides from the parked car. He froze, spun back, and she could hear his voice carrying through the old walls, sounding anxious, maybe even angry, though she couldn't hear exactly what he was saying. He was shaking his head now, talking faster, the open flaps of his jacket shifting with his rapid movements.

He paused directly under the exterior light, and Clea had a clear view of him. Fairly young. White shirt. Dark suit, rumpled and ill-fitting. No overcoat. No headset. No earpiece. He spun, kept talking, and she had an unimpeded view of his opposite side. No headset there, either. So he wasn't talking on a cell phone.

". . . your keeper . . ." He turned away, his movement muffling the sound. Then his voice rose, agitated, and she caught snatches of his conversation. ". . . you'll do as I say . . . stay in the car!"

Bolstered against the raised counter, she leaned forward, trying to see to whom he was speaking. There was no one else there. No one in the car. No one beside the car. He was definitely alone.

He made a great show of locking the doors with his remote, stabbing one finger toward the window, the remote, and back again. Then he spun and sprinted to the motel office, shoving the door open so it slammed back against the wall with a sharp *crack*. His lips were drawn down in a grimace, and his eyes darted wildly back and forth.

Catching sight of Clea, he strode to the counter and slapped his palms against the old, stained Formica.

"A room," he said in a low growl. Spittle flew across the countertop, landing in a frothing white blob about an inch from Clea's baby finger. She jerked her hand down to her side and stepped back, more than a little grossed out. The guy smelled like stale sweat and fear. "Gimme a room."

"That'll be $35." She tried a smile, but something in his eyes stopped it cold. "We only take cash."

He frowned, as though he didn't understand her words, then said, "I need one at the far end of the motel. With a lock that works. I'll pay you in the morning."

"Our . . . umm . . . Our policy is cash up front." Clea wrapped her arms around herself as a chill prickled her skin. She wondered if maybe just this once she should make an exception. Give him a key just to get him out of the lobby and away from her.

"I don't have cash! Who the fuck ever carries cash?"

Who indeed? He had a point, but Mr. Beamish refused to pay a fee to the credit card companies. He said it was a matter of principle.

The guy was breathing fast and heavy, darting glances at the front window and at the car. The *empty* car.

Unless . . . There was someone in the trunk. . . . She shook her head. Oh, frig. She didn't need this. Not tonight.

"Maybe you should go up the road, sir. Just head east.

There's a brand-new motel where the bypass meets the main highway." She tried a little bribery. "They have coffeemakers in every room." Like the guy needed caffeine. He already looked like he was ready to jump out of his skin. "And they're set up for credit cards."

Glancing over his shoulder, he stared hard at the window, through it, out into the night. Clea followed his gaze but still didn't see a thing. "I need a room. I just need a room," he said dully, still staring out the window. "With a door that locks. *Fuck*."

Clea frowned, wondering if he'd actually heard anything she'd said.

His voice rose abruptly, making her jump. "Gimme a goddamned room. You have no idea—"

He turned then. Clea met his gaze and shivered. Cold. His eyes were so cold. Dead. Like he had given up hope a long, long time ago.

She swallowed, glanced at the window, wondered what it was he thought he saw out there that had twisted him up so tightly and beaten all the hope out of him.

Shaking her head, she stiffened her resolve and snaked her fingers to the phone. Less than two seconds to dial 911. She knew. She'd timed it.

Of course, the Blue Bay was way out here on an isolated stretch of road to the north of the city. It had once been a busy thoroughfare before they built the bypass. Now, the area was deserted. It would be at least twenty minutes before help arrived, but that was something she *so* did not want to think about.

For an endless moment, he held her gaze, those dead, dead eyes boring into her, giving her the creeps.

Creeped out, yes. Genuinely afraid, no. She stared

him down. Over the years, Clea had learned that she could defend herself against just about any threat.

Well, maybe not exactly defend *herself* . . . but there was *something* inside her that wouldn't let her come to harm. Some kind of weird psychic thing she'd had since she was a kid. Her insides would coil as though squished by a belt drawn too tight, and a burst of light would flare from her body, knocking back whatever threat had summoned it. A drunken frat boy who hadn't seemed to understand that no meant no. A bunch of girls who'd swarmed her in high school.

That light had been strong enough to save her life the night the crash had killed both her parents. But she'd never talked to anyone about the light, not even Gram.

Heck, she'd watched reruns of the *X-Files*. Every episode. At least three times. She had no desire to end up locked away in some secret lab, prodded and studied and tested.

With a strangled cry, the guy broke eye contact and lurched from the office, arms waving wildly as he continued his argument with whatever imaginary companion he had left locked in the car. Clea shivered as he turned back toward her, staring at her through the glass, his face a mask of sorrow and regret.

His emotions seemed a little extreme. All she'd done was deny him a room.

She hitched in a nervous breath, watched him yank open the driver's side door and climb into the vehicle. As he pulled out, she let go her breath in a gusty sigh.

Slowly, she sank into her seat. She'd been working here at the Blue Bay for five years. Easy work. A night job that paid on time, and she could study while she earned enough to keep her and Gram off the streets.

Gram.

Clea swallowed, battling the sharp bite of fresh grief.

Old man Beamish had sent a sympathy card, and he'd offered her the night off. But she couldn't imagine anything worse than going back to the empty apartment tonight. All alone. With Gram gone.

So she was sitting here instead. All alone. Behind the beige Formica reception desk of the Blue Bay Motel, with an old wood-framed picture of Gram beside her for company.

Wishing she could numb her thoughts, her emotions, she rummaged through her overstuffed knapsack and pulled out her ragged copy of the *Photographic Atlas of Human Anatomy*. She was beginning to see a theme here. She'd spent half the night talking to a picture of Gram.

Who was dead.

And now she was staring at pictures of dissected cadavers.

Who were dead.

Laying the heels of her hands against her forehead, she pressed. Hard.

Yeah. Definitely a theme.

Clea stared at the atlas. She needed to study. Midterms were less than a week away.

"Okay. Left subclavian artery from the arch of the aorta," she muttered. "Gives rise to the vertebral artery that ascends within the transverse foramina of the upper six cervical vertebrae . . ." Her voice trailed away, and she sighed.

Yeah, she needed to study, but her heart wasn't in

it. Medical school had been Gram's dream, and for a long time Clea had thought it was her own, as well. So after high school she'd worked for a couple of years until she'd saved up a bit of an education fund, and then she'd earned an undergraduate degree in biomedical science. Worked for another year. Been accepted to med school. She'd made it through the first two years, agonizing every step of the way, knowing for certain that she wanted to help people but wondering if medicine was really the way she wanted to go.

The truth was, she liked her life nice and neat and ordered and safe. Medicine was perfect in a way. People got sick, no matter what. People needed doctors, no matter what. She couldn't pick a safer career. She'd always be needed, wanted.

Still, med school somehow felt *wrong*.

The past few months, she'd been sleeping badly, eating next to nothing. Her gut told her that her uneasiness was more than the horror of seeing Gram through her final days, more than just symptoms of stress. It was a feeling deep inside of her. A restlessness. An edginess. Almost like there was a part of her that was struggling its way to the surface.

Just thinking about it made the feeling shift and grow inside her, like a live snake winding through her, within her, around her bones, between her muscles, winding, twirling, making her feel like she was going to jump out of her skin.

Like the weird, wired guy who'd just been in here.

Nice.

Now she was creeping herself out.

Chapter 2

*B*LUE SMOKE CURLED FROM THE GLOWING TIP OF a cigarette that hung over the edge of a scarred wooden table. Darqun Vane leaned his chair back on two legs, away from the acrid smell, and glanced toward the pool table to his left. The owner of the cigarette, a twitchy guy who looked like he could use a shower, was carefully lining up a shot. With a thought, Darqun broke the guy's concentration and white ball followed green into the side pocket. Perhaps the arrogant pup would learn to ask before he inflicted his disgusting habit on someone else.

Or perhaps not. His mouth curving in distaste, Darqun lifted the cigarette and dropped it into an overflowing ashtray.

Settling the chair back on four legs with a solid *thud,* he scanned the smoky interior of the bar. The place was crowded, mostly a rough crowd, peppered by a few young professionals with a taste for living on the edge.

He almost laughed. They had no idea where the edge really lay.

Certainly not in this crowded bar, with its warped pool tables and cracked stairs, its pretense of danger. Slinger's was downtown, in a place partway between trendy and dive. Closer to dive, if truth be told. Which was the draw for this particular crowd. The occasional biker or wannabe gangsta might stumble in, and that gave the place a certain cachet.

Darqun liked it because the bar was always busy, rain or shine. Packed like a sardine can. Noisy. Stinking of booze and sweat and smoke and perfume. He needed that, needed the crackle of loud music from cheap speakers, the swell of boisterous laughter and overloud conversation. He'd spent too long alone, so alone, without a single living thing to break the silence.

He glanced at the wide front doors with their fogged windows, the BUD LIGHT sign glowing neon. Sleet and rain had been beating against the glass since he'd arrived, but now it looked as though the weather was showing signs of improvement.

The chair to his left scraped across the floor, drawing his attention as Javier Saint swung it to face backwards and straddled the seat. He was dressed in his usual snappy style. Hand-sewn Italian shirt. Perfectly pressed slacks. Darqun shook his head. Give him a T-shirt and ratty jeans any day.

Leaning bent elbows on the table, Javier began to count a pile of cash, his white teeth flashing against the dark, carefully cultivated stubble that shaded his jaw.

Darqun nodded at the other sorcerer's winnings.

"What the hell, Jav? Where is the pleasure in beating a mortal?"

With a low laugh, Javier raked a hand through the straight dark strands of his hair. "I played like a mortal. No magic. I still won." His smile faded. "So, is he coming?"

"Yeah. Ciarran's on his way."

That he'd agreed to meet them was strange. That he'd agreed to meet here, in a bar packed with mortals, was stranger still. Ciarran preferred his solitude. But Darqun had made it clear that the information he had to share was better spoken in person, and better spoken *here*, where Ciarran could see things for himself.

"Oh, he's gonna love this place." Catching the neck of the bottle between two fingers, Javier lifted his beer and took a long, slow pull. The sarcasm in his tone was unmistakable.

Darqun knew what Javier meant. There had been a time when Ciarran would have enjoyed mortal company as well as any of them, availed himself of the amusements the human world offered. But no longer. He'd made a mistake two decades past on a deserted road to the north of town. Darqun knew how it had been, demon stink heavy in the air, the remains of dead mortals strewn across the ground. . . . Ciarran had lost a piece of himself that night, and he'd never found a way to gain it back.

A blast of cold air cut through the smoky haze as the front door of the bar opened, closed. Darqun caught a glimpse of Ciarran, scuffed leather jacket glistening wetly under the bar's yellow lights, sun-shot hair hanging in damp strands to his wide shoulders.

Ciarran's gaze focused on the table where Darqun

and Javier sat. As he moved through the throng, bodies shifted to let him pass, opening a path. He touched no one, looked at no one, his attention never wavering from his goal. And no one made a move to get in his way.

Then a human male laughed drunkenly and lurched to the side, his shoulder bumping Ciarran's back. The sorcerer turned slowly, his expression cold. The drunk took one look, and even his sodden brain recognized danger. His gaze flickered, and he held up one hand as though to ward off an attack, though Ciarran did nothing more threatening than stand there looking down at him. With a mumbled apology, the man stumbled away, and the sorcerer resumed his trek.

"Hey," Javier said by way of greeting, as Ciarran approached.

"Jav. Dar." Ciarran gave a curt nod, cast a disgusted look at the dirty ashtray. "And you two chose this place because . . . ?" he asked in a low growl, glaring at Javier and jerking a chair away from the table.

The dragon current crackled with a whisper of dark energy, and Darqun's gaze shifted to Ciarran's gloved hand.

"It's strong tonight, huh?" Javier asked, his tone edged with concern.

Ciarran paused midmovement and acknowledged the other sorcerer's question with a tilt of his head. His mouth shifted into a cold smile, and his fingers tensed on the seat back. When he spoke, his voice was low, the tone laced by a sneer. "Don't worry, Jav. I've got it under control."

"I know, man. No worries." Javier rose, clapped him

on the back. As he let his hand drop, he paused to assess Ciarran's jacket. "Sweet."

Darqun grinned at Ciarran's bewildered look. The guy really needed to get out more. "He means he likes it."

"Yeah, I got that." Shrugging out of his leather jacket, Ciarran slung it over the back of the chair and sat.

He was about to speak when a waitress appeared beside them. "What can I get you gentlemen?"

Leaning back in his chair, Darqun let his gaze slide over her tiny belly-baring top and the scrap of black cloth that pretended to be a skirt. "You're new," he said.

She blinked, smiled, studying him in obvious appreciation. "Yeah. My first night." She held his gaze as she ran her tongue along her lower lip. "So . . . what can I get for you?"

"Tequila."

"My favorite." She glanced at Ciarran, and her eyes widened, but not in appreciation. Darqun had seen it time and again. While he might be handsome, Ciarran had a definite edge to him, more than a hint of menace. Some women were drawn to that danger. Any woman with the smallest sense of self-preservation avoided it.

Cocking her head, the waitress took a step back and asked, "And, um, for you?"

Smart lady, Darqun thought, and ramped his smile up even brighter.

"Leave us," Ciarran said on an exhalation.

Her brow furrowed in confusion—an expression Darqun found incredibly cute—then she turned and slowly walked away.

"Nicely done, Ciarran. You know she won't remember my tequila now," Darqun complained amiably. He'd remind her. Later. Hell, if he could wrangle an invitation to her bed, he'd take a bottle of tequila with him as a gift.

"You can reorder when I'm gone." Ciarran crossed his arms over his broad chest and waited, his eyes scanning the room, ever watchful. Shaking his head, Darqun looked around. A woman stood toying with a pool cue, staring at him, her expression sultry.

"It might not be a bad idea for you to let off some steam, my friend." Darqun waved a hand toward the woman by the pool table. If Ciarran tried a genuine smile, he might not scare the pants off her. "A place like this, you can have your pick. It will hurt no one."

Ciarran studied him in silence, his eyes glittering, his jaw tight. He leaned in close, one side of his mouth curving in a dark smile. "Won't hurt anyone, Dar? How do you know?"

Yeah. That was the million-dollar question. Darqun's gaze slid to Ciarran's gloved hand. Nodding, he acknowledged the point. He *didn't* know, had no idea what Ciarran might be capable of.

The worst of it was, neither did Ciarran.

A second ticked past, and another.

Javier cleared his throat. "So, uh, what's with the smell of brimstone, Ciarran? You trying it out as a new cologne?" He took a pull on his beer.

"Yeah, eau de demon," Ciarran muttered.

The beer almost came out Javier's nose. "Holy shit. Was that a joke?"

Darqun was less verbal but equally incredulous. Humor wasn't Ciarran's strong point.

"Yeah." Ciarran glared. "Go to hell."

Javier snickered. Darqun smiled. It almost felt like old times.

"Ten minutes ago, I smoked a cluster of *hybrids* in the alley outside," Ciarran said.

So that explained the faint smell of brimstone that clung to him.

"They're getting bolder, and I've got a hunch as to why." Darqun waited, knowing Ciarran would sense what he had sensed, what Javier had missed. He wasn't disappointed. Ciarran scanned the room, his posture subtly alert, looking for something; then his gaze slid to Darqun's, one brow raised questioningly. Darqun gave a barely perceptible nod of acknowledgment.

"You guys wanna share?" Javier asked, narrowing his eyes. "I know there's something off beam, something wrong with the *continuum*. I didn't notice it right away. Just woke up a couple of weeks back feeling, I don't know, out of sorts. But it didn't go away, you know. Just kept nagging at me like a sore tooth."

Darqun exchanged a look with Ciarran. As if a sorcerer, even a young one like Javier, would live with a sore tooth.

Rolling his eyes, Javier continued. "You know what I mean. It was just an analogy." He leaned in to punch Ciarran's shoulder, thought better of it, and whacked Darqun instead. "You feel it, right? I'm not the only one."

"I feel it," Ciarran said. He sat almost perfectly still, powerful, deadly, the slow drumming of his gloved fingers on the table his only concession to his dislike of the noisy crowd that flowed around him.

"And I want to know what the hell it is." Darqun's voice was low and hard.

"A shift in the *continuum*. A betrayal." Ciarran held up one hand as the other two stared at him. He shook his head at Javier's questioning look. "No, I have no more idea than you. But there *is* something wrong, something—" He paused, fisted his hands, searching for the right description and failing to find it. "Something that must be investigated with both haste and care."

"That's the reason I asked to meet *here*. . . . Do you sense it?" Darqun's lip curled as he inhaled. "The stink?"

Sniffing his sleeve, Ciarran asked, "Worse than my brimstone?"

Javier groaned. "Don't plan on making a living at stand-up."

"I smell it." Any pretense at humor faded. "Asag." Ciarran said the name like a curse. "Demon of plague. He has been here, in this bar, days past. He left a trail. How long?"

"Less than a mortal week," Darqun replied, his gaze sliding away to follow the swinging hips of a tall brunette. Possibilities, possibilities.

Ciarran drummed his fingers a little harder. Darqun shot him an apologetic grin, then continued. "He was here. I was here. But I didn't figure it out until after he was gone. Frigging Asag, in the same damned bar, and I missed him." A fact that was unbelievably strange. Darqun had sat only yards away from a demon both ancient and evil, one whose mere presence should have raised every hackle. And somehow he'd missed it, missed the stink of demon. Which meant that Asag had been walking the human realm for decades, long enough to mask his presence, to take on mortal guise. Likely he'd been

loose, here, in the world of man since the night he'd cost
Ciarran his hand.

"And has he been back?" Javier asked, leaning forward, his expression intent. "Could you follow the remains of the trail?"

Ciarran opened his senses and searched for a clear
path, but the trail was weak, diffuse. His gaze shifted
to Javier. The boy was young, true. A mere three hundred years old. But he had good instincts and even better
control. Ciarran remembered himself at that age, puffed
up and ready for a fight. Always ready. Not bothering
to think before he leaped. Perhaps Javier was a better
sorcerer than he. For all his youthful exuberance, Jav
always thought a situation through, weighing the value
of every action.

Which was why he was still in possession of all his
limbs.

Beneath the table, Ciarran flexed the fingers of his
ruined hand, tamping down the malevolent buzz that
swirled through him to coil round sinew and bone, and
weave into his veins, into his very thoughts like putrid
smoke. Restlessly, he rubbed his palm against his thigh,
battling his own private hell, the darkness within.

"We have two problems," he pointed out. "The first, a
disruption of the *continuum*. Dark magic. Demon magic.
I feel it."

"Yeah." Javier grunted. "It feels like the dragon's got
gas."

Sorcerers called it the *dragon current,* the perfect
blend of negative and positive, darkness and light. Humans who sensed the earthly tributaries that fed the
infinite river of the *continuum* called them *ley lines,* be-

lieving them to be lines of magnetic force. By whatever name, the *continuum* was the flow of raw magic that connected all realms but one. The demon realm. And that was what worried him. There was a smear of darkness in the current, a disgusting hint of demon spoor.

"Problem two is Asag"—Ciarran looked slowly around the bar—"walking here in the human realm without a keeper, and therefore without constraint."

He sucked in a slow breath, narrowed his eyes. "So how is it that Asag, a demon of uncommon power, walks unbound, unfettered by his summoner?"

"Not just Asag." Darqun leaned in close. "Yesterday I found a minor demon pawing through garbage in a back alley. It had no keeper."

"No frigging way." Javier slapped his palm against the table.

"Way," Darqun grunted.

"I think our two problems are really one," Ciarran said. "Demons can't walk around without their summoner. And yet, all of a sudden, they can. Last month I found a minor demon sucking on rat carcasses in a condemned building. There was no sign of its keeper. And today, I'm sitting here breathing Asag's stink."

Drumming his fingers once in a slow roll across the tabletop, Ciarran fell silent for a moment. "He's feeding, growing powerful, preparing himself for something."

"He's gonna try to bring over the Solitary," Javier said.

Darqun snarled and came halfway out of his seat. "And he's gonna fucking fail."

"Yeah. Yeah, he is." Ciarran rose, slid his leather jacket back on and turned to go. He paused, glanced

over his shoulder at Darqun as the other sorcerer got to
his feet.

"Two *hybrids*. Booth at the back," he said. "Which
means Asag made you the night you were both here,
Dar, my friend. Made you, and evaded you, and now he's
sent his lackeys to watch you." Ciarran smiled. "Time to
clean out the vermin."

"Ciarran, wait." Darqun caught him by the arm as he
began to walk away. "You've already had your fun for
the night. Leave the two *hybrids* for Jav. How's the kid
ever going to learn to use his power if we don't let him
practice?"

A snort of derision escaped Javier. "At least I can
move without my joints creaking," he muttered.

"There's a third problem." Darqun paused, his expression intent as he met Ciarran's gaze. "The grandmother. She died. Cancer. Funeral was this morning.
The girl, Clea, she's alone now." Something flickered in
Darqun's eyes, memories, ghosts. "I thought you'd want
to know."

"Yeah. Thanks." Ciarran bit back a curse. Just what
he needed, a responsibility he'd never sought but one he
could not deny. He'd check on her. Make sure she had
enough money to survive. And then he'd leave her the
hell alone.

The girl had lived, and a piece of him had died. And
the only one he had to blame was himself, for making a
careless mistake in the face of a cataclysmic disaster.

"You know what Sunday is?" His gaze met Dar's.

The other sorcerer nodded, his mouth drawn in a grim
line. "Yeah. I know."

"I'll take care of it." Ciarran turned away, anxious

now to get the hell out of the bar, away from the people, the scent, the dark temptation to do something he would regret. He was going to get on his bike and ride north, see if he could find the demon he'd been tracking for the past three nights.

He shoved open the door, turning his face into the cold wind, welcoming the bite of it.

She's alone now.

Alone.

Except for him.

And Sunday would be the twenty-year anniversary of the day she'd witnessed the start of his trip to hell.

Chapter 3

CLEA CAREFULLY CLOSED HER ATLAS. WITH A shiver, she glanced at the front door of the motel just to make certain it was closed, a dark feeling of unease gnawing at her. She felt cold, and hot, and a little sick.

Made sense. She probably should have eaten something at some point in the last twenty-four hours, but somehow, food hadn't been a priority. She'd been too busy with the arrangements and the funeral, and trying to figure out how to scrounge together the money to pay for the plot.

Slapping her palms against her thighs, she pushed herself upright and headed to the back office to check the thermostat. It felt like a morgue locker in here.

As she cranked the heat a few degrees, the sound of a heavy footfall drifted to the back office, making the fine hairs at her nape stiffen and rise. A doorknob rattled; then something scraped across the floor with an eerie rasp. Clea's heart flipped over in her chest. There was someone out front. Oh, man, she hoped it wasn't the wired guy.

Forcing her feet to take one step and another, she walked slowly through the office door, back to the reception area. With a gasp, she froze, pressing the flat of one hand against the base of her throat.

"Gram?" The word escaped her on a whisper.

Gram. There she stood, at the far side of the lobby, staring out the window, her ash blond hair streaked with gray, tied in a loose bun at her nape, her slim body clothed in black pants and her favorite green sweater, looking tall and strong as she had before the cancer had done its worst, eating away at her from the inside out. Only . . . it wasn't possible. Gram was dead.

And buried. Buried just that morning, beneath an overcast October sky and a damp blanket of light rain. And the dull thud of wet earth.

Clea made a soft noise, low in her throat, half groan, half sob. It was enough to grab Gram's attention, and she turned, smiled.

Smiled. A straight smile. Even. The sides of her mouth curving in perfect symmetry.

The smile wasn't right. Not Gram's smile.

Gram's mouth had sagged a little on the left thanks to one of the tumors, the one on the facial nerve. Cranial nerve VII, Clea thought absently. She'd looked it up in her neurology text when Gram's face had first started to change.

She studied the woman by the window. Not Gram's eyes . . . Gram's eyes had always been warm and loving, even at the end, even after the cancer had done its worst.

"You're not Gram," Clea whispered. "You aren't real. I know that."

"Right. And wrong." The voice was terrifying, not quite human, and Clea felt it sink into her and grab hold, like a barbed hook snagging a fish. "Not your Gram. But definitely real."

The air shimmered and twisted, like cool breeze hitting sun-baked pavement; and then the illusion of Gram was gone, gone, her image replaced by—

Oh, God, the thing that stood in her place—

Clea stumbled back, one step and then another, a scream locked in her throat, adrenaline pumping through her system. Her foot caught the swivel chair, knocking it back, nearly sending her to her knees. She recovered, clawing at the wall as she backed up, faster now, her fingers scrabbling for balance, the hideous thing before her filling her vision, stalking her.

"Think of me as the Big Bad Wolf." Its voice was like ground glass. "You should have believed the vision. Things would have been easier that way. Easier for me."

Her breath coming in sharp, harsh gasps, Clea spun and barreled into the back office, slamming the door shut behind her and shoving the bolt home. *Where to go? Where to go?*

There was no other door. Heart pounding, she leaped for the small window at the back of the office, her hands shaking as she yanked on the lock. *Come on. Come on.* It released, and she curled her fingers under the handle, jerking up with all her might.

Come on!

The window didn't budge. Her nails tore as she

clawed at the old paint that formed heavy blobs on the window frame. Sealed tight.

A strangled sob escaped her. She was trapped, and it was there, right behind her. She could hear the dull thud of its steps.

The familiar heat that heralded her strange power uncoiled in her belly, and she hitched in her breath, waiting, waiting. The burst of light that had saved her from harm more than once was there, just beneath the surface. It shimmered and writhed, and she felt the tips of her fingers tingle, like she could shoot sparks, and then . . . nothing. It did *nothing*.

"Nooooo." She exhaled on a desperate moan.

The door splintered with an ugly crunching sound, and Clea spun, her back pressed against the cool metal of the filing cabinet, her heart beating so hard that she could feel it banging against her ribs.

A clawed hand reached through the hole in the door, long, pointed nails scratching at the knob, thick gray fingers closing around it, twisting slowly, slowly, to the right.

Her heart hammered. The taste of vomit burned the back of her tongue.

The door swung open.

OhGodOhGodOhGodOhGod—

The thing before her was a monster. Its skin was rough, cracked, and gray as death, like asphalt pavement that could have used replacing years past. And its face—Oh, God—its face was twisted and cruel, and all she could see was a huge gaping maw and row after row of sharp, jagged teeth. It reached for her, hands like reptilian claws coming toward her, the nails curved and blackened, and she could smell sulfur and the stink of rotting meat.

Terror sifted through her body, so sharp and stark she weaved dizzily from the force of it. Every breath a harsh, desperate rasp as she battled her fear, she sank to the floor, her legs giving way from under her.

Reaching behind her, she frantically traced her hand across the linoleum tiles, looking for something, *anything,* she could use as a weapon. Her fingers contacted cold floor, and dust, the leg of a chair, and—yes—something sharp. She snatched at it, dragged her hand up, glanced down. A thumbtack.

Useful.

Not.

She was breathing so fast and hard, she felt lightheaded. Not good. Not good. *Slow it down, Clea.* Breathe nice and slow. In through the nose. Out through the mouth. *Stay in control. In control.*

The thing took a step forward, moving leisurely, as though it enjoyed her terror.

And that pissed her off.

Focusing every thought, every fear, she pushed outward, trying to channel the power inside her. Now would be a very good time for it to make an appearance.

Because whatever this terrifying . . . terrible . . . *thing* was, it wasn't getting her without a fight.

Gliding through her veins with a surge of pain, the power rippled and stirred, a sharp heat, but she couldn't make it gather, couldn't guide it the way she so desperately needed to. She'd never tried to summon it before. It had always just come, without effort, without thought. Maybe that was the problem.

The gray beast took another step closer, and the smell pummeled her, stronger than before, fetid and dank.

"Don't fail me now," she muttered to herself, closing her eyes, focusing her energy, fists curled, nails digging into her palms, hoping that sheer will and determination would bring forth the power. "Come on!"

Closer. She could feel the thing stalking her, feel its cruel intent and the heat of its breath, smell the stink of decay.

She kicked out at it, and it laughed, an ugly, wet sound. Her blood roared in her ears. Scuttling back a bit farther, she wedged herself behind the dubious barrier of the filing cabinet.

The sound of a masculine voice, low and smooth, drifted from the lobby, making her head jerk up and her pulse catch. "Demon. Where is your keeper?"

The monster turned away from Clea, toward the speaker.

She pressed the back of her hand against her mouth, trying to hold back a panicked cry, not wanting to do anything to call the monster's attention back to her. As it moved away, she flung herself to her feet and ripped open the desk drawer, her fingers closing around a gold-leaf letter opener that bore the crest of the Blue Bay Motel.

"Where is your keeper, demon?" Again that voice, so calm, so confident. "Have you been left to your own devices?"

With the demon focused elsewhere, Clea spun toward the sound of that voice, brandishing the letter opener, breathing heavily as she peered through the open office door into the lobby.

She saw a man, broad-shouldered and sleekly muscled, clothed in faded denim and well-worn black leather. He was surrounded by a glow of light, or maybe it was coming from him, silver strands of moonlight that fanned out and around him, glittering, liquid, bending and twirling. . . . The sight seemed familiar somehow.

His face was both magazine-cover perfect and ruthlessly cruel as he stared at the thing that stalked her.

Demon. He'd called it a demon.

I want to wake up. I want to wake up. Clea reached down, her hand shaking so badly she could barely make it do her bidding, and she pinched her thigh. Hard. Only she didn't wake up, and through the open office door she could see that vile gray beast circling, circling, and the man, oh, God, the man just standing there, waiting for it to come.

Opening her mouth, she tried to call a warning, but panic trapped the words in her throat.

"Ciarran D'Arbois," the demon hissed. "You meddle where you have no place, sorcerer."

Ciarran D'Arbois. Sorcerer. Clea frowned, chasing a memory, or perhaps a dream, but it eluded her.

She sank her teeth into her lower lip, choking back a cry as the demon lunged, claws curved and raised in deadly intent, mouth hanging open to bare endless rows of razor-sharp teeth.

The filaments of light surrounding the sorcerer glowed stronger, rippling as he stepped aside, a fluid movement of grace and speed.

"You think to stop me?" The demon laughed, the sound soggy and loose, like a beast slurping at a carcass.

"The conduit must be returned to the gate. Tonight, the great master of us all, the Solitary, comes."

"The great master of us all?" Ciarran laughed, a low, menacing chuckle. "Not *my* master."

Lashing out, the demon raked the tip of one claw along Ciarran's arm, cutting through leather and cloth, leaving a thick line of red, red blood that welled and dripped to the floor.

He was injured. Bleeding. Clea stared at the blood. Terror surged inside her, escaping in a short, sharp cry as the thing lunged once more. And still Clea couldn't make herself look away, uncertain if it was worse to watch or to hide, not knowing what was to come.

She thought of the Discovery Channel special about the sharks. Of the way the shark's teeth tore through flesh and bone. This thing, this *demon*, would do that to this man, Ciarran, this beautiful, terrifying man who was about to be killed in front of her.

And then the demon would kill *her*, make her bleed just like Ciarran . . . *oceans* of blood. . . .

RunawayRunawayRunaway . . . Only she couldn't. Her legs were like noodles, and she couldn't make them bear her weight as she tried to stand.

Besides, the guy had come to save her. She hoped. The least she could do was watch his back.

With her gold-leaf letter opener.

Because it seemed that the power inside her that had saved her butt more than once over the years was definitely not making an appearance tonight. With a hiss of frustration, she closed her fingers tightly around the edge of the desk.

"Tell me you aren't so brain-dead that you think I'll

let the Solitary pass the gate." Ciarran smiled, a curving of masculine lips that held far more threat than humor. He didn't even glance at the nasty gash on his arm.

"You cannot stop it, sorcerer." The demon's head swiveled, and it pinned Clea with its burning gaze. "*This* conduit is strong, stronger than any that has come before, laced with *your* magic." The demon laughed again. "And for that, I thank you."

Ciarran shook his head. And then he moved. At least, Clea thought he moved. Suddenly, the lobby was full of glittering, sharp-edged strands that swelled and swayed with lethal beauty, catching the demon about its arms, its legs, its throat.

Filaments of woven light.

A light very much like the one she had tried to call forth, only bigger, brighter, stronger. Controlled. She blinked. Ciarran could channel the power. It didn't rush out of him in a stuttering unrestrained burst, the way it did from her.

His light, *his* power, flowed and danced.

It was beautiful, calling something inside her that she couldn't quite grasp.

"Go find your keeper, demon. I offer you this one chance."

"My keeper is weak, and I am strong. Strong enough to stand separated from him by miles. Strong enough to feast on you, sorcerer." The demon circled, watching his opponent.

"Then you *will* join your Solitary this night." Ciarran shifted the palm of his right hand up, sending a ripple through the shards of light. "But your meeting will be on the far side of the gate, demon. Enjoy your trip to hell."

Staring in frozen fascination, Clea felt her stomach turn a slow, sick roll as the deadly filaments sliced through cracked gray hide, spewing blood-drenched pieces of demon all over the walls, the floor, the ceiling. A bit landed on her cheek, and she slapped at it, panting now, flapping her hand at her skin as it sizzled and hissed. She could feel it burning. She looked around, her mouth opening and closing in soundless terror as the other bits crackled and fizzed and smoke curled up, the smell so bad that she gagged and gagged again.

"Clea." Soothing, so soothing, Ciarran's voice was like the rich red wine. Two-hundred-dollar-a-bottle wine.

She pressed her palms to her face, hiding her eyes as she pressed the backs of her thighs against the desk for support.

"Clea Masters." Okay. He was talking to her, though how he knew her name was a mystery.

Slowly, she let her fingers move apart, peeking from between them. Ciarran loomed over her, staring down at her, and she blinked, searching for the razor-sharp strands that had haloed him earlier.

But they were gone. All gone. And he was just a man. Who had shredded a demon like Parmesan cheese.

He took a single step closer, and she made a low sound of protest, snared by his gaze, unable to look away. His eyes widened slightly as he studied her. Silver. Blue. Green. Gold. Beautiful eyes.

"Are you hurt?" he asked.

A memory tugged at her: the stink of fire and the crashing waves of pain, a smooth voice, and bright, warm light. The hazy recollection darted away.

She shook her head as her hand strayed to her burned cheek. His gaze followed her movement to her cheek, then dropped to her mouth. The breath left her in a rush.

Unable to resist, she touched him, a light caress of her outstretched fingers along his hard, leather-clad forearm, just to be certain he was real. Heat sizzled through her, and she dropped her hand with a sharp hiss.

His features were an impossible blend of masculine perfection, strong jaw accented by a whisper of stubble, high cheekbones hollowed by dark shadows, straight nose with just the hint of a bump at the bridge. And his hair, sun-kissed and thick, hanging in loose waves to his shoulders. She was staring. She knew she was staring, but she couldn't make herself stop. The heat of him, the power, the luscious scent . . . everything hit her with the force of a physical blow.

For the first time in her entire life, Clea understood—really understood—the meaning of the words *animal attraction.*

"Oh. My. God." She couldn't breathe. Could barely think. Her body felt like it was on fire, and she had the desperate urge to press her palms to the firm jaw of the man who was before her, to touch her mouth to the decadent curve of his lips, to taste him and draw on him.

It was beyond insanity. Everything was beyond insanity. She'd lost it. She'd lost her ever-loving mind.

Ciarran. Even his name was sexy.

All she could think about was chemistry . . . and not the kind she'd studied as an undergrad. No. This was another breed entirely. This was hot. Wet. A dull ache between her thighs. Sexual chemistry. Everyone talked about it. She'd never really believed it existed. Until now.

She frowned, glanced down. There was a large chunk of . . . of . . . *demon* that was stuck to the floor, spitting and smoking as it slowly disintegrated, taking her control right along with it.

Tearing her gaze from the terrible sight, she focused instead on the stranger before her.

"How tall are you?" she blurted. Nice segue into conversation. But from where she sat in a nervous huddle perched on the edge of the desk, he looked like he was seven feet tall and packed with enough muscle and power to take down a house.

Certainly enough power to take down a demon.

He blinked, shot her a puzzled look. "Six foot four."

Okay. Good. He seemed inclined to answer questions. And she had a ton of those. "What are you? What was it? What the hell is going on here?"

"You are the conduit." He watched her closely, as though his words ought to have some meaning. *"Christe."*

Leaning forward, he braced his hand against the desktop beside her right thigh. He was wearing a glove. Black leather, like his jacket, supple, the fit tight to his hand. She hadn't noticed it before, but she noticed it now because . . . he wore only one. On his left hand, but not his right.

His warm breath fanned her cheek, and she forgot about the glove. Her head jerked up, and her pulse ratcheted up a notch. With his gaze locked on hers, he reached out, almost touching her burned cheek. Almost. Strong, masculine fingers just a whisper away from her skin.

She could feel the heat of him, smell the clean scent of his skin.

God. The way he looked at her. *God.*

He was looking at her as though he were starving and she was an all-you-can-eat buffet.

"I believed I was hunting a minor demon," he said softly in that poured-honey voice.

His mouth tightened. A little cruel. A lot sexy. She wanted to taste his mouth. She wanted to taste more than his mouth.

Raw sexual chemistry, she thought numbly. Just another part of this crazy mixed-up dream.

"But I was wrong," he continued. "The demon was incidental. It was *you,* Clea Masters. All along, I was hunting *you.*"

Chapter 4

I DON'T UNDERSTAND," CLEA WHISPERED, HER breath hitching in a sexy little catch that made Ciarran's body tighten. And then she dragged the tip of her tongue along her lower lip, just begging him to take a taste. "What do you mean . . . you were hunting me?"

Ciarran smiled darkly. His blood pumped, rich and hot in his veins, and a pulsing coil of lust settled in his groin.

Christe.

They needed to talk. He had much to say, but not here, not now. Since the demon was dead, his keeper would survive only a short while, and Ciarran knew he must be found before his life force expired. There were questions the demon-keeper could answer, and Ciarran needed those answers.

"Say *something*," Clea muttered. "Maybe tell me to click my heels three times and wish myself back to Kansas."

He frowned, uncertain of her reference, and she shook her head.

"Never mind." Watching him warily, she tightened her grip on the small gold weapon she was holding.

Ciarran reached down and took the blade from her hands, careful not to touch her skin, unnerved by the sizzle of magic that passed between them even at this, a casual contact. With a murmured sound of denial, she first held, then surrendered the weapon. She looked up, studying him.

She had beautiful eyes, the color of dark, polished mahogany, thickly lashed, tilting up just a touch at the corners, scrutinizing him with intensity and intelligence.

And heat and need that matched his own.

Such a link, instant and strong, was an impossibility. Yet he could feel the impossible surging inside him, urging him to taste her and take her, and pleasure them both. Distance seemed the wiser course. He took a step back.

He felt a glimmer of admiration for her as she watched him, her body tense, her gaze dropping to the blade he had taken from her hands. She had been prepared to battle a demon with her puny weapon.

"Brave." He thumbed the edge of the blade and frowned. Dull. "What is this?"

"A letter opener." Her voice did not waver. This human female was daring, indeed.

"What did you plan to do with it?" 'Twould not have even scratched the demon's hide.

She raked her fingers through the tousled waves of her brown hair as she exhaled, the sound a flowing sigh that touched him as surely as a caress. He wanted to run his hands over her naked body, to draw that sound, and others, from her lush mouth.

Madness. He'd descended into madness. These thoughts, *this* woman, were dangerous to him. When Clea Masters had been a child, she had demonstrated the inexplicable ability to drain his magic. His subsequent inattention had cost him both his hand and a chunk of his soul. Getting close to her now ought to be the last thing he considered doing.

He let his gaze travel over her. Clea was no longer a child.

"The—uhh—the letter opener?" Her voice wavered just a little now. "I was going to use it to defend myself against that . . . thing." She hesitated, then continued. "I cheated death once, a long time ago, and I had no intention of giving in to it tonight."

Cheated death. An apt description. Yet death had claimed a forfeit, and he well knew the price that had been paid.

She held his gaze. He found her unutterably attractive, this human woman who would battle a demon unto death.

This human woman who was cloaked in impossible magic.

"You cheated death a *long* time ago," he echoed, unable to keep the trace of amusement from his tone. "How old are you?"

Again, she wet her lips. He followed the subtle movement of her tongue. "Twenty-eight. Last Tuesday."

"Ah." He turned the letter opener in his palm, then snapped it neatly in two.

"How—"

Glancing back at her, he found her staring at his hands.

At his leather glove. Supple leather, lined in flexible metal alloy, woven with protective magic. A relatively effective cage, bolstered by tattooed wards.

She would do more than stare if she saw what lay beneath it.

"Good thing you didn't need to use your weapon." He shrugged, held up the broken pieces. "Plastic."

Perhaps he expected her to cry. Bury her face in her hands and sob. Or perhaps he expected her to look at him blankly, shock and fear numbing her to reality. She did neither.

Her dark eyes widened, and her brows rose. A snicker burst forth, and another, until her laughter swelled and filled the small space.

"Plastic!" She gasped, pressing one hand against her belly. "Oh, that's priceless. And perfect." She held up one hand, palm out. "No. Really. Perfect."

Not the laughter of hysteria, but true mirth. She found amusement here. He was startled to feel his own lips twitch in response.

Her gaze collided with his, and her laughter died, sharp and quick.

She looked away, arched her back, rolled her shoulders, as though stretching out a kink, her movements pulling the light blue knit of her thin sweater tight across her breasts. He could see the outline of her lacy bra etching its pattern in the cloth.

A smart, no-nonsense girl, wearing a simple sweater and conservative jeans, her dark waving hair cut in an uncomplicated, low-maintenance style. No makeup, save for the last remnants of her smudged mascara. And underneath, against her smooth skin, lace. His gaze dropped to her hips as he tried to imagine her underwear. Lacy underwear. Sexy underwear.

The girl was a study in contradictions.

And what the hell was he doing thinking about her underwear?

Looking away, he focused his thoughts on the task at hand. He needed to pursue the demon-keeper, to seek answers before the man's final fate sealed off that avenue of information.

"I feel like I've been shoved through a meat grinder," Clea muttered, drawing his gaze back to her.

Mistake. Big mistake. Her back was arched even farther, hands braced just behind her on the desktop, her breasts straining now against their cotton covering, leaving little to his imagination. She rolled her head slowly to one side and the other, sending waving strands of dark hair tumbling along her shoulders.

Ciarran didn't think; he just moved. Two steps and he was close enough to catch a shimmering curl between his thumb and forefinger. With a gasp, she turned her head, her brown eyes bright as she studied him. She didn't pull away, and he sensed her confusion. She could not understand her body's call, the desperate drive to touch him, the half-crazed need that gnawed at her.

Hell, he barely understood it himself. Such was the stuff of legends, of faded dusty tomes from a time before the *Pact*, before even his time. This link between souls could only happen between two of magic synergy. But Clea Masters was human. . . .

She could not possibly be other than human.

For thousands of years, the Compact of Sorcerers had guarded the realms, standing against the demons, holding fast to the *Pact*—the agreement of protection forged between ancient beings so powerful that they defied even Ciarran's understanding. Long-dead tribes had called them *gods*.

Sorcerers were not human; they *protected* humans. In all his life and all the lore, Ciarran knew of none who had walked over the line from human to immortal. A child of two sorcerers was born a sorcerer. Such a birth was a rare and unusual occurrence.

When a sorcerer procreated with a mortal—an equally extraordinary occurrence—the child was invariably human. A kernel of magic might bloom, the faintest spark that might allow for a small amount of precognition, but the child was *mortal*.

Which made Clea Masters something of an impossible anomaly. She was human. And *not* human.

He still held the glossy strands of her hair, and she still held his gaze.

Surprise, he thought wryly. He'd come north in pursuit of the minor demon, Darqun's mention of the dead grandmother and the girl a vague, gnawing issue that Ciarran intended to deal with once the immediacy of the demon-keeper was addressed. Now it turned out that the two concerns had melded into one.

Christe. Clea was the damned conduit.

The minor demon had not meant to *feed* upon her; it had meant to take her to the gate. She was the instrument, the key. This was no surprise. He had surmised as much from the demon's babble.

No. The surprise was inside her. And inside him.

He *knew* her, was part of her. Certainty bubbled through him. On a dark, deserted road with death hanging heavy in the air, he had made a mistake, a miscalculation. Not enough to damn the world. Just enough to damn himself.

Just enough to cost him his hand. And a chunk of his sanity. He flexed his fingers in their leather-and-alloy prison.

Slowly, he let go the strand of Clea's hair, and she exhaled on a sigh. Shifting his touch to her cheek, he healed the burn with a thought and a subtle touch of magic, felt the smallest quiver in her body. Not fear. Desire. His touch made her tremble, and he felt the answering tension low in his gut.

How could he explain this to her? How could he explain it to himself?

Clea Masters was *his*. His by right. His by ancient claim. His by the bond that pulsed between them, hot and wild. And his because she wanted it so. She allowed this attraction to him, which made his own need swell.

He had marked her, branded her with one rash act when, in a reckless moment of lost concentration on an empty road some two decades past, he'd broken every rule of the *Pact* and saved a human child from death.

No, that was not the truth.

The truth was that the human child had reached out, seeing what she should not possibly be able to see, catching his magic in her tiny hands, dragging it from him, using it to heal wounds that should never have healed.

Stealing his power while he watched, dumbfounded.

The human child had saved herself, while he had battled an ancient demon. And lost.

And now the grandmother had died, and Darqun had sent him to find the child.

Only she was no longer a child. Here she was, all grown-up, sitting on the edge of a rickety desk, watching him with a sultry hunger that made him feel a dark and aching lust.

Clea Masters. The conduit that could open the gate between dimensions, the key that could unlock the end of the world.

He had saved her. His magic. His power.

He had doomed her.

And he wanted her with a fierce and primitive need that raced through every cell in his body, making him burn.

Stepping back, he did them both the small kindness of allowing a little distance between them. The action was in direct opposition to his inclination, the primitive, clamoring part of him that wanted to drag her up against him, touch her, taste her, bury himself inside her right now, right here.

The way she looked at him, like she wanted to run from him. Like she wanted to thrust her body against him, take him deep inside her, score his skin as she moaned her release. He was scorched by her heat, and it confounded him, lured him, made him feel the gnawing sharp edge of desire.

Gathering himself, he glanced at the remnants of the dead minor demon, which still sizzled and smoked, clinging to the walls and floor around them.

"I was hunting *you*, Clea Masters," he repeated softly, returning his gaze to her.

"And now you've found me." She caught her lower

lip between her teeth, rolled it slowly back and forth, an instinctive gesture of nervousness, an unintentionally sensual action. He wanted to lick her full lower lip, to catch it between his own teeth.

"How do you know my name?"

He chose to dissemble. "There was a name plate by the registration desk." The truth, but 'twas not how he knew her name.

The air left her in an indelicate rush, her disbelief apparent. "And you just happened to stop and read it before you followed me back here to shred that . . . that . . . thing?"

Smart. Insightful. He liked that. Liked her. Yet another danger to add to their smoldering attraction.

With a glance at the last place the demon had stood, she shivered, brought her gaze back to his. "Are you going to do *that* to me . . . cut me to pieces?"

"No." The thought made his gut wrench in angry denial. Nothing would harm her. *Nothing*.

"And I believe you because . . . ?" She paused, blew out a breath and answered her own question. "Because if that was your intent, you would have done it by now."

Her gaze slid over him in a slow, sexy perusal. Like she was studying him, measuring him, and definitely liking what she found. She was afraid of him, but her fear was weaker than her need.

Ciarran's heart rate escalated, his blood pounding. Such had not happened to him. Ever. For centuries he had walked the earth, High Sorcerer of the Compact, coolheaded, rational, never bowed or swayed from his cause. The many times that he had chosen to materialize, to allow a human female to see him, to be pleasured by him and to pleasure him in return, he had always remained somewhat detached. He had enjoyed physical release, but in an aloof and distant manner, never allowing strong passion to overcome his control.

This intense, vibrant arousal, so sharp and sweet that he was hard as a rock, this unbridled *lust* was unfamiliar to him.

Clea's gaze slowly shifted the rest of the way up his body, until she was looking directly into his eyes.

"So do I get some answers?" she asked, squaring her shoulders and tipping up her chin.

And he could think of only one answer he wanted to give her, the kind found in hard, wet kisses and pounding release.

Chapter 5

D R. ASA PALEY PULLED THE DOOR OF THE EXAMI-
nation room in the ER shut behind him, closing
out the hum of activity outside. St. John's was a busy
ER, but tonight was quiet. Turning to greet the small
woman who sat on the gurney, arms wrapped around her
narrow chest, layers of filthy clothing warding off the
chill, Asa sent her a professional smile, meant to encourage and allay fear. She smiled back guilelessly, her eyes
trusting, almost childlike.

He recognized her. She'd been in the previous month,
but she had snuck off when he had left the room to at-
tend to another patient.

"Hello," he said. "I'm Dr. Paley."

She nodded. "Okay. Hello." Holding one arm in front
of her, she whispered, "I got worms in me."

Worms. "Well, let's take a look"—he glanced at her
chart, reminding himself of her name—"Louise." An-
gling a stool a little closer, he took a seat and waited as
she carefully rolled up her grimy sleeve.

Slowly, she turned her hand palm up, and he saw a large laceration, an old festering wound, the edges of the skin dark and brittle. He adjusted the light and picked up a pair of tweezers. The *shush* of the door opening and closing behind him hailed the arrival of a nurse. He frowned.

Something in Louise's wound moved, an undulating shift, and the nurse let out a startled gasp. Asa sent her a reassuring smile over his shoulder. "Shawna, can you hunt down some containers please? I have a feeling we'll need a few. Urine specimen bottles should do the trick."

Shawna sent a wary glance at the woman's blackened arm and nodded, her momentary startlement pushed aside by her professionalism. "Certainly, Dr. Paley."

Asa turned back to his patient as Shawna slipped from the room. "Louise, I'm so glad you came back to see me."

She looked up at him, the lank curtain of her hair falling back, and she smiled trustingly as she nodded.

Taking a deep breath, he savored the smell of her. Unwashed skin and clothes. Rich earth. Subcutaneous tissue rank with the festering wounds that marked her. And deep inside of her . . . yes . . . a lovely secret treat.

Just a whisper, but it was there, glittering like a jewel.

He was almost strong enough. Almost. Each day his energy, his power, grew.

Last week, he had been most pleased with his progress as he trolled the downtown clubs. He had sensed one of the Compact, one of more-than-moderate strength, before the sorcerer had sensed him, and he was certain he had escaped undetected. Such would not have been possible only a few months past. But he had been careful. Choosing his meals with optimum enhancement in mind. And his sacrifices, his forfeits, were beginning to pay off.

Tonight he was even more pleased. He had been strong enough to sense the failure of the minor demon tonight, strong enough to feel the ripple of magic as it had been destroyed. Somewhere close. Very close. Foolish being, to attempt to bring the Solitary before his time. The minor demon deserved its destruction, just reward for its audacity.

Asa fully intended to greet the Solitary himself, to take his rightful place at the great being's side. There was so much to be done, and for the tasks ahead, he needed strength.

"Got worms in me," Louise said again.

He smiled. Worms. Oh, there was so much more than worms inside of her. She was an unusual creature, one who had some sorcerer ancestry that had provided the seed for a tiny spark of magic. Enough to turn Louise from a mundane morsel into a sumptuous feast. Enough to ratchet up Asa's power several notches.

She was a rare and wondrous find, his Louise. A delicacy to be savored. "Tell me about the worms, Louise."

"Worms inside of me. In my arms. In my legs. I put them there to protect me from the others, the ones in my dreams. The ones inside me are small still. But I know they'll get bigger, and . . ." She leaned closer, her eyes rolling in fear, her body tense. "The worms in my dreams'll eat me. From the inside out. I'm food for them. And they're evil. Bad. They come into my dreams."

"Have you been taking the pills that Dr."—he glanced

at the chart—"Langford gave you the last time you saw him, Louise? The ones in the brown bottle?" Asa asked gently, taking his time as he closed the tweezers around the slithering worm at the opening of her wound. An earthworm. Keeping his expression neutral, he pulled it out and dropped it in the metal pan on the tray by his side.

Louise shook her head. "No. No. No pills. They won't help. I got worms in me. Worms in me. Worms in me." She began rocking back and forth, one hand still held in Asa's grasp, the other lying limply at her side. "Worms in me . . . worms in me . . . worms in me . . ."

"Oh, my," Shawna said from behind him, as Asa closed the tweezers around a second earthworm and pulled it from the wound. She opened the specimen container, but Asa shook his head and dropped the worm in the metal pan.

"I think we can easily identify the organism with a visual confirmation, Shawna." He masked his annoyance at her quick return. He wanted Louise all to himself. Delightful, succulent Louise, who had no husband, no children, no known family, no one to notice when she simply . . . disappeared. And if her friends who lived with her in cardboard boxes beneath the Bathurst Street Bridge happened to report her absence, who would listen? "It seems we have no need of specimen bottles after all."

"Louise, how did this happen?" Shawna asked. "Did you put these worms in your arm?"

"Yep. To carry 'em. Like a mama kangaroo carries her babies in a pouch." Louise kept rocking. "Worms in me. My friends. They keep the other worms away. The ones that are eating me."

Rising, Asa guided Shawna a few steps away. "She has no family? You are quite certain?"

Shawna shook her head. "I double- and triple-checked last time she was in, just like you asked me. Called social services. She has no one." She tipped her head, her eyes shimmering as she looked at him with adoration. "You are so great, worrying about a poor homeless woman, all upset last time when she left while you were called to a different room. But you were right. She came back. Just like you said she would." She ran the tips of her fingers along his sleeve, watching him from beneath lowered lashes, then dropped her arm with a little laugh. "I'm glad it was you she saw tonight."

Oh, so was he. So very glad.

"Thanks. I've got this now, Shawna." Asa smiled, that practiced, perfect smile that made him so damned attractive to these human females. The irony was a small secret pleasure. If they could see him as he truly was . . . He caught her gaze, held it, pouring the smallest glimmer of his will into her.

"I'll . . . I'll just go," she said, her expression puzzled. "I . . . I'll go." She walked slowly from the room, pulling the door closed behind her.

He turned back toward Louise, who was humming quietly to herself, or perhaps to her worms.

Damn, he loved this job. The smell of blood. The mayhem. The suffering—

Louise looked up, met his gaze, and her eyes widened as he dropped his façade.

—the food supply.

Chapter 6

AS SHE FOLLOWED CIARRAN OUT OF THE BLUE BAY Motel, Clea noticed that the day's drizzle had cleared, leaving the night sky dark and star-speckled. Pretty. Gram would have pointed out the Big Dipper. Clea's breath hitched at the thought.

Turning, she locked the door behind her, then held out her hand for her backpack. With a half smile, Ciarran slung it over his shoulder and walked on. The air was sharp, and Clea wrapped her arms around herself to ward off the October chill, her cotton-and-lycra sweater doing a poor job of it. She stared at Ciarran's broad back, let her gaze drop to his long-legged stride. Strong. Purposeful.

Sexy.

She exhaled sharply.

It seemed he had places to go, people to see, and he had every intention of taking her with him. He hadn't given her a great deal of choice, and even if he had, she'd have chosen to go with him.

Because the guy had just saved her from a demon.

A *demon,* for frig's sake.

Someone needed to explain *that,* and for lack of a more cooperative candidate, she nominated Ciarran.

Which meant they weren't exactly at cross-purposes. He wanted her with him, and for now, the idea had merit. It was the best way for her to get the information she wanted.

Back in the motel, she'd asked him, and he'd stared at her for an infinite moment, his eyes hot. Hungry. For a second she'd been afraid he would kiss her . . . or maybe she'd *wished* he would. What was it with that?

She sighed. Later, she would find another opportunity to ask questions. Demand replies. Something other than the monosyllabic grunts she'd gotten thus far. And if sticking to Ciarran like a fly to flypaper was the only way to get those answers, then that was exactly what she planned to do.

Except, maybe that wasn't the best analogy. Flies on flypaper invariably ended up dead.

Following him around the side of the building, Clea stopped short at the sight of the sleek black motorcycle sitting in the pallid circle cast by the dim overhead light. The emblem read DUCATI. She didn't know anything about bikes, but this one looked like it could break the sound barrier.

Which meant she was not getting on that thing. Definitely not. She'd survived one horrific crash, and she had a firm policy against inviting another.

"I think I'll take my car," she said. If it started. There were never any guarantees.

He paused but didn't turn, and she thought she saw his shoulders tighten just a little. "No, you'll stay with me."

And he sounded none too thrilled about that.

She thought about climbing onto that bike, pressed up against him. Nope. Not a plan. In a choice between Ciarran and Ciarran's motorcycle, she wasn't sure which was more dangerous.

"Okay," she agreed. "I'll give you a ride in my car." Problem solved.

He did glance at her then, and the look he gave her spoke volumes. "There is no longer anyplace that is safe for you."

"No longer anyplace that is safe for me? You do realize how melodramatic that sounds?" Clea waited for him to laugh, to clarify his point. Of course he meant that the Blue Bay wasn't safe, because that horrible gray *thing*, that demon, might have friends. That must be what he meant.

"There is *no* safe place, Clea." His voice was low and rough. Intense. A shiver chased along her spine. "Not here at"—he glanced at the sign—"the Blue Bay Motel. Not in Toronto. Not here in Ontario. Not anywhere in the mortal world."

"What?" She sucked in a breath, her mind spinning as his words sank in. She lived in a typical city, with its boxy malls, megaplex movie theaters, and a skyline that boasted the tallest freestanding tower in the world. The crime rate here was a bare two shades above zero. And he was telling her it wasn't safe? What did he mean? That there really was no place safe?

That was a horrible thought.

He shook his head, exhaling a hiss of air from between his teeth. "I am your only safe place now."

That thought was only marginally less bad.

Just as she was about to protest, he added, "That minor demon wouldn't work alone. Others are likely to follow."

Okay. That got her attention. Made her weigh her options.

Demon . . . bike . . . demon . . . bike . . .

She opened her mouth to argue in favor of her car, but catching sight of the glint of steel in his expression, she decided against it. Hadn't Gram always taught her that strength lay in choosing one's battles?

"Bike it is," she said, forcing the words out. The decision wasn't an easy one, no matter how glib she tried to sound.

Ciarran nodded, settling her pack on the back of the motorcycle and strapping it in place before he turned to face her.

"The man who was here earlier, the one you called Wired Guy, where did he go?" he asked. She'd mentioned that encounter in a babbling torrent of words as he'd questioned her about the moments before the demon arrived.

"I sent him up the road to the Motel Seven." She shrugged. "I don't know if he went, but if he's the one you're looking for, it's a place to start."

The wind swirled down from the north, biting through her thin sweater, and she shivered. Frowning, she cast a glance over her shoulder at the front door of the motel. She had a coat, didn't she? Or had she forgotten to bring one? She thought back through her day, the cemetery, the wet dirt that was pushed into Gram's grave, the dull ache in her heart. She'd gone back to the apartment to change for work, and, yeah, she'd forgotten to bring a coat.

"Put this on. It will warm you." Ciarran slid his sculpted arms out of the sleeves of his leather jacket. Buff. The guy was buff. Hooking one finger under the collar, he held out his hand, offering her the jacket.

There was a tattoo on his left forearm, a dragon. Its head stretched toward the black glove, its body winding upward, aligned with the bulge of his muscle. The tail meandered up and around above the elbow. In this light, the dragon looked black, but its scales seemed to shimmer with a hint of blue and green. And its eyes were bright, a turquoise of incredible luminosity.

Oh, man, she'd always been a sucker for a well-drawn tattoo, and this one was absolutely gorgeous.

The black T-shirt Ciarran was wearing left nothing to the imagination. She could see every ridge of his toned abdomen, and his low-slung, washed-out jeans made her want to catch her fingers in the belt loops and haul him just a little closer. No. A lot closer. If warming her was his goal, that would be a great way to go about it.

When she made no move to take his jacket, he stepped close, and she couldn't help it. She leaned forward, inhaling the scent of him, almost touching her face to the base of his throat.

Trembling, she stood unbearably still, every nerve sensitized, every cell alive as he stepped around behind her and settled the jacket over her shoulders. A scent teased her, tantalized her. Masculine. Seductive. A little spicy, a lot sexy. God, the coat smelled like *him.*

She shivered, slammed her eyes shut. She was losing it. *Losing* it.

"What about you?" she asked, her voice thick. "You'll be cold."

Yeah. Right. She could feel the heat of him at her back, and she moved without conscious thought, tipping her head to one side, letting his breath warm her skin. She sensed him leaning in, his lips inches from the side of her throat. Inches. A sweet, sharp tingle of awareness sizzled through her. If she leaned back just a bit, she could rub against him, feel the solid wall of his body. She wanted to do just that, wanted it more than she ever could recall wanting anything.

And that yearning frightened her.

God, he was the most singularly sensual man she'd ever seen. And she was so hungry for him. She craved him with a wet, throbbing ache that made her press her thighs together and wish with all her heart that she was naked and he was naked and that they were on any reasonably comfortable horizontal surface.

The asphalt parking lot would do.

"I'm having a bad day," she said. Maybe that was the explanation. Grief, loss, stress. Maybe she just needed to have crazy, mindless sex with him, to reaffirm the fact that she was human, that she was alive. Too much death and sorrow and fear for a single day, the culmination of watching Gram slowly fade away for months and months.

Not to mention the fact that demons and magic and filaments of light were a little outside her normal scope of experience. Oh, she'd always known she had some kind of mojo, some kind of weird protection thing going on. But a dead demon . . . shredded by razor-sharp ribbons of light . . . It was way too much.

"I know about your bad day. I am sorry for your loss." His voice was a smoky rumble beside her left ear. Her insides twisted in response. It didn't help that she could sense his arousal, feel his desire pulsing from his hard body. It definitely didn't help that she knew he wanted her just about as much as she wanted him.

Because she didn't think that *her* having a bad day explained *his* passion.

"How do you know? About my bad day? And how did you know to come here just when the demon arrived? How—" The words caught in her throat as he raised his hand, the one with the glove, and ran a leather-encased finger along her jaw.

Something stirred deep inside her, twining, writhing, light and power, reaching out toward his hand as though called. She turned her face into his touch.

He made a sound low in his throat and jerked back.

"Later," he said, his voice tight. "I will explain later. But now we must find the keeper, before it is too late."

"Wired Guy . . . He's the one you're calling the keeper?"

"Yes."

"Keeper of what?"

"Keeper of the minor demon that I terminated."

Of course.

She hesitated, almost asked him, *too late for what?* But instinct told her he wouldn't answer, so she gave it up.

His broad chest expanded against her back as he inhaled. He was so close. So big. Solid male muscle and barely leashed power. One taste. One brush of her lips across that hard, luscious mouth. She just wanted, no, *needed*, one taste of him. She started to turn toward him, felt him stiffen.

He moved then, three strides, and he was back beside the motorcycle, and she felt the loss of his heat, his presence, like a physical blow. The power inside her shriveled, drawing into itself. She was left with the strange thought that somehow she was tied to him, linked to him, that the inexplicable force inside her was lured by the ribbons of light inside him.

Or perhaps not lured to the light but to the darkness. Because she did sense darkness. No. More than sensed it. *Knew* it was there with a cold and sharp certainty.

The thought gave her pause.

But darkness or light, or some terrifying combination of the two, he was the one who could explain the power that pulsed inside her. The one who could explain the demon, the light filaments, the magic.

And, according to him, he was her only safe harbor.

"Okay. Let's do this your way," she said. "Let's find the keeper, and once he's found, you give me some answers. Agreed?"

"We need to leave." He straddled the bike, muscled thighs framing the seat. The sight of him, harsh features softened by the fall of honey brown hair, the golden skin and taut muscle, the look in his iridescent eyes . . . he made her mouth grow dry.

Eyeing the bike, she battled back her wariness and climbed on behind him, her thighs forming a notch that cradled him, her hips tight against worn denim, her breasts pressed to his T-shirt-encased back.

He gunned the engine, and as she felt the powerful hum against the insides of her thighs, she realized that he hadn't agreed to a blessed thing.

Not a single blessed thing.

Chapter 7

THE BIKE BLAZED DOWN THE ROAD, THUNDER-OUS power and unleashed speed. Clea locked her arms around Ciarran, holding so tight she thought she might melt right into him, become a part of him. Terror sluiced through her, rough and dark, and all she could do was watch over his shoulder as the white lines painted on the road sped past at an unbearable rate. No helmet. No protective gear. Just unfettered speed.

Her worst nightmare.

She wondered if—no, *wished*—the cops would stop them.

She let out a high squeak of protest as Ciarran disengaged his right hand from the grip, the sound snatched by the roaring wind. Then he closed his fingers around hers, warm and strong. Her terror receded, just a little, just enough to let her breathe, let her think. And then they were pulling into the parking lot of the Motel Seven.

She was still alive. Blessedly alive.

Stumbling from the bike, she shot a glance at Ciarran.

He'd shredded a demon in front of her, destroyed any notion she had that her world was good and safe, then dragged her onto the back of his bike and made her face her greatest fear. Frig.

Breathe. Nice and slow. In through her nose. Out through her mouth. God, she'd never practiced this much relaxation breathing in her life, but this night was different. Tonight she'd been slapped with enough stress to make her an expert.

Her panic reined by a tenuous thread, she looked up to find Ciarran studying the cars in the lot. He shot her a close-lipped smile, as though challenging her to comment on the ride.

"This way," he said, and walked across the parking lot toward the end of the row of units, like he knew exactly where he was going. With a mental shrug, she followed.

Keeping her behind him, he turned the handle of the motel room door and pushed it open. Remembering how insistent Wired Guy had been about a door with a lock that worked, Clea couldn't imagine that he hadn't checked and double-checked his security.

Which meant one of two things. Either they had the wrong room, or locks posed no barrier to a sorcerer.

She blew out a breath as he led her inside, keeping his body angled protectively in front of hers.

Not that there was much to protect her from, she realized as she scanned the interior. Wired Guy wasn't here. The only occupant of the room was a wizened old man who was stretched out fully clothed atop the generic brown bedspread, his breath rattling in his frail chest.

White shirt. Dark suit. She frowned at the strange familiarity of it.

Clea dragged the edges of Ciarran's leather jacket tight and glanced around the room. A dresser with a TV bolted in place. Dull brown curtains. She shivered. It was cold in here. Frigging cold.

Colder than it was outside.

She wondered if the old guy had accidentally cranked the air conditioner instead of the heat.

"It's not him," she said. "Wired Guy was younger, by about five decades—"

The man on the bed turned his face toward her, and she caught a glimpse of his eyes. Cold. Dead. There was a loud buzzing in her ears, and she felt like she'd slipped on the ice and fallen on her butt, hard enough to knock the air out of her.

". . . or maybe not," she whispered, watching the man's eyes widen in recognition as he stared at her.

And she recognized him, too. Wired Guy's eyes were looking out at her from the wrong face.

She knew. Ciarran could tell by the look on her face, the sudden loss of color, the rapid, panting breaths.

Smart girl. It had taken Clea less than ten seconds to figure out that Wired Guy had aged fifty years in the past fifty minutes. And from the look of her, she was determined to hold it together in the face of yet another earth-shattering discovery.

He felt a burst of admiration for her. Clea's world was all but falling apart, and brave girl that she was, she was fighting to take it all in. To believe what, for her, must be unbelievable. To stay sane while she figured it out.

He liked her for it. Respected her courage.

She was a warrior, his Clea.

His Clea.

Christe.

He had no room anywhere in his life for this human woman. No room for liking. No room for wanting. She was a distraction he could ill afford.

Distraction was his deadliest adversary.

His maimed hand tingled, the darkness writhing and twisting, searching for release. Gritting his teeth, he clenched his ruined fingers in their leather-and-alloy prison, and he pulled it back, leashing the snarling beast. Yeah, that was the price he had paid for distraction. The loss of a damned part of himself, and the gain of his eternal millstone, the demon seed that gnawed at him, threatening to take the whole of him if he let it.

"Sit," Ciarran ordered, leading Clea to the chair in the corner, relieved that she let him. He had no wish to waste time on useless argument.

He crossed to the side of the bed and stood watching the rise and fall of the old man's chest.

"Hello, demon-keeper," he said, keeping his hands fisted, his power in check.

"If you've come to kill me, you're almost too late." The keeper pushed himself to a sitting position, slowly, painstakingly. "I'll be dust in another few minutes. Nothing but dust." He sounded infinitely relieved, almost glad, as he said it.

Ciarran nodded, recognizing the man's acceptance of his fate. "Your demon has been terminated, demon-keeper."

"Don't call me that!" The man looked down at his

age-spotted hands, the translucent skin showing a network of blue veins. "Matthew. My name is Matthew." He drew a deep, shuddering breath. "Demon-keeper? More like *it* kept me."

"Did you summon it by choice? For longevity?" Ciarran glanced at Clea as she made a small sound of confusion. She was perched on the edge of the chair, her knuckles white as she clutched the armrests, her eyes wide. He turned back to the keeper. "For riches?"

Matthew stared at him blankly for a moment. "For my wife," he whispered, his breath rattling in his chest.

Without the demon's dark magic, the keeper was aging at an accelerated rate, rapidly losing the youth and vigor he had enjoyed as the demon's companion.

"Tell me," Ciarran commanded. "Tell me all. Quickly."

He wanted the man's story, in all its detail, to sift through and study and, hopefully, find a clue. There was something amiss between dimensions, a smear of filth in the *continuum*. Darqun had felt it, too. And Javier. Only once before had Ciarran encountered such discord, and the end result of that occasion had been eating at him for twenty years. His gaze flicked to Clea and back. Absently, he ran the back of his gloved hand up and down along his thigh, trying to still the twisting, winding buzz that thrummed through the ruined sinew and bone.

"Diphtheria. My wife had diphtheria." The keeper's voice was thin, weak. "I went to the church to beg God for her life, because there was no man who could help her. She was dying. Choking to death on a thick gray membrane that grew in her throat and clogged her every breath. I would have promised anything, traded anything, even my own life, to save her." He shuddered. "Traded my soul."

Matthew fell silent, and Ciarran heard the creak of the chair as Clea shifted.

"There was a book there. In the vestry," Matthew said. "One I'd never seen before. And as I opened it, the words were clear to me, though I knew not how to read. I said them, once, again, each recitation more fluent than the last, and on the third time, it came. One moment I was alone, and the next, I was in the company of a great gray beast with teeth as sharp as any ravening dog's."

Matthew turned his head toward Clea. "You know the beast. It came for you."

She was shivering, huddled in the depth of his leather jacket, and Ciarran figured part of the problem was the frigid temperature in the room, and the other part was shock. For an instant, he thought she might succumb to her fear, but then she raised her head and met his gaze, visibly mastering her agitation.

Brave, strong Clea.

His Clea. Emotion hummed through Ciarran, vibrating with strength and certainty. The urge to claim her, to protect her, was unbelievably strong.

Unnerved by the intensity of his thoughts, he dragged his gaze back to the keeper. His gloved fist burned, white-hot pain, the evil restless, so restless tonight.

With a grunt, Matthew fixed his gaze on Ciarran, studying him. "You're just a kid. What? You're maybe thirty? Thirty-five? Do you even know what diphtheria is? Hasn't been around much for decades."

A kid. Ciarran almost laughed. "Tell me about the demon."

"Ah. The demon. He was to be my sweet wife's savior, and mine." The old man gave a long, panting laugh, but the sound was rife with bitterness and regret. "He said he'd spare her life. And all I had to do was say the words one last time. Bind him to me so he could leave the church, follow me to my home. I did it. For the love of my wife, I did it. Said those cursed words and bound him to me. Sold my soul."

"Demons know no honor." Ciarran had heard this story, in its varied and sad versions, for centuries. He had heard, too, of those who summoned a demon for power and riches and life eternal. Either way, the outcome was the same. The keeper became the kept, slave to the ever-growing evil of the demon that was released.

Matthew coughed, the sound wet, fluid building in his lungs as his heart slowly gave way, its pumping action growing ever weaker. He coughed again, and his body convulsed as though he was in great pain.

"Water." Clea leaped from the chair, took a step forward, her face a mask of concern. "Would you like some water?"

Compassion flowed from her, and Ciarran wondered at her willingness to be kind to a man who had brought her destruction to her. Matthew was the one who had obeyed the demon, who had brought it into Clea's life. And Ciarran had no doubt that she knew it. Yet she was not immune to the man's suffering, willing to ease it despite what he had done.

He was not certain how he felt about that. Perhaps a little awed.

"No. No water." Matthew raised one hand weakly, then let it fall back against the coverlet. "I'm fine. Fine."

After a moment, he slowly raised his head and stared at himself in the mirror that hung across from the bed, above the cheap pasteboard dresser. "Not three hours ago, I looked as young as you, sorcerer." With a wheezing sigh, he fell back against the mattress, his reserves depleted.

"Appearances can be deceiving." Ciarran smiled grimly in acknowledgment of the dark, bitter venom, the putrid rot that ate away at him from the inside out. Only *he* knew the strength of the darkness that was his daily battle. Not even his comrades, the Compact of Sorcerers, knew the worst of it.

"Hnn." Matthew nodded. "So it is gone? Killed?"

"Your demon is terminated, bound to you no longer."

"And so I am free. I knew it. Sensed the very instant it was gone." Matthew looked at Clea, pausing to take a rasping breath. His words were punctuated by shallow gasps for air. "You are the woman from the motel. I wanted a room. And the demon wanted you."

"I know," she whispered. "I found that out pretty quickly."

"I tried to lock it in until I could get to the city, to an alley. Let it feed on a pimp or a murderer." He paused, sucked in a rattling gasp of air, and when he spoke, his voice was faint and labored. "I couldn't stop it, not completely, but over the years I gained some knowledge, learned how to cast wards. In a room with a lock."

As though reminding her that she had turned him away, he nodded at Clea. "I had some say in its prey, and I tried to make it choose where I willed it."

The man's voice was so faint as to be almost inaudible. Ciarran leaned closer. "The demon broke from me tonight, proving that I had deceived myself. So long as I was close enough to maintain the link, it could move from my side. I had no power over it, no true influence." Labored breath, a rattling whisper. "It only chose to let me believe I did. Until tonight. Tonight its lust for her was stronger than its desire to trick me." He paused, made an obvious effort to rally his strength. "I am glad she is unharmed."

"As am I." Ciarran's gaze strayed to Clea, his gut wrenching at the thought of what might have been had the demon succeeded in capturing her. He slapped back the unfamiliar intensity of the emotion. He should have long ago stopped feeling anything. A soldier. A killer. He was an instrument in a battle between dimensions. Nothing more. And if he told himself that often enough, maybe someday it would be true.

He had never learned to stop caring altogether. Every death, every moment of grief that he sensed in the humans he protected, rubbed his senses like pumice rock. But this, this inexplicable anger, this feeling of utter rage at the thought of the slightest harm befalling Clea Masters, this was outside his experience.

My Clea, he thought. And the darkness inside him shifted restlessly, as though it, too, laid claim to her. An unsettling thought.

"I wanted to die the day after I summoned it," Matthew said, his voice thin and reedy. "You know, it was true to its word. It promised to take away the diphtheria, to save my wife. And it did. She got up from that bed as though she'd never been sick." He closed his eyes, and for an instant, Ciarran thought he would speak no more.

Clea shifted her chair closer, took the dying man's hand, offering what comfort a human touch could.

Fingers fluttering weakly, Matthew gave a wheezing sigh. "We loved and laughed and made foolish promises, and for the space of a whole day and a night, I thought I'd made such a fine bargain. Tie myself to a demon, let it stay here on earth, and in exchange I got my wife's life."

"And what happened after a day and a night?" Clea's voice, low and soft.

Matthew's head wobbled from side to side, too much weight for his rapidly failing frame. "In the morning, it ate her. My wife. Tore her throat open. Right in front of me. Her blood running in rivulets along the earthen floor, soaking the ground, turning it black." Tears coursed down the man's cheeks, and Ciarran could feel the pain wafting from him, still fresh and stark after so many decades.

"Ate her?" Clea whispered, her words edged with horror.

"I grabbed an axe, tried to kill it, and when that failed, I tried to kill myself. But I couldn't die. We were one. Bound as one. And that meant that *I* had killed my wife. Killed her. Not saved her." The breath left him in a rush. "In the early years, the demon ran amok. But later . . . later, I learned a little of how to keep it in check. I tried not to let it prey on innocents."

Kill him. The darkness writhed inside the glove, slithering restlessly. *Kill him.*

Ciarran's head jerked up. Clea was staring at him, eyes wide, as though she sensed the terrible swell of power.

Kill him.

Out. It wanted out, to kill and maim. To feed and grow stronger and take over all that he was.

With a low growl, his gaze locked on Clea's, Ciarran pushed back against the foul tide, and for the first time since the demon had taken his hand, the agony, the fight, was almost bearable. He frowned, confused.

Matthew coughed long and hard, blood welling from his lips. Ciarran cast his power with his right hand, wrapping the old man in magic, easing his pain.

"Matthew, have you seen others of your kind? Other keepers?" he demanded.

Matthew studied him, ancient blue eyes heavy with regret and the memories of a century of horror. "I've yet to see another. We were heading somewhere close, though. The demon would tell me nothing, but I sensed its growing excitement the farther north we moved. It was *called,* I am certain of it, leading me, talking of strength and numbers and the wall between dimensions. The realm of fire. The plane of man."

Clea was moving now, inching her way around the bed to shift closer, as though seeking his proximity. Leaning toward her, Ciarran let the side of his arm brush her shoulder and felt the instant surge of energy that spiked between them. She made a choked sound, surprise, perhaps dismay. But she did not break the connection.

"Go on." Ciarran bid the keeper, biting back his frustration. There was nothing new in the man's revelations. Nothing of use. He had hoped for more. Hoped for an explanation of the hum of threat and wrongness that spread through the *continuum,* an explanation for the reason that full demons, albeit minor ones, were walking unfettered in the human plane, unmatched by keepers. Alone, like the ones he had found in the alley some weeks past.

"We were going to open some sort of portal." Matthew rallied, his voice a little stronger, his words coming in a rush, as though he was driven to get them out before it was too late. "The demon said that with the help of the conduit, their leader, the Solitary, would come through the breach."

"Not while the Compact of Sorcerers guards this dimension. Even a conduit would not be strong enough to open the realms," Ciarran said, feeling Clea lean a little tighter against him. "Tell me the rest. How? How will it come to pass?"

A sinister dread rose up in him, even as he spoke the question. And suddenly, he knew. Knew with a horrific certainty, his own words supplying the key.

Not while the Compact of Sorcerers guards this dimension.

But what if they chose not to guard? What if the *Pact* was broken?

"Open the portal." Gasping, Matthew closed his eyes. "With the help of the conduit," he whispered. "And with the help of a sorcerer."

A betrayal.

"One of your own betrays you, sorcerer." Wheezing words whispered in a raspy voice. "One of your *own* summons the Solitary."

Chapter 8

CIARRAN SAT ON THE BENCH IN FRONT OF CLEA Masters's run-down tenement, watching the sun inch up over the horizon, pink and orange and red. Beautiful. Like Clea.

And he was pretty much crazy. He shook his head, wondering why he was so tied up he couldn't think straight.

He'd gotten her home last night, taken her to her apartment, to her bedroom, used a whisper of his power to cast her into much-needed sleep. Tugged her quilt up over her fully clothed body. He hadn't dared undress her, hadn't dared touch her.

Christe, just the thought of brushing his fingers over her soft, soft skin made him hard.

Leaning forward to rest his elbows on his knees, Ciarran watched a lone jogger approach from the west, chuffing along, moving east without so much as a glance in his direction.

No surprise. Ciarran was bending light, refracting and

reflecting its rays. To the human eye, he simply wasn't there.

And Ciarran desperately wanted to believe that *he* was looking for something that wasn't there. A traitor.

One of the Compact of Sorcerers.

One of his own.

Rage uncoiled in a powerful wave, and he steadied himself against it, feeling the demon parasite inside him revel as the black emotion gathered strength.

The demon-keeper's words ate at him. The thought of such betrayal revolted him, but he couldn't make himself doubt the truth of the old man's last warning. Everything made sense. The increasing arrogance of the *hybrids*. The sensation that something was wrong in the *continuum*. Minor demons stalking the earth without keepers, like the one he'd found in the alley slurping rat carcasses, and the one Darqun had found rifling through garbage. Lesser demons. Weak. But here in the world of man nonetheless.

Such things should be impossible; that they were happening only served to increase his certainty. There *was* a traitor within the Compact who was deftly slicing the wall, just enough to let advance minions through but not enough to raise an alarm.

Ciarran needed to find out who the hell it was.

The air stirred beside him, a small forewarning. The only one he needed.

"Twice in two days. If we keep meeting like this, I'm going to think it's lu-u-u-v." Darqun settled on the bench beside him, stretching his legs out in front and crossing them at the ankles. "Hope you know what the hell is going on here, 'cause I sure don't."

"You know as much as I do, but my gut is telling me we're in for a mess of trouble." Ciarran glanced at the other sorcerer. He'd already told Darqun all he knew, making a quick phone call to fill him in on the salient points before giving him Clea's address. Ever careful, Ciarran had considered the possibility that Darqun was the traitor and discarded it. Darqun was loyal.

Which left who? Javier? Baunn, with his quips and his jokes? Could he possess the skill and cunning to betray his own? Dain, the illusionist, with his love of showmanship?

One of his own contemporaries? A sorcerer? The thought made Ciarran sick.

Absently, he drummed his fingertips on his thigh. "You took care of the *hybrids* from the other night?"

"Not me. Javier. He insisted." Darqun laughed, a low sound, devoid of any real humor. He shot a glance at Ciarran. "You take care of the granddaughter?"

"Clea. Her name is Clea." Closing his eyes, Ciarran pictured her, a brave and valiant warrior clutching her plastic letter opener before her. "Yeah. I—" He pushed himself to his feet, paced, then turned and jutted his chin toward the building. "That's her apartment. Fifth floor."

Darqun looked around. "Why'd you bring her here? We're in the middle of *hybrid* heaven."

"She wanted familiarity. I figured that after what she'd been through, it wasn't a bad idea." At Darqun's blank look, Ciarran rubbed the back of his neck and shrugged. There had been limited choices. Bring her here or to his home. He had a distinct predilection to avoid long-term guests, preferring his solitude. No, *needing* his solitude, for the times that it took all he had to control the demon within. "She's safe. I cast wards to shield her. And as long as one of us guards her, none can reach her."

Darqun frowned at him, clearly bemused. "Okay. Where are *you* going?"

Now Ciarran smiled wryly. "Clea's a little nervous about the bike. I figured I'd switch it for a car."

His gaze slid away as Darqun lifted a brow incredulously.

"And she, uh, likes coffee, you know? I thought I'd get her some coffee," Ciarran muttered as he strode away, Darqun's whoop of laughter trailing after him like a tail.

Weird dreams. Clea threw her forearm across her eyes, shielding them from the light that streamed through the window of her bedroom. She could feel the warmth of the sun's rays on her skin and felt a pang of sadness, wishing that yesterday had dawned as bright and clear as today. It had been so hard to say good-bye to Gram with the sky dark and sullen, and the thin mist falling on the fresh grave. Gram had loved the sun.

Snuggling deeper under the thick quilt, Clea let her thoughts bounce around like a pinball off the bumpers, the morning's light helping to put everything in perspective. Gram. The funeral. That part had been real.

Wired Guy. The demon. Not so real.

And the sorcerer. *Whooo.* She *wished* that he'd been real.

Rolling to a sitting position, she realized she was still wearing her clothes. Nice. She didn't even remember falling into bed last night. All she remembered were the nightmares.

She'd dreamed of the crash, dreamed of the fire, the terrible sound of rending metal, then the silence. Pain. So much pain. And the feeling that she was never going to get up off the cold, wet ground.

Then she'd dreamed of him, Ciarran, there with her, cloaked in light and glimmering filaments.

In her dreams, he'd been at the Blue Bay, too, last night, the only thing standing between her and a demon with its rows of jagged, razor-sharp teeth. Same guy, different nightmare. Ciarran D'Arbois. The sorcerer.

She sucked in a breath, almost believing she could smell the delicious, sexy scent of his skin, remembering the way the aroma had wrapped her in its luscious embrace as she hugged his leather jacket around her. Shaking her head, her palm pressed flat against her lips, she told herself it was crazy. There was no guy.

Rising, she hesitated, clenching and unclenching her fists. In two steps, she was at her closet door, yanking it open and riffling through the contents. No butter-soft, megaexpensive leather jacket, even though she could swear he'd settled it over her shoulders to keep her warm. She gave a snort of laughter. Of course. There was no jacket because *there was no guy.*

It was all just a weird dream, the product of a grieving mind. Her angst-ridden, overwrought, grief-stricken mind. Funny, she'd never thought of herself as the hysterical sort. Solid, rational, uncomplicated Clea Masters. That was her. Except for the rare occasions when her insides spun themselves into a knot, and a flare of energy erupted from her body, protecting her from harm.

That part wasn't so rational or uncomplicated, but

given the rarity of its appearance, she figured she could overlook it.

Raking one hand through her hair, she wandered barefoot along the hall to the tiny kitchen, yanked open the cupboard door, searching for the coffee can. The sun streamed through the yellowed lace curtain, filling the old kitchen with light, dancing across the countertop. She glanced around and spotted the empty can in the pile of recyclables that needed to be carried out.

Damn.

She tapped one finger on the counter.

Actually, it was a perfect day to be out of coffee. A walk in the sunshine to the corner market would do her good. Clea felt her spirits rise, just a little.

She was tempted, so tempted, to splurge on a caramel corretto with whipped cream. Closing her eyes, she could imagine the delicious taste, the creamy texture. But that was nuts. Cash was so tight. She still owed half the money for Gram's burial, and her next installment payment for tuition was coming due. For what it would cost her for a single corretto, she could buy a whole tin of coffee that would last for weeks.

Forget the corretto. The momentary thrill wasn't worth the price.

In a few minutes she was showered, scrubbed clean, dressed in jeans and a bright pink sweater. She felt like she really needed that punch of color. Crossing to the front door, she paused, wistfully studying the framed photo of her and Gram. Her gaze shifted to the vase of old dried flowers that were slowly disintegrating, leaves and bits of petals breaking off to dust the small tabletop.

Kind of like her life.

Bits and pieces falling apart. Gram dead. Medical school feeling more wrong every day. The bills piling up like autumn leaves under a maple tree.

She needed to make some decisions, but not right now. It wasn't like her to procrastinate. Usually, she faced her problems, made a decision, and moved on. But she supposed it was a smart woman who realized that she might be pushing it a little too close to the edge. So right now, she just wanted to do something normal, something uncomplicated, like going out to buy coffee.

Shaking her head, she unlocked the dead bolt and opened the door.

Shock sent her heart skittering to a stop; then it started beating again, so hard she could feel it knocking against her ribs. With a gasp, she pressed one hand against the doorjamb for support, taking an involuntary step back.

He was there. The sorcerer, Ciarran, right outside her door, the weight of his powerful body resting on one shoulder as he leaned negligently against the wall. His honey gold hair was loose around his shoulders, and dark sunglasses hid his stunning iridescent eyes.

Man, oh, man. He was everything she'd thought he was, and more. Clea swayed, feeling light-headed. She wet her lips. Not a dream. God. He wasn't a dream, which meant none of it was a dream. Not the gorgeous guy. Not the dead demon. None of it. He was real, so real that she felt his presence in every cell of her body.

Using his leather-encased index finger, Ciarran pushed the sunglasses down the bridge of his nose and looked at her over the rim. He studied her for minute, unsmiling.

"I brought caramel, chocolate, and vanilla. Oh, and a chai latte." He shrugged, pushed away from the wall until he was standing upright, filling the doorway. She realized he was holding a cardboard tray with four enormous cups of coffee, the aroma wafting toward her, making her mouth water. "I didn't know what you'd like."

You. I'd like you.

As though he read her thoughts, he smiled, the edges of his mouth curving up, slow and sexy. That mouth was unbelievable. Hard. A little cruel. Promising passion, inexplicable delight, the fulfillment of any dark fantasy.

A sharp coil of desire slid through her, shocking her, scaring her. She'd never been attracted to dominant, aggressive men, but, oh, the way he was looking at her, his gaze so hot, dragging her from a slow simmer to a rolling boil. Promising that he would have her, and she would have him. And it wouldn't be sweet and slow and gentle.

She swallowed. Suddenly, dominant and aggressive were looking damn good.

Oh, man. She wasn't just losing it. She was so far gone along the path that she had no chance of finding her way back.

"So, can I come in?" That rich, smoky voice held her in thrall.

"Sure." She stumbled back a step, and another. "Come on in." No sense in denying him. She had a feeling that even her dead bolt wouldn't hold up long if he decided he wanted in. Besides, if he'd wanted to hurt her, he would have done it last night.

Her gaze dropped to his gloved hand and the cardboard tray. He'd brought her a caramel corretto.

He filled up the entryway, carrying the rich aroma of coffee and caramel and chocolate with him.

Balancing the tray first in one hand, then the other, he shrugged out of his leather jacket, glanced around, and hung it on a peg behind the door. Then he reached up and drew off the glasses, folded them, and tucked them into the pocket of his coat.

Catching her looking at him, he flashed her what he must have thought was a reassuring smile, white teeth and curved lips and that sexy crease carving one cheek. Her knees almost buckled. When he looked at her like that, she didn't find it reassuring in the least.

God, he was gorgeous.

Clea blinked, wondering for a fraction of a second if he would disappear, a figment of her imagination. But, no, he was still there, and he took her breath away.

She turned, led the way into the kitchen, and lowered herself into a chair, watching him warily as he methodically removed each cup from the cardboard tray and set them on the table in a perfectly straight line. His movements were deft, his fingers long and strong. She stared at the leather glove on his left hand, curious, a little unnerved. A prickle of unease skittered along her spine.

"You ever take that off?" As soon as the words left her mouth, she felt terrible and wished she could call them back. It was none of her business.

He glanced at her. "No." His tone made it clear that the topic was off-limits. He waved his hand to encompass the coffee, and said, "Which one is your favorite?"

"Caramel." The word came out as a sigh.

Sinking down on the second chair, he slid one of the cups along the table toward her, his eyes glittering.

Gorgeous eyes. Blue and gray and gold and green, deep-set, framed by sinfully long lashes.

She dropped her gaze. He'd splayed his legs, knees apart, a purely masculine posture. She realized he was wearing different clothes than he'd had on the previous night, darker jeans with a tattooed pattern and a chocolate brown shirt with a subtle design in a slightly lighter shade, open at the top to reveal the solid column of his throat and a hint of muscled chest. Dark brown suede boots. She wasn't much for fashion, lacking both the finances and the inclination, but it didn't take a genius to realize he was probably wearing the equivalent of what she earned in a month.

He made a sound, drawing her attention.

"Sorry," she said as she glanced up. "I didn't even ask which one you wanted. I like the chocolate, too, so if you want the caramel, I don't mind."

"You do mind. But if I choose the one you want, you'll find a way to make do."

She opened her mouth to reply, then closed it. What to say to that? He was right. She always found a way to make do. Gram had raised her to find a path even in the roughest terrain.

A little flustered, she pressed her lips together. He'd known her less than a day, and yet he *knew* her.

"Go ahead. Sometimes you need to take what you want." With a half smile that made her think of forbidden fruit and really naughty secrets, he pushed the cup a fraction of an inch closer.

Sometimes you need to take what you want. Is that what he did? Took what he wanted?

"If you're certain . . ."

"Having sampled none of the options, I can't claim a preference."

"Oh." That surprised her. She was sitting in her kitchen with a man who hunted demons, and she was taken aback because he'd never tasted a corretto? Popping the lid off the coffee in front of her, she pushed it back across the table toward him. "You don't know what you're missing. Try it. You'll love it."

He blinked, closed those long, strong fingers around the paper cup, and took a sip. His brows rose, and his gaze shot to hers.

"Sweet." He sounded affronted, as though coffee should be anything but sweet.

With a laugh, Clea accepted the container as he handed it back to her. Her fingers brushed his. Less than a second. But, oh, the heat that poured through her from that innocuous contact. Her pulse sped up, and she spoke in a rush.

"You should taste it with whipped cream on top. Now that's sweet. I was fantasizing about it just this morning." *Fantasizing.* Maybe not the best word choice. Nervously, she pressed her mouth to the paper rim and tasted the coffee, only to realize that she had put her lips on the exact spot he had placed his.

She looked up to find him staring at her mouth, and she knew he hadn't missed what she had done. A bolt of heat shot through her.

"I was unaware of your preference for whipped cream." He turned his hand, a careless gesture, and a pulse of light shot from his finger, touching the cup, winding round it from bottom to top.

"Oh, my, God." There was a healthy pile of whipped

cream gracing the corretto, cream that definitely hadn't been there a second ago. "Oh, my, God."

She carefully set the cup on the table. *Breathe. Nice and slow.* She'd already known he wasn't quite human, had already watched him save her from a demon. But somehow, as they sat face-to-face in her homey little kitchen, with its familiar yellowed curtains and small wooden table, his trick with the whipped cream seemed enormous.

"What *are* you?" Clea whispered, pressing her palms flat on the table to keep her hands from shaking.

"I am High Sorcerer. Guardian of the wall between dimensions and all the human realm."

"All at once, huh?" She nodded slowly. "How about you explain that in plain English?"

He studied her for a long moment, and said, "I kick demon ass. I save the world."

His words seemed to come at her from far, far away.

"I don't believe you," she blurted.

"I don't do parlor tricks," he said flatly. "The whipped cream was a small demonstration because I figured you'd be disinclined to believe what you recalled from last night. We need to talk."

She thought about that for a minute and nodded. "Yeah, I guess we do."

One side of his mouth turned up in a sardonic smile, and there it was again, the long deep crease in his cheek that was so sexy it made the pit of her belly do a slow drop that left her breathless and more than a little flustered.

Without thinking it through, she reached out and touched his face, laying her fingers on his warm skin, feeling the rough stubble of his beard under the sensitive tips. His eyes widened, but he didn't pull away. She traced his jaw, dragged her fingers over his lower lip, and almost moaned aloud at the intensity of the heat that crashed through her.

There was a low hum in her fingertips, then a buzz, and finally it grew to an itch, like radio static converted to a touch. A surge of energy flared from Ciarran, and he jerked back, away from her fingers, the expression on his face as shocked as if she had punched him.

Heart pounding, she looked down at her hands, at the thin crackle of light that fanned from her fingertips, and she raised her eyes to his, a little awed. More than a little scared.

Moving so fast it made her gasp, he rose and came to stand in front of her, his muscled body towering over her as he closed his hand around her upper arm and drew her to her feet. A jolt of excitement and electricity sizzled through her, leaving her breath coming in short, sharp huffs through her parted lips.

"Christe," he said, his eyes dark and hot. Heavy-lidded.

He dragged her up against his solid body, heat and power swirling around them like a storm. A thrill shot along her veins, reckless exhilaration that burned away common sense and reason. All she wanted was his kiss, the taste of him, rich and warm on her tongue.

Catching her chin between his gloved fingers, he tipped her face and brought his mouth to hers, a light brush of his lips; then his tongue touched her, making her wet. Clea arched into him, a whimper of pure feminine pleasure pouring from her as he pushed inside and kissed her deeply, lips and tongue and teeth, a little rough, a little urgent, and so hot she felt singed. He was inside her, the luscious velvety stroke of his tongue sliding into her, tasting her.

Oh, God, his mouth. The way he moved it on hers, the heat of it, the carnal pleasure.

She sucked him deeper, her fingers twining in the long, silky strands of his hair, and she was half-crazy with wanting him, a burning hunger gliding through her, pooling between her thighs into an ache so strong it bordered on pain.

Dimly, she was aware of his light, his power, and hers, that thing inside her, coiling up, weaving from her into him, and him into her, joining them, a sharing as sensual as their kiss. And then she felt something else, a slow hiss of menace, something dark, something dangerous, slithering through him, a whisper of movement like a shark in still waters. Breaking the connection, she jerked back, eyes wide, and clamped her fingers around the chair back, certain she would collapse but for its solid support.

Chest heaving, she stared at him in confusion.

"What—" She couldn't ask, didn't know what to ask.

He looked down at her, eyes hard and bright, his breath coming harsh and fast. Swallowing, he backed up a step, his gaze shifting to his leather-gloved hand as he turned it slowly palm up, then palm down.

Power arced between them; then he pulled it back, leashing his magic. She knew it, sensed it, felt him slamming a door against her.

"Perhaps you asked the wrong question, Clea," he said, his voice rough. "You asked what *I* am." His gorgeous face grew deadly earnest, and his eyes, his beautiful, long-lashed, iridescent eyes watched her with a wary respect. "The better question might be, what exactly are *you*?"

Chapter 9

*C*IARRAN SQUELCHED A PANG OF REGRET. HE HADN'T meant to ask the question quite so bluntly, but he was unused to the ways of mortals, the need for carefully chosen words and layered meanings.

The better question might be, what exactly are you*?* Nicely done, D'Arbois. Glib. Well-spoken.

He hadn't meant to kiss her, touch her, either, but his regret was tempered by a swell of masculine satisfaction. The temptation to kiss her again tugged at him. Putting a careful distance between them, he returned to his side of the table, folding his tall frame to fit the wooden chair. Clea stared at him for an endless moment with those wide, dark eyes, assessing, measuring. She followed his lead, trying for a veneer of normalcy as she took her seat.

What the hell had he been thinking?

Nothing. He'd been thinking nothing, only feeling, wanting her with a fierce ache that gnawed at him, drove him. He wanted her still, wanted to take her there against the wall, pin her with his weight, sink inside the heat of her with her long legs wrapped around him, the sound of her pleasure singing in his ears.

He blew out a slow breath, shifted on his seat. Hell. He was a thousand years old, and kissing her had left him feeling as jacked as any teenager.

Leaning back in his chair, he watched emotions play across Clea's features. Confusion. Disbelief. Perhaps even fear.

And lacing all of it, the shimmer of sexual awareness that had yet to abate.

She picked up the cup of coffee, buying time to get her thoughts in order, he figured. Watching him over the rim, she took a sip. Her hand trembled just a bit.

Wise girl, to try to figure things out. She was a thinker, a planner, and a stark regret nagged at him because everything that had happened to her since he'd walked into the Blue Bay Motel had happened without giving her much time to think or plan or even adjust. But she had rolled with it, swayed and bent, letting the tide swirl around her. She was a survivor.

And he . . . well . . . he should have done a bit more thinking. For twenty years he'd thought of that night every time he looked at his damned gloved hand, but he hadn't spared a thought for the child he had healed. In a turmoil of pain, his body and emotions ravaged by Asag's attack that night, he had trusted Darqun to ascertain that with her parents dead, there was someone to raise her. A grandmother. Responsibility met, he had put her from his mind, never contemplating the fact that the child who had siphoned his magic on a blood-drenched road might grow into a woman who would carry that power for eternity. A woman who could purloin not just one filament, but half his magic, or more, linked to him, taking what was his, what was the sole protection of all her kind.

The more she drew, the weaker he became, leaving him open to the insidious swell of the demonic parasite that ate at him.

No, he had not considered it, because such a thing had never happened. Sorcerers were rare, a breed born of *two* sorcerer parents. When two of magical bent imprinted one another, their power joined as well, flowing between them, stronger, bigger. Their child would be a sorcerer, coming to full power at the completion of puberty, aging until full adulthood, then aging no more.

The offspring of a mortal-sorcerer match might have a kernel of magic, a whisper, just enough to give him or her what humans called a sixth sense, but not enough to draw on in the manner of a full sorcerer. He had never heard of a human child pulling power from a sorcerer. An impossibility that had become reality for him the night he lost his hand and Clea her parents.

He had thought such connection impossible.

She had proved him wrong. Whether she willed it or not, she had the capacity to draw from him as a bonded sorcerer would, yet because her power did not match his own, she had nothing to give back.

She would weaken him. Slowly. Inexorably. She would take his magic, steal his barriers and protections against the demon seed that writhed and twisted inside him.

And he'd be completely to blame. What had happened just now when he kissed her, when he molded his mouth and body to hers, was proof enough of that.

He'd reveled in it. In her response. In the mewl of utter pleasure that had escaped from her mouth into his. In the pounding of her heart and the way her fingers had tangled in his hair, pulling him closer, tighter. But their connection, the way she'd called his magic, both light and dark, was perilous.

He wanted her to want him, to crave him, to burn for him with a fierce and lush intensity. And he wanted her safe. Which put him in direct opposition with himself.

Beautiful, brilliant, sensual Clea Masters.

His emotions swirled as he stared at her, and something swelled inside him, whispering, demanding, just as it had last night.

My Clea. Yes. He wanted to claim her.

His ruined hand tingled, and a slow, shadowy burn spread through him. He knew she'd sensed it, felt the dark coil of menace that he fought so hard to hold in check. It had frightened her.

Smart girl.

He'd been living with it for twenty years, and the way it had swelled, snaking out toward her, wanting her . . . hell, it had almost frightened *him.*

She took another sip of coffee. Anything, he thought, rather than focus on him. She was wary now, her gaze skittering from his.

Blood pounded through him, hot and thick, as he watched her lick whipped cream from her upper lip, her tongue making a slow sweep that he longed to follow with his own tongue.

Everything about her turned him on. Her plain, conservative sweater hiding a sexy bra beneath. Inexpensive jeans with a low-rise waist. He'd caught a glimpse of her black thong underwear as she'd moved around the table to take her seat. He wanted to see her in that thong—and nothing else.

The hum of desire buzzed through him, and riding it, the sharp edge of darkness writhing inside the leather-and-alloy glove, trying to wriggle free. It wanted out. It wanted her.

Christe. What the hell was he thinking? He couldn't have her. The risk was too great.

"So you're what? Some kind of magician?" Clea set the cup down on the table with meticulous care and raised her eyes to his.

Ciarran jerked, clenching his fist as he battled the urge to reach out and touch her. She'd called him a *magician.* He ought to be offended, but he wasn't sure he cared. He just wanted to touch her.

"So last night, at the Blue Bay, when the . . . uh . . . demon came after you, it scratched your arm through the leather of your jacket. I watched you bleed." Her attention shifted to the skin of his arms, unmarked, unbroken, and she frowned. "I *saw* you bleed. Which means that you're human and that whatever you did was some kind of trick, right?"

"I am no magician, Clea. I am High Sorcerer."

"Isn't that the same thing?"

"No."

"Okay. So you are High Sorcerer," she mused softly, repeating his earlier explanation as though trying the words on for size. "Guardian of the wall." She cocked her head to one side, and a frown etched small creases between her brows. "So then you can tell me now"—she held one hand in front of her, trembling, sparking faint

filaments of light, and she spread her fingers wide—
"*what exactly am I?*"

She raised her gaze to his, eyes slightly narrowed,
such a serious, intent look, but instead of the terror and
confusion he expected, there was only interest. Watch-
fulness. A huge dose of curiosity. He wasn't surprised
to find that Clea focused on learning rather than being
afraid.

"This light, my light . . . is it . . . magic?" she asked.
"Like yours? Will it do what yours did"—her voice
caught—"to that demon? Do I have to be worried that
I'll be walking through the grocery store and end up
shredding things?" She shivered. "Shredding people?"

He threw back his head and laughed, an amazingly
rich, sinfully appealing sound. Clea closed her eyes for a
moment and just listened, letting it wash over her, stroking her senses.

"Bloodthirsty, are you?" God, when he smiled like
that, she didn't think she'd ever seen anything more
dazzling. He didn't look as tough or menacing when he
smiled.

And that just made her wonder what the hell she was
doing, thinking of climbing all over a guy who had to be
the scariest human being she'd ever met.

She looked at him, considering his question. "Not
even slightly bloodthirsty. No, I just want to understand
the big picture. Get an idea of where I fit in."

"Ah. A sensible approach."

Yep. That was her. Sensible. Which was why it made
no sense that she was sitting in her kitchen, actually

believing he was some sort of . . . what? Warlock? Sorcerer? Protector of all mankind?

Because she'd seen that demon last night. Smelled it. Felt the burn of its flesh on the skin of her cheek. Absently, she raised her hand, ran her fingers along the skin of her face, and felt . . . nothing. No burn. No scab. She remembered Ciarran touching her cheek and the sensation of electric energy arcing into her.

What in heaven's name was going on here? Her idea of reality was doing a quick about-face, and she had the feeling that she didn't have much choice in the matter.

"So what's really going—"

Ciarran's eyes narrowed, and he held up his ungloved hand, his movement and the harsh expression on his face cutting short her words. Tension laced his features, as though he was listening for some almost imperceptible sound. Rising, he spun a slow circle, his body beginning to glow, first with a faint light, then stronger, and stronger still. The look on his face was intense. Dangerous.

Clea's stomach took a long, slow roll, as it always did when her power swelled. A shiver of nervousness twitched through her body. The faint lights dancing across her fingertips snapped and popped, and suddenly, she was on alert, sensing some unseen threat. She had a suspicion that Ciarran knew exactly what it was.

"We must leave, Clea. Now." He held out one hand toward her, and even at a distance, she could feel the raw energy sparking from his fingertips. "This apartment is at the center of a *hybrid* warren."

She didn't understand any of this, and something inside her balked. "*Hybrid* warren?" She stared at his hand warily, uncertain if she should take it or not.

"I had not thought they would dare come for you with me here. Perhaps I overvalued the deterrent presented by the presence of a sorcerer." The corner of his mouth lifted in a self-mocking smile.

Slowly, she got to her feet, her gaze darting to the door of the kitchen, and somehow, despite the sunlight that streamed through the window, she felt the darkness, the threat. Suddenly she wasn't just wary. She was afraid.

"I set wards this morning before I went in search of your coffee, but it is better if we leave. The strength of the spells fade with time, and they have been in place many hours."

"Wards? What—"

"Too late," he muttered. Closing his hand about her wrist, he yanked her behind him.

Clea pressed up against Ciarran's back, her heart pounding, her mouth dry. His muscled body was taut, vibrating with energy even though he stood perfectly still. Heart slamming against her ribs, she made a quick decision. Whatever they were about to face, she'd let him take the lead. He definitely had more experience at this than she did.

Because how many third-year med students who worked night shift at a motel knew anything about demons and *hybrids* and magic?

Ciarran's power swirled around her, warm, strong, and she felt her insides coil and twist, as though moving in synchronicity with the glowing strands. She closed her eyes, focused on the steady thud of his heart. While hers was pounding wildly, his was not. Maybe sorcerers didn't get scared.

Without thought, she pressed tighter against his back, drawing comfort from his warm solidity.

A dark pain snaked through her, gliding, twirling, and she gasped at the intensity, so much stronger than she'd ever felt before. Razor-sharp agony bit through her skin from the inside out, and her power burst from her, doubling her over, spewing in every direction in a haphazard pulsing wave of light and strength.

She heard a crash as a chair flew back and hit the wall; then the three untouched cups of coffee followed suit, splattering corretto and chai latte wildly across the pale wall.

"*Christe.*" Jerking away from her, Ciarran dropped her wrist as though she'd burned him. "Pull it back, Clea."

Pull it back? Was he talking about the pulse of light that was hacking through her like a butcher's cleaver?

"I don't know how," she cried.

With a low moan, she pressed her forearm against her belly, struggling to stand upright, and the light just kept pulsing out of her in haphazard spurts. She was breathing in a pattern, two short gasps in, one long slow push out, concentrating, focusing on that instead of on the pain.

Her body felt clammy, cold, despite the hot wave that poured out of her. She wanted it to stop. It had never done this before. Never. The light usually pulsed out once, only once, knocking back whatever it was that threatened her, and then it would slide away, back to wherever it had come from. But this was different. Stronger. More chaotic. This constant throb, the feeling of unbelievable intensity, was new. With concentrated effort she stuck with her breathing pattern, swaying, but managing to stay on her feet.

With a glance at her over his shoulder, Ciarran reached out, as though to touch her again. And then he made a sound of frustration and dropped his hand back to his side.

There was no movement, no sound, but suddenly Clea knew they weren't alone anymore. Certainty swelled within her, bitter and cold. Something was coming for them.

Her head jerked up, and she stared at the kitchen doorway, waiting, her blood frozen in her veins, her heart beating in an erratic dance. There was a sharp bang as her front door slammed against the wall. The sound of heavy footfalls carried from the hallway. For some crazy reason, all Clea could think of was short, round Mrs. Garfinkle in the apartment downstairs and how the noise would upset her.

A current of air swirled through the kitchen doorway, thick and pungent, carrying the stink of death and decay, the smell reminiscent of the demon last night, but not quite as strong.

She couldn't breathe. Her chest felt tight, blocked.

Two men slunk toward them, and behind them two more. She registered the appearance of the man closest to her, thick and barrel-chested, his face brutal. Then her eyes locked on his, and in that instant she realized he wasn't a man at all. His eyes were bottomless pits, soulless, the entire socket filled by a round black marble with no white showing, no color. Whatever it was, this thing wasn't human.

A chill of certainty scurried across her skin. It was here for her.

Well, bully for him, because she had no intention of letting him get her.

With her forearm pressed tight across her belly, she backed up a step, and another, toward the counter and the butcher block of knives. Her breath chuffed in and out. No. Not a knife. She needed something heavy she could wield. Gram's rolling pin.

Ciarran glanced at her, his body tense, and when he moved, it was so fast, she could do little more than let out a startled squawk. He yanked her hard against him, wrapping his arms around her, half-carrying, half-dragging her across the kitchen. Then he leaped, catapulting them both up and over the ancient counter, his booted feet punching through the window above it.

A wild, terrified cry escaped her. Clea was aware of the sound of breaking glass and splintering wood, the shards that flew in all directions, the steady thud of Ciarran's heart; then they were falling, hurtling through air and space, the ground rushing up to meet them.

Chapter 10

CLEA WAS AWARE OF COLD AIR ON HER FACE AND the frantic blur of windows and brick wall rushing past. Spinning them in midair, Ciarran twisted beneath her to take the blow as they landed with a heavy *thump* on the grass. A wave of nausea crashed through Clea, the impact forcing the breath from her lungs.

Five stories. They'd fallen five stories.

He had to be dead, or smashed to pieces. And *she* ought to be dead.

"Come on," Ciarran snarled, pushing himself upright. Blood dripped from his shoulder, running down his arm.

Words tumbled out of her in a wheezing rush. "*OhMyGodOhMyGodOhMyGod—*"

He yanked her to her feet, and as she swayed, he glanced up at something behind her. With a muttered curse, he hauled her against his side and sprinted forward, half-carrying, half-dragging her to a sleek black car parked illegally at the curb. The landlord, Mr. Koschitsky, would have a fit if he saw that.

Ripping open the door, Ciarran shoved her in and bolted to the other side. In the mirror, she watched the men. . . . were they men? She didn't think so because no one could have made it down the stairs that fast. God. Whatever they were, they cleared the front door of the building just as Ciarran rammed the car in gear and peeled away from the curb.

Clea's hands shot out, the right one digging into the grab-handle, the left grasping at the console as the car flew along the street. Trembling, she uncurled her fingers and fumbled with the seat belt, taking three tries before she finally got the pieces to snap together with a solid *click*.

Ciarran glanced at her, his gaze running over her from crown to toes, as though assessing any damage. Apparently satisfied, he returned his attention to the road.

Swallowing, she stared at the blood trickling down his arm, at the brutal scrape on his shoulder. He'd been hurt because of those *things* that were after *her*. The realization made her light-headed. Leaning forward as far as the seat belt would allow, she lowered her head between her knees.

The roar of the engine filled the car. Sitting up just in time to wish she hadn't, she tried to decide what was worse, watching the scenery whiz past or hiding her head in the sand like an ostrich. She let out a startled squeak as Ciarran nosed the front bumper about a centimeter away from an enormous truck that lumbered along in front of them. Obviously unhappy with the delay, he did a smooth lane change into the path of oncoming traffic.

She couldn't help it. She screamed. Long and loud.

"Shh." He shifted back again, into the proper lane, only now they were in front of the truck.

"Oh, my God." He was going to get her killed. Clea let go of the console and slapped her palm against the dashboard, pressing her right foot hard against the floorboards as though slamming on the brakes. Only it didn't have the desired effect. The engine roared, and the car went faster, leaving Clea wishing that they were on the motorcycle he'd driven last night. And how crazy was that? But at least Ciarran had shown some respect for the speed limit when he'd been driving the bike.

The four . . . *hybrids*. Were they back there? Following them? The thought made her stomach do a sick flip. Her palms were slippery on the interior leather, and her hand skidded across the dash as she twisted around in her seat to look out the back window. Her fingers slammed against the volume control of the radio, and suddenly the car was filled with the pounding beat of some death metal band she couldn't name.

Which did nothing for her nerves. Her heart was pounding, and her temples were throbbing.

Through the back window, she watched the outline of her apartment building growing smaller and smaller in the distance, and in front of it, something that looked suspiciously like her beat-up, rusted-out 1979 Chevy Nova.

The one she'd left at the motel last night. The one she definitely hadn't driven home.

Her attention jolted from her car to the road.

"I don't think they're following us," she yelled, then

shook her head and reached over to turn down the volume. "Maybe we can slow down."

Her mouth as dry as a protein bar, she tried to steady her nerves. A full-blown panic attack would not be a good thing just now, but she really, really hated to be in the passenger seat, and she hated it even more when the driver was reckless.

Ciarran glanced at her and smiled, his left hand holding the wheel in a relaxed grip, his right hand on the shifter. Maybe that was why he wore the leather glove. For driving.

He caught the direction of her gaze, and something flashed in his eyes, something not quite frightening. But almost.

She shivered, studied his grip, his posture. Okay. So the driver wasn't reckless. He was driving way too fast, but for some reason, her fear was diminishing to a manageable level. Which was crazy, because she had a healthy respect for cars, recognizing them for the weapons of death that they were.

"You're fine, Clea. I can't get in an accident," he reassured her, his expression somber.

"You can't? Because of your insurance rates, you mean?"

He laughed, the sound rich and deep. "No. Because it is not possible for me to make that sort of miscalculation. Accidents are errors in human judgment. I am not human."

Okay. A reassuring thought. In some ways. The "I can't get in an accident" way. Not so reassuring in the "I'm not human" way.

"You never make mistakes?" she demanded, not even trying to temper the incredulity that laced her words.

His gaze shifted to his gloved hand, then back to the road. For a heartbeat, he said nothing, then, "Yeah. One."

His tone killed any intention she might have had of asking which one.

Okay. Next topic. "So . . . um . . . what were they, those things . . . ? You called them *hybrids*."

"They were human, once. But no longer. Think of them as converts to the cult of the damned. No soul. Just darkness."

"Yeah. I picked that up." She shuddered, thinking of their eyes, devoid of life or warmth. Windows to empty, hollow shells. No conscience, no remorse. Deader than Wired Guy, and she had thought at the time that he was the bleakest it could get.

"But you—umm—said that you're not human, so . . . are you the same thing that they are?" Oh, that was such a not good thought.

The look he shot her spoke volumes. Next question.

"So, how did they just show up in my kitchen? And why today?" She focused on him, on the thick fall of sun-shot hair and the profile too perfect to be real. Because if she looked out the window, at the rapid blur of buildings and trees flying past, it was going to put an end to any hope she had of hanging on to her control.

She'd been hunted by a demon.

Filaments of light shredding demon hide, leaving only oozing, sizzling remains.

Hunted by *hybrids*.

A window. They'd jumped out a fifth-story window.

Kissed by a sorcerer.

God. No one had ever made her feel like that.

All in the space of twelve hours.

"Demons cannot cross planes without a portal, so at times they send *hybrids* to do their dirty work. *Hybrids* can travel in the human realm at will, but they lack true magic. They are walkers."

Of course. That explained everything. "So how are *hybrids* different than demon-keepers?"

"Demon-keepers are those who summon while they still have life. They are chained to a demon in the human realm. *Hybrids* are those who summon at the time of death. They lack the life force to bring the demon over, so instead, they are"—he drummed his fingers on the dash—"*infected* by a demon. That would be the easiest way to describe it."

"So demon-keepers are alive and *hybrids* are half-dead?"

He shot her a glance. "Close enough."

"And they showed up in my kitchen because . . . ?"

"Because of you. The demon failed to obtain you last night, but he left a trail, so they knew where to look. The Blue Bay Motel." He downshifted, slowed just a little, and her breath came just a little easier.

"How did they find my apartment?"

"One of two sources. You keep your insurance in the glove box?"

She nodded.

"Then they got your address from that, or from your employment record in the motel office."

She could only wonder why his explanation made her panic less rather than more. The fact that the walking dead *hybrids* were stalking her was terrifying, but, oh, she had a reasonable explanation of how they had found her, and that made her feel so much better.

Staring out the front window, she watched the scenery change from the crowded low-rise tenements of her neighborhood to open highway. Gray blocklike industrial buildings flanked them.

Demons. Magic. She glanced at Ciarran, trying to figure it out, figure him out. Why was a—what had he called himself—a High Sorcerer driving a man-made vehicle rather than using magic to transport himself from one place to another?

With a frown, she realized how crazy it was, sitting here in a car that was going way too fast for health or safety, wondering why a man who wasn't quite human was driving said car. A shaky little laugh escaped her.

"So . . . why are you driving? A motorcycle? A car? Why don't you . . . I don't know . . . just ride some kind of wave to get where you want to go?"

She leaned a little to her left, just enough to get a glimpse of the speedometer, and immediately wished she hadn't. They were flying. *Flying.* She was a woman who never drove a single mile over the speed limit, and here she was, clinging madly to the grab-handle of a car that was eating up the road in hungry leaps.

Sucking in a breath, she pushed down on the door lock. Better late than never.

"Ride some kind of wave? Like a surfer?" His smoky voice was laced with humor.

"Can you do that?" she asked.

"What? Surf?"

She sent him a quelling look, and he laughed again,

the sound tumbling over her, decadent as a long, hot shower.

"There is the issue of, well, let's call them unwanted hitchhikers," he said. "*Hybrids* can steal transport on the trail left by magic. But if I travel by human vehicle, they must do the same. They possess few enhancements of magic, but they are adept at utilizing the remnants that others leave behind."

"So they're like scavengers."

He smiled darkly. "In more ways than you imagine."

Which brought all sorts of disgusting images to mind.

"But you *can* travel on magic?" she asked.

"Yes. But you can't." He paused. "Not yet."

Chapter 11

Y OU HAVE DISAPPOINTED ME." ASA PALEY WALKED
a slow circle around the four *hybrids,* reveling in
the scent of their unease. They were afraid, all of them,
and the one who had led them on their ill-fated retrieval
mission, Baal, was most afraid of all.

Pausing behind the group, Asa studied them, their
posture, the faint trembling of their limbs. His fury escalated, and he embraced the feeling, the strength of it.
They had failed him. They knew the price of failure.

If he let such behavior pass unaddressed, then other
hybrids would dare to let small failures grow, dare to put
forth less than their best efforts. Such could not be toler-
ated. The Solitary was due to arrive soon, and all must
be in perfect readiness.

Hybrids were disposable. Replaceable. Their value
determined only by their weakest link.

This small group had thrust themselves into the spot-
light, put themselves in his sights, and so they became
his prey.

Asa circled them, slowly, slowly, inhaling the sharp metallic scent of their terror. Not one of them had the courage to so much as glance at him. They stood, feet planted shoulder-width apart, arms at their sides, bodies rigid. Their posture might have been military, save for the fact that they dared not look straight ahead. None dared raise his eyes from the floor.

With a thought, Asa dropped the temperature in the cavernous space, the inside of the warehouse growing frigid. The *hybrids'* breath came out in white puffs, and the trembling of their limbs escalated until they were shaking from the cold.

Their physiology was more human than demon, and they were subject to many human weaknesses. Cold. Heat. Fatigue.

Pain.

Asa knew their limitations. He enjoyed exploiting them, had counted on them when he chose the place of their meeting, a deserted warehouse in a run-down industrial park. There were no neighbors to question any *unusual* sounds. Perfect for what he had in mind.

He glanced at the row of *hybrids*, inhaled the lovely scent of their growing panic.

Sometimes, only the harshest of lessons would do.

He had set them the simplest of tasks. Walk in the world of man. Find one woman, a particular woman, special, unique. In that, they had succeeded.

Bring her to him.

In that, they had failed.

Perhaps not such a simple task after all. Clea Masters had proven wilier, more slippery than the *hybrids* had expected. An adversary of some worth. Which only escalated the excitement of the hunt.

He knew she was no easy prey. He knew much about her, pretty, sweet Clea, with her tender heart and even more tender flesh.

Far in a corner, a drop of water hit the concrete floor with a distinct *ping*. Then another. And another. Asa measured his tread, slow, steady, drawing out the moment for his maximum pleasure as he walked past each quivering underling and moved to face the leader of the small group. In the silence, the sound of the dripping water was a steady marker of the passage of time, and he knew they found the sound inordinately loud. Frightening.

He stopped in front of Baal, a squat, barrel-chested *hybrid* with battered features. In his human life, he had obviously been a man who lived hard and rough. In his *hybrid* life he had been ruthless, cruel. They were wonderful characteristics, but the man was also stupid and overly arrogant, rather unpleasant qualities that had been minimally balanced by his ability to understand and follow instruction. Until now.

Asa reached out and laid the palm of his hand on the *hybrid*'s head, a gentle movement. He stroked the short strands of hair, enjoying the texture, enjoying Baal's shudder of sheer terror even more.

"You know you have disappointed me, Baal," he said, leaning in so that his quiet words were spoken directly beside the *hybrid*'s ear, yet the echo reverberated through the empty space, clear enough for the others to hear.

"My most humble apologies, my lord. I will not fail again." The *hybrid* kept his eyes downcast, and in his voice Asa heard genuine regret. And fear. Terrible stark fear.

Lovely.

"No. No, you will not fail again." Asa's skin slithered along his frame like discarded clothing, and he let the mirage fade away, his handsome features melting and changing, leaving a dreadful visage. He laughed, hot demon breath scorching the skin of Baal's ear and cheek.

With an unintelligible cry, the *hybrid* jerked back. Asa smiled, releasing the full impact of his rows of jagged, razor-sharp teeth, and he let his claws elongate where he yet rested his hand on the *hybrid*'s head. The sharp talons sank into Baal's scalp, through skin and fascia and the thin layer of muscle that covered the bone, and yes, there, with a horrible scraping sound, they went through the bones themselves.

Exquisite. The sensation was superb.

Baal squirmed, moaned, a fish on a hook, struggling desperately for freedom.

Two of the three remaining *hybrids* skittered sideways, away from Baal, away from the river of blood that they knew would soon stain the cracked concrete beneath their feet. The third *hybrid* held his place, eyes glued to the floor, body rigid as the sounds of his comrade's desperate thrashing swelled and echoed in the vast empty space. Asa's smile grew wider. He was well pleased by the third *hybrid*'s actions. Perfect. The small group had a new leader, and once they had acclimatized to that fact, he would round out their number with a new recruit.

Or he would kill them. He had yet to decide which option suited his pleasure.

"Watch," he commanded. "Watch, and remember." What they would see was his insurance of their continued efforts on his behalf. The threat of slow dismemberment was strong influence indeed.

Their terror, their horror, would only add to his delight.

One of them sank to the frigid concrete floor, his legs giving way beneath him. The other two managed to stay on their feet, trembling, sweating.

But they all followed his directive. None of them dared look away.

Holding his captive in place with the claws of his left limb, Asa unsheathed those on his right. Long and pointed and sharp, they gleamed in the thin light that filtered through the grungy windows set high up in the wall.

With careful attention and barely contained relish, Asa proceeded to carve the main course.

Slowly. Deliberately.

Until, finally, the screams stopped and the only sound that remained was a soft *slurp* as Asa sucked the last of Baal's blood from his fingers.

Chapter 12

I NEED TO STOP AT A GROCERY STORE. AND I NEED TO get to a kitchen. And—" Clea stopped abruptly and looked around the interior of the car. She'd grown quiet after he'd answered her questions about traveling on waves of magic—a strangely apt description. He'd figured she needed to sort things through, so he'd turned on an all-news station and let her be.

Now, all of a sudden she started talking again, fast and a little breathless. "My purse. I don't have my purse." She sounded panicked. Genuinely distraught.

Ciarran glanced at her. There was glass in her hair. Hell. He'd done that to her, taken her through a double-paned window. Slowly, he reached out and freed the glittering shard from a silky brown curl.

"What is it you need, Clea?" He would get it for her. Anything. Everything.

"My purse. It has my money. And today's the third Saturday." She said the words as though they ought to mean something to him.

Dark eyes wide, soft pink lips slightly open, glossy hair tumbled and mussed, she looked like she'd just climbed out of bed. And he definitely should not be letting his thoughts drift in that direction.

Her attention dropped to his bloodied shoulder, and she frowned. "I should see to that. Clean it, at the very least."

"Unnecessary." Ciarran passed his hand over the wound, cleaning it, partially healing it, repairing the shirt that covered it. He still felt the pain, still needed to heal from the inside, but magic did a good job of clearing out the worst of the wound's appearance.

"Wow. Okay. Wow." She swallowed. "That was . . . wow."

Her reaction made him smile. She faced demons and *hybrids* without flinching, but he used the most basic magic, and she was impressed. Maybe he ought to drag a rabbit out of a goddamned hat.

He returned his attention to the road, knowing that if he kept looking at her, her sexy, pouty mouth, her rumpled curls, her big, expressive eyes, he would pull over onto the wide, paved shoulder that ran along the side of the road, drag her across the center console, into his arms, into his lap, put his mouth on hers, his tongue inside her.

Christe. She was making him crazy.

And she deserved better. She was grieving for her dead grandmother. She was facing a reality so far outside her normal experience that it was as if she'd just been launched into the stratosphere. Her world was coming apart at the seams, and he was coming apart with sheer, hard-edged lust.

Wonderful.

One would think that in a thousand years, he would have learned some self-control. But that was the problem. He did have control, perfect control. Only, apparently it was less than perfect, because five minutes alone with Clea Masters wiped it out completely.

It had been a long time, years, since he had been with a woman. Not that he didn't enjoy sex. He did. But joining with a woman by necessity required a certain deliberate vulnerability, a lowering of his guard, an exposure he was unwilling to chance.

After he lost his hand, he'd taken that chance only once, and the memory of the girl's terrified face as she shrank from him, pressing herself back against the headboard, made him sick. She had invited his touch, pleaded for it. In an unguarded instant he had failed to hold the darkness at bay, and she had somehow sensed what he was. He swallowed, forcing the ugly recollection to the furthest corner of his mind.

The memory was a bitter tonic, the only saving grace the fact that he'd held it together long enough for her to get the hell out of there before he had a chance to do any harm. *Would* he have done her harm? *Could* he? Questions he could not answer. The experience was not one he had chosen to repeat. After that, all his energies remained focused on maintaining his rigid control, on holding back the venom that writhed inside him, seeking release.

Then, last night, he had seen Clea Masters, watched her move, fluid grace and bright intent, seen deep inside of her, valor and intellect and sheer guts. He'd been amazed at her courage, the way she'd grabbed a plastic blade to fend off a demon, the way she'd seized her own fear and wrestled it to the ground, climbing on his motorcycle despite a terror so strong he could feel it pulsing from her in waves. He had wanted her with a near overpowering urgency.

His desire for her had only grown. Sitting here next to her, the scent of her—vanilla and a little bit of caramel—teasing his senses, he wanted to taste her again so badly it hurt. And that had nothing to do with darkness and everything to do with light. Her light. The one that shone from her soul. Goodness and kindness and mercy. An old cliché, but one that applied. Clea Masters knew nothing about the malevolence, the evil, the soulsucking ugliness that was his constant companion.

He flexed his ruined hand, aware that she was watching him, waiting, expecting some reply.

"What's so special about the third Saturday?" he asked, shifting gears and lanes to pass slower traffic.

"I have to feed them. Louise and Maggie and Brian. Everyone. They'll be waiting for me. Expecting me. Gram and I have been doing it for years." Tucking a curl behind her ear, she paused, then pressed her palm against the dash and leaned forward to look out the front window, a frown creasing her brow.

"Okay." He had no idea what she was talking about, but it was obviously important to her. Which, oddly, made it important to him.

"There." She pointed at the big blue Wal-Mart sign. "Let's go shopping." Her voice was high, too bright. Definitely too brittle. "Oh, my purse . . . I have no money."

His Clea sounded like she might be getting a little too close to the edge. He pulled into the parking lot, eased the car into a spot, turned off the ignition. "I have money," he said, and waited.

"Thank you," she whispered. "I know I should be telling myself that I *can* do this. Force myself to keep it together, you know?" Her hands were clasped tight in her lap, the knuckles white, as though she was afraid to let go, her body language saying she was determined to keep it together, no matter what.

He recognized that in her. Valiant, calm, controlled Clea. Maybe that was part of the attraction. Part opposites attract, part like to like.

She hadn't lost it when a demon attacked or when *hybrids* broke into her home. Because that was how she coped. She dealt with it, whatever "it" happened to be.

Just like she dealt with the crash that had killed her parents. Just like she dealt with nursing her grandmother through a cancer that took years to release her finally into death. Clea didn't lose it.

He liked her. Admired her.

Wanted her.

And she was looking at him with those big dark eyes, so serious, so scared.

"You're okay, Clea." There. He was certain he'd sounded reassuring.

"No." She pursed her lips, considering his assertion, then shook her head. "No, I don't think I am, and I don't think I *can* do it. Because there's just too much . . ." A breathy sigh escaped her, and she narrowed her eyes as she stared at him. "My car's gone, isn't it?"

He opened his mouth to reply, struggling to keep up with this odd conversation.

Holding out her hand, palm forward, she stopped him.

"No. Don't answer. I know it. Those *hybrids,* they stole it, right? They used *my* car to hunt me down in *my* home. I saw it parked out front of my building." She made a sound of annoyance. "And it's only insured for collision. And the rent's late on the apartment, because I had to use it to help pay for the funeral. And I can't pay tuition. But actually"—she paused, sucked in a breath—"that's good, because I don't want to be a doctor. I really don't. Which means I don't have to pay the rest of the tuition, because I'm not going back."

She stopped, stared straight ahead out the front window. He figured she was having a bit of a meltdown. Justifiable, in his estimation, and he wanted to gather her close, and hold her, and chase away her demons. Literally.

"And I don't believe in magic, never have," she continued, the words pouring out of her. "At least, not since I was eight years old and my parents were killed in a car crash. What kind of fairy godmother lets that happen? Only, *you're* here, and you're not human. You're—what?—some kind of sorcerer, right? Which means that either I've had a psychotic break, or you're real, and those guys were real, and that thing from last night, that demon, was real, and there's something weird going on with me and with you. I felt it back there. In the kitchen."

She looked at him then, her body vibrating with tension, her eyes wide. "And I *can't* do this, not right now. I can't look for explanations, because I don't want them. I'll want them later, in an hour. In a day. But right now, if I'm going to stay sane, I just want to do something *normal.* I just want to *cope.* Not watch you slice up a demon with filaments of light. Not jump out my fifth-story window and land without so much as a scrape. Right now I just want to go into *that* store, right there, and shop for enough groceries to make hot soup and sandwiches for the people who live in Box Town, just like Gram and I have done every third Saturday for the past eight years."

Slumping back in the seat, she followed her rapid-fire monologue with a deep, cleansing breath that filled her chest, then whooshed from between her puckered lips in a rush.

Box Town. The cardboard box homeless community under the Bathurst Street Bridge. She wanted to go feed the homeless. Even though she had nothing left.

"Okay," he said.

"I'll pay you back." Her breath hitched, and she laid her hand on his arm. His muscles jerked as he felt the contact rocket through him. She stared at him for a long minute. "Please. I need to do this."

"Okay." He had no intention of accepting repayment, but this was not the time to argue. For a second, he tried to imagine what it was like to be her, at this moment, in this place, everything she knew about the world tossed in the trash like so much garbage, while she tried to come to terms with a new reality.

She was unbelievably courageous.

And all he wanted to do was keep her safe. The gut-wrenching yearning he felt every time he looked at her was probably her biggest peril, which meant that the best way to keep her safe was to get her as far from him as she could be. Turn her over to Darqun or Baunn or some other sorcerer.

Yeah. Like he would let that happen.

One of your own betrays you, sorcerer. One of your own summons the Solitary. The dead demon-keeper's claim ensured that trusting Clea's long-term safety to another was not an option.

Closing his eyes, he felt the pull of her, the draw on his magic, their close proximity offering a unique complication. She could drain him, tap into his power, and she had no clue. *Christe,* the energy she'd pulled from him back there in her kitchen had been enormous, and she had no idea how to channel it, how to guide it or pull it back. She'd just siphoned it from him, and then let it burst out of her like fireworks. If he let her drain him, how the hell was he supposed to protect her? And if he kept her with him, how was he supposed to keep her from sucking him dry?

He glanced out the window, toward the crowded supermarket, then back toward her. "That's fine, Clea. We can get whatever you want."

A part of him wished he could give her what she must *really* want. Her life back the way it was before she found out that monsters actually *did* live under the bed.

Looking into those amazingly luminous brown eyes, he couldn't help himself. He reached out, let the side of his finger graze her cheek. Her skin was soft, so soft.

She inhaled sharply but didn't pull away. Her eyes widened, darkened, and he trailed his finger down along her cheek, her jaw, her throat, feeling the wild leap of her pulse.

His gaze drifted to her mouth, her lips parted and moist, and he felt a hard kick of desire. He wanted her, any way he could get her. Wanted her enough that he'd risk draining his power just to have her.

He was in so deep, he didn't have a hope in hell of swimming his way to the surface. He was centuries old. Old enough to know better. Old enough to recognize primitive attraction. And this wasn't mere lust. Which made it something more, much more. Something incredibly dangerous.

My Clea, his soul whispered again, more insistent than before, and this time he didn't ignore it. This time he let the feeling wash through him, terrible and terrifying and wonderful, and he slid his fingers to the base of her skull, tangling them in the silky curls that tumbled to her shoulders.

Clea couldn't breathe, couldn't think. God. He was looking at her, hard, intent, so sexy she was sure she would burst into flames. She wanted to touch him, to tunnel her fingers through his gorgeous sun-shot hair, to pull him close. She wanted his mouth on hers, hot, wet, taking whatever he wanted.

And he knew it. Knew every crazy, lascivious thought that was pumping through her brain, pumping through her blood, making her throb and ache and squirm.

She wanted those strong, muscled arms around her, holding her close, keeping her safe. He'd kept her safe. Last night. Today.

And he'd turned her world upside down.

She needed air. She needed out. She needed . . . him. Oh, God.

"Don't kiss me," she whispered desperately, knowing that she wanted him to, wanted it almost more than she could bear. The way she ached for him was terrifying. She'd been attracted to men before, sure. A teenage crush. A mild attachment. There'd been a doctor at St. John's. He'd asked her out after they met in the cafeteria, but she'd hesitated, somehow unsure about him. A few conversations over tepid cups of coffee, and she'd known he wasn't for her.

But this, *this* was different. Ciarran was different. She felt like she had *known* he would come, had waited for him her entire life. How crazy was that? Fate. Karma. But still, she felt the choice was hers, to accept him or reject him. Her free will.

She couldn't believe she was actually considering having a relationship with a sorcerer.

Relationship? Could she call it that?

She was the queen of safe. She'd spent her entire life trying to build a nice, secure environment where the most exciting thing that ever happened was when the garbage truck changed pickup days to accommodate a long weekend.

In the space of a day and a night, that had all changed. She'd just leaped out a flipping window to escape inhuman assassins.

Ciarran definitely was *not* safe. He lived in a world of demons and *hybrids* and magic. And suddenly, so did she.

He was watching her, his expression inscrutable, his hand resting on the nape of her neck. His fingers were strong, massaging her muscles lightly, drawing a sigh of pleasure from her lips.

The power that had arced between them in the kitchen was dormant now. She felt only his touch, warm, enticing. The frightening spike of electricity, of magic, was absent, as was the shimmer of darkness she'd sensed deep in his soul.

That darkness frightened her. It had woven through his light, then through her, into her. And it had left her afraid.

"Please don't kiss me," she said again, stronger, firmer. "If you kiss me, I won't stop. And I can't do that again, feel that again, the light, the heat. The pain." She drew a slow breath. "The shadows inside of you that flow into me."

His eyes widened. The most stunning eyes she had ever seen. Multifaceted, rich with color, vivid against the golden cast of his skin and the dark frame of his lashes.

"Are you afraid of them? Of the shadows?" she asked, and at his faint hiss of breath, she wished she hadn't. She wanted to think he wasn't afraid of anything.

Sometimes, deep inside, she thought she was afraid of everything.

He pulled away, dragging his fingers along the curve of her jaw, her lower lip, and then he broke the contact entirely. She sighed, half-disappointed, half-grateful for the respite. *Don't kiss me.*

Because he would steal her breath, steal her sanity, steal her heart.

Oh, man, she was in such trouble.

Chapter 13

T WO HOURS LATER, CLEA FELT HALFWAY NORMAL, standing in the shadow of the Bathurst Street Bridge, handing out a late lunch to the residents of Box Town.

"Hey, Terry," Clea greeted the woman before her. She'd known her forever. An old friend of Gram's who had fallen on hard times, Terry was the reason they had started coming to Box Town all those years ago. She was older now, her straight blond hair wilted to gray, her blue eyes faded, her face weather-beaten. But her smile was still Terry's laughing smile.

"Much obliged." Terry accepted a Styrofoam cup of hot soup that Clea poured. She blew on it, took a careful sip, and selected a sandwich from the huge tray that sat perched on top of the toolbox in the open trunk of the car. Ciarran's generosity. Thermoses and preprepared hot soup to fill them, trays of sandwiches and fruit and cookies. When Clea had protested the cost, saying that it was much less expensive to buy the ingredients and prepare the food themselves, he'd laughed, a low, sexy sound that set her every nerve tingling.

"I'm not inclined to head back to your kitchen right now," he'd said.

Thinking of the *hybrids,* she hadn't been so inclined, either.

He'd insisted on buying triple the amount of food that Clea usually prepared, saying that he figured the people at Box Town wouldn't mind the leftovers.

She'd felt strange, buying the meal rather than making it with her own hands, but she hadn't been able to argue with his logic, especially when they'd gotten to the register and he'd pulled out a wad of cash thicker than a paperback novel.

Now, Clea's gaze slid to Ciarran, where he stood not three yards away, distributing blankets. Just looking at him kicked her pulse up a notch. His dark jeans hugged his muscled legs, and his shirt was rolled up at the sleeves despite the chill of the October wind, revealing forearms thick with muscle. Lean and powerful, he was so comfortable in his skin, perfectly balanced, cloaked in danger. A warrior. Even here where she could imagine no possible threat, he was alert, watchful, expecting an attack.

"How's Pickles?" she asked, forcing her attention back to Terry.

"Pickles is doing just fine. She's a good girl, aren't you, Pickles? Aren't you?"

The tiny Chihuahua poked her head out of the pocket of her mistress's baggy black overcoat and gave a single, sharp yap. A smile tugging at her lips, Clea tore a crust from the edge of a sandwich and, leaning forward, offered it to the dog.

"Fine weather we're having today, but I smell winter. Won't be long before it snows," Terry said, glancing at the clear blue saucer of sky; then her expression shifted, growing distant and wary as she focused on something over Clea's shoulder.

Slowly, Clea straightened, frowning as a ripple of awareness stroked her skin, making the hair at her nape prickle and rise.

Glancing over her shoulder, Clea found that Ciarran had stepped up behind her. She had known it, sensed him drawing near. She shivered at the realization. Connected. They were connected, and it was growing stronger every minute.

He was studying the little dog, his expression intent; then he held out his hand for the animal to sniff. Pickles licked him, yipping ecstatically, and Ciarran smiled as he extended his free hand toward Terry, the handles of a large plastic bag held in his fist.

"Dog food," he said. "And biscuits."

Terry just looked at him, startled, soup cup poised halfway to her lips, then blinked rapidly, her eyes filling with tears. Carefully, she lowered the cup, her expression pensive, as though she was trying to decide if he was for real. She reached out, looping the plastic handles of the bag over her forearm while she balanced her plastic plate and soup.

"Thank you." Her voice was thick, and she looked as though someone had just gifted her with a lottery win.

"You are most welcome." Ciarran inclined his head. His gaze slid to Clea, wandering over her in a slow caress, lingering in turn. She blinked, sucked in a sharp breath, feeling as though he'd actually touched her. A masculine smile curved his lips, sexy, knowing, and with just that look, he made her think of his mouth on hers. Slow, sucking kisses. Rough kisses and frantic need. She shifted her weight from one foot to the other as he turned away.

She watched him walk, loose-limbed and elegant, back to the box of blankets he'd been distributing a few moments past, and she thought that he was definitely a sorcerer, in more ways than one. With a glance, he worked some kind of crazy enchantment on her. And she liked it. Liked the feeling of her blood rushing hot and thick through her veins, liked the feeling of her breath catching in her throat as she looked at him and he looked at her and she thought of him touching her, taking her.

Whoo. Control. Breathe in. Breathe out.

Turning back to Terry, who was hugging the plastic bag close against her chest, Clea felt her heart warm at Ciarran's kind gesture. She'd mentioned Pickles while they were buying the sandwiches, and Ciarran had insisted on picking up a bag of dog food.

"You doing okay, Clea?" Terry asked. "We're all missing your grandmother something fierce. I can only imagine you must be missing her worst of all. I'm real sorry, you know. We all are."

"Thanks, Terry. I know you are."

"That man of yours . . ." Terry glanced at Ciarran, where he stood by the open box he'd hauled out of the trunk. He was holding out an assortment of blankets in three different shades for an older woman to choose from, his expression inscrutable.

His broad shoulders were set at just such an angle, his lean hips cocked in a way that claimed the world. Acts of kindness aside, Ciarran D'Arbois was a dangerous man. Remote. In control.

Clea swallowed. He was also savagely beautiful. Unbelievably sexy. And she ought to be running as fast and as hard as she could, in any direction other than the one he was in. If she was smart. Which she'd always thought she was.

Smart, sensible Clea.

Only suddenly, she wasn't so sure exactly what sensible meant.

A long, lazy hiss of air escaped her. She just didn't know what to make of him. Or herself.

"He's okay, you know," Terry said. "Your man. He's okay."

Pressing her lips together, Clea poured another cup of soup and handed it to the next woman in line. Ciarran wasn't exactly her man. And he wasn't exactly okay. He was—

She handed out more soup, stared at him a little longer. He turned to look at her, his gaze hot, and she shivered.

"Where's Louise?" Clea asked, dragging her attention back to Terry. Louise never missed the third Saturday of the month. She had a sweet tooth, and Clea always brought dessert.

At her question, Brian shuffled forward, leaning heavily on his cane. He'd been a construction worker. Successful. Owned his own home. Had a wife who loved him. Then the scaffold he'd been working on had failed, and he'd ended up with a crushed leg. He'd lost his house to medical costs. Lost his wife to the drinking that he'd started to try to numb the pain. Lost his only son a year later to a hit-and-run driver. And slowly, bit by bit, he'd lost his grasp on reality. He still had his lucid days, but they were few and far between.

"Louise ain't coming back. Not unless she comes as an angel," he muttered, filling a plate with sandwiches.

He turned to go, but Clea stopped him, his words settling inside her like sludge at the bottom of a dirty lake. "Brian, has something happened to Louise?"

"She's dead," he said bluntly. "Dead. Died there. At St. John's."

His words dripped down on her like a cold rain.

"Tssss." Terry shook her head. "She went to St. John's for her arm. You know the one. The infected arm you warned her about last time you were here. She listened to you, took it serious, went over to the ER. And she never came back. It's not like her to wander off. . . ."

Clea felt Ciarran come up behind her, and he rested his hand on her shoulder, solid, strong. She had the crazy thought that he was offering support, that he knew something terrible had happened to Louise, a woman he'd never even met. Just like Clea knew, with a dreadful certainty. Nausea churned inside her, poisoning her stomach, crawling up her throat. Brian was right. She sensed it, felt it.

Louise was dead.

"Maybe she came and went. Maybe you missed her." Clea wrapped her arms around herself, hugging close the jacket Ciarran had picked up for her when they went into the Wal-Mart.

Swallowing a mouthful of soup, Terry shook her

head. "Nope. Brian went looking for her. He asked at the desk over at St. John's, and they told him she wasn't there, that she never was admitted, that she left from the ER. He didn't believe them. He thinks she never left, 'cause she woulda come back here. He thinks she died." A shudder wracked her solid frame. "He thinks she was killed."

Cold fingers of dread chased along Clea's spine.

Brian leaned closer and lowered his voice. "They're covering it up. It's a conspiracy."

"Who's covering it up, Brian?"

"The government, that's who. Never trusted the damned government. Never," he said as he turned and shuffled away.

"He's upset." Terry made a sound of sympathy. "Louise gone and disappeared. And only two weeks ago, Nala gone, too."

Clea jerked in surprise. "What? Nala?"

"Yep. She got bumped by a car crossing Main Street. Said she was fine, but right then I saw she was already bruising something terrible. I took her over to St. John's myself, but they wouldn't let me go in with her on account of Pickles. So I sent her in by herself, and we haven't seen her since."

"Nala's wandered off before," Clea pointed out. "Last year she took off for a month."

Terry shook her head, her overlong bangs flopping down over her eyes. "I'll tell you something. I get hurt, no way am I going there. I don't care that the other hospitals don't like us homeless folk. I'll go to one of them for certain." Her mouth tightened. "Call my daughter if

I have to. But no way am I stepping foot in St. John's. Something bad going on there. Something real bad."

"Where did Louise live?" Ciarran asked, his gaze moving intently over the rows of cardboard boxes that served as makeshift homes. He stilled, focusing on one sagging box tucked right up under the bridge. "There," he said.

Terry shot him a startled look. "Yeah. How'd you know that? What you got? ESP, or something?"

His mouth curved in a tiny, dark smile. "Or something."

A blighted seed, Ciarran thought. Clea's Louise had had a tiny spark of magic, diluted over generations. Somewhere in her past was a sorcerer progenitor. The spark was not enough for her ever to recognize it in herself, not enough to make a difference in her life. Just enough to be a danger to her if a higher demon sensed it.

Ciarran laid his hand on the box that had been Louise's home. There was nothing amiss. No trace of demon trail or danger. Only the whisper of a very faint remnant of magic, days old, left behind the last time Louise slept here.

He had no way to be certain, not yet, but if Louise had disappeared from St. John's Hospital, it was a good bet that it had something to do with her blighted seed and an even better bet that a demon was responsible.

Too many coincidences. Too many demon sightings and *hybrid* attacks. The bar that Darqun favored, Slinger's, was a mere two blocks from here and another three blocks from St. John's Hospital, in the opposite direction.

Asag had been at that bar, and Ciarran had a strong suspicion that he'd been at St. John's.

Turning, he looked at Clea. He could feel the low hum of contact between them, the draw as she pulled magic from him. Even from this distance, the connection did not fade. She was stronger than he had thought possible. More dangerous than he could have imagined, draining him with a slow, steady draw that she didn't even realize she was exerting.

As though she sensed his thoughts, he felt Clea tug hard on his magic, dragging it from him, into her.

He wanted to put more than magic into her.

He wanted to push inside of her, into the warm wet heat of her. *Christe.* He remembered what it was to want a woman, to feel the hard, sharp kick of desire, to want to touch her and kiss her and bury himself inside her. He'd had such thoughts, vague, impersonal imaginings that gnawed at him despite the relief he sought in the pleasure of his own fist.

Twenty years of solitary release. Twenty years to regret what he had allowed to happen, the loss of his hand. The loss of a piece of his soul.

Twenty years. A mere moment in his ancient existence. An eternity to his lonely heart.

But whatever yearning he had thought dogged him with sharp and bitter barbs was nothing compared to the thought of losing her. Clea. He wanted her with a dark and erotic need, and, yes, with a gentle care.

She was his poison.

She was his cure.

Which left him between the proverbial rock and a hard place. If he stayed with her, she threatened all he was. She could drain him to the point of weakness, to the point that he might no longer be able to hold the darkness at bay. What value would he have then as guardian, as High Sorcerer?

But the alternative did not bear consideration. To leave her alone, unprotected, untutored in the use of her own magic . . . he could not even think of it.

Asag would find her. He would use her. He would—

Emotion churned inside him, alien and strange.

If Asag sank his talons into her, he would warp her power until she threatened the whole damned world.

Chapter 14

DIMLY AWARE OF HER SURROUNDINGS, CLEA roused from a doze as Ciarran pulled up in front of her apartment and parked illegally at the curb. How long since they'd left Box Town? She glanced out the window. Long enough for dusk to fade to night. She stretched, working the kink out of her neck from having let her head fall to the side as she slept. Running the back of her hand over her lips, she had the thought that she might have snored. Or drooled. *Great, just great.*

She slanted a glance at Ciarran. His hands rested on the wheel, and he was frowning, staring straight ahead. Something was on his mind. She could sense it. Something more than the fact that he thought she was crazy, and yeah, probably stupid, for insisting on coming back here tonight.

Louise? Was it Louise's disappearance? She couldn't imagine why he should care about the fate of a woman he had never met, but his distraction had started when he had walked over to investigate Louise's home at Box Town, and it had not abated since.

"Hey," she said, and he turned to look at her, his eyes glittering in the darkened interior of the car. The shadows were as kind to him as the light, accentuating his chiseled features. She raised her hand, almost touched him. And then she caught herself. *God.* If she touched him, even once, she wouldn't want to stop.

"We're in, then out," Ciarran said, his gaze watchful as he glanced at the apartment building, then scanned the area for any threat.

"I know." Clea stared straight ahead, blinking against the sudden sting of tears. They'd had this discussion before they left the Bathurst Street Bridge. She knew it was dangerous for her to go into her apartment, and how horrible was it that she wasn't safe in her own home? It seemed that she had barely had time to assimilate one loss, one change, before another rode in on a crashing wave that nearly knocked her to her knees. "I just need my photos of Gram and Mom and Dad. Two minutes."

Those pictures were her last tangible link to loved ones she had lost. Really, they were her only possessions of value. Not monetary, but of untold worth to an orphan's isolated heart. If she had those photos, her touchstones to anchor her in a chaotic world, she'd be fine. She'd find a way to be fine. She looked at him then and attempted a wobbly smile. "I promise I'll stay so close you'll think we're attached at the hip."

Something flared in his eyes, and she realized that maybe she hadn't chosen the best reassurance. Attached at the hip. At the pelvis.

Whoo. Don't go there, Clea.

He scanned the area once more, returned his gaze to her. "Your home is directly in the center of a *hybrid* warren—"

"You mentioned that this morning. What is it?"

"An anthill." He smiled, a slow disquieting curve of hard, masculine lips. "With *hybrids* instead of ants."

"Oh." A reassuring thought.

"Two minutes. In and then out, Clea," he said brusquely. "The *hybrids* are a wily breed. They may be waiting for your return."

"But you don't think they are." She could hear the confidence in his voice, and the censure. He definitely thought this was a bad idea.

"No. I do not think they lie in wait." He pushed open the driver's side door.

"So we're . . ." She hesitated. "We're safe?"

He slanted her a sardonic glance. "As long as you are by my side, you are safe."

Safe. She'd spent her whole life trying to build a wall around herself, trying to be safe. Every decision she made. Every action she took. All for nothing, because it turned out that the world wasn't anything like she'd thought it was.

He climbed from the car, walked around to her side, and offered his hand to help her out.

A wistful smile blossomed inside of her as she studied his hand. Such courtly, old-world manners. Slowly, she raised her eyes to his, her smile fading. Old-world. A shiver coursed through her, and with it, a strange premonition that his definition of time was far different than hers.

She pressed her tongue against the back of her top

teeth. Too much, too fast. She hadn't wanted answers earlier, but now, suddenly, she wanted those answers. Needed them. Demons. *Hybrids*. Why an all-powerful sorcerer was stuck to her side like a burr. Why she felt unsettled and strange, twitchy inside her own skin. Why the power she had known since childhood, the force that had protected her from harm, had changed now, grown, evolved.

She was almost afraid of herself. Definitely wary of what she was quickly coming to recognize as magic grown from a seed to a sapling. Why her? Why now?

Ciarran stood waiting, watching her, his expression remote, and yet she sensed his interest, his focus on her. She was changing because of *him*. Somehow, they were linked.

Swallowing, she took Ciarran's outstretched hand, let him help her from the car, felt the sizzle between them. Attraction. And something more. Something dangerous. Frightening. Light, yes, but darkness, too. She dropped his hand. Whatever this sensation was, it was getting stronger, had been building all day, until she thought it might burst out of her in a flash of exploding skin and flesh and bone, and she was certain it was coming from him, into her.

Arms wrapped tight about herself, she stepped back. Despite the dark edge she sensed in him, or perhaps— God help her—because of it, she wanted to be close to him. Touch him. Run her hands over his muscled frame. Smooth, hot, golden skin. The image of him, looming above her, naked flesh and pulsing heat, features taut with passion, filled her mind.

She sucked in a breath. Turned away. Began to walk

toward her apartment building. He moved so fast, she gasped. One second he was standing beside the car, the next he was firmly planted in front of her, towering over her, his expression harsh.

"Joined at the hip, Clea." He leaned in close until his warm breath fanned her cheek, and his lips moved against her ear. "You move, I move. You breathe, I breathe."

Oh, God. The feel of him, so close, so warm, was halfway to ecstasy, and despite the menace in his tone, the sound of his low, rough whisper poured through her, igniting every cell. She'd never responded to anyone the way she responded to him, hot and shivery. Chemistry, yeah. But something stronger, deeper, a primal link, and she didn't understand it.

How could she fight something she didn't understand?

He moved back just enough to look into her eyes, so close she could count every long, lush eyelash, highlighted in the pallid glow of the streetlight. Her heart slammed against her ribs, and her every nerve went into overdrive.

"Yeah," she muttered, thinking about the two of them, moving together, breath intertwined.

His eyes narrowed as he studied her; then he shifted to the side. She took a step forward. He fell in beside her, matching his pace to hers as they approached the building.

"I don't have my key," she said a few moments later, pausing in front of her door. Or her money. Or her purse. She'd locked the door from the inside that morning and hadn't had time to gather her belongings, hadn't had time to do more than gasp before they left by way of the window. She shuddered at the recollection of hearing the glass shatter, feeling the wind whistle past her as the ground rushed up to meet them.

"Not a problem. I doubt the *hybrids* locked up after themselves this morning." Ciarran reached out and turned the knob to open the door. Unlocked. Of course.

Ciarran moved in front of her, going through first. She figured he wasn't taking any chances that they might encounter *hybrids,* but his body language was relaxed, leaving her fairly certain that nothing lurked in wait.

As they entered her apartment, she sniffed delicately. An unpleasant aroma wafted through the space, like she'd left the garbage can open in the kitchen. Flicking on the light, she gasped in dismay and grabbed Ciarran's arm, her fingers digging into solid muscle. Her home was a mess, violence and rage marking the furniture and walls. Her twenty-year-old TV was smashed. The cushions of her sagging tweed couch were slashed open, the stuffing pulled deliberately from the gaping holes and left strewn all over the floor. Through the narrow archway that led to the kitchen, she could see a rectangle of linoleum flooring dotted with garbage, the source of the nasty smell.

The picture of her and Gram that had been on the table in the hall was lying facedown at her feet amid the jagged shards of the small vase, broken now, the dried flowers crushed to powder. The photograph of Mom and Dad that had hung on the wall by the kitchen was nowhere to be seen.

A sick horror welled inside her.

"What were they looking for?" she asked, her voice trembling as she bent and carefully lifted Gram's picture from the debris. "What did they hope to find?"

"Nothing. They were looking for nothing. This destruction is an expression of their fury." Ciarran rested one hand on her shoulder, and she felt her emotions spike, along with the crackle of their connection. His sympathy almost pushed her over the edge, and she blinked against the sting of tears.

Wanton destruction. Rage. A frenzy of spite. Yes, she could feel that, the crushing weight of it. They had done this for no reason other than to destroy.

For an instant, she thought her heart would break.

Things. They were only things. She turned the frame in her hand faceup. There was a long jagged crack running from one corner to the opposite one, but underneath, the photo was unmarked.

Her head was swimming, and she leaned her back against the wall, resting her weight on the solid surface, closing her eyes for just a second, only long enough to gather her emotions.

When she opened her eyes, she saw Ciarran's leather jacket, hanging on the peg behind the door where he had put it that morning. He had left it behind when they'd gone through the window.

The soft leather hung in tatters, long strands hacked and torn, jagged, ugly.

"Your jacket. Ciarran. I'm sorry—"

"*You're* sorry? It is not your failing to be sorry for. The fault is mine." He was there, in front of her, his gaze focused, his jaw tense. "I'll make it better, Clea," he said, his voice tight.

Running his gloved fingers along her arm, he made a gesture with his free hand, and in an instant the room was filled with light, bright, sharp, and when it dulled, everything was in its place. The smell of garbage gone. Cushions whole on the couch. Dried flowers in their vase on the table.

All was as it had been.

Only *nothing* was as it had been.

That morning, the *hybrids* had driven her from her home; then they had decimated it. Despite the fact that Ciarran had returned everything to its original state, in her mind's eye she would forever see the needless, spiteful demolition, feel the personal violation.

She let out a measured exhalation, focusing on the feel of the air escaping her puckered lips.

"This doesn't make it better," she whispered, making a loose gesture that encompassed the now-pristine room. "Actually, it makes it worse. You wave your wand, but I still *know* what they did. I know they were here. You can't just lift the corner of the rug and shove the mess underneath"—her voice cracked—"because the mess is just too big."

Her gaze locked with his as the moment stretched. His jaw clenched, and he looked away to scan the room. Panic washed through her, a cold rain. He wasn't going to understand that his magical fix was superficial, shallow. How could he understand?

"You made it go away, but it's only cosmetic." She forced the words past the tightness in her throat. Just like he'd made the demon go away last night, but that hadn't really fixed anything, either, because today more demons, or *hybrids*, or whatever they were had come and done *this*. She sighed. "Underneath, the ugliness is still there."

"Ugliness under a pretty surface, huh?" He gave a

short laugh, laced with self-derision, and she had the disconcerting thought that he wasn't talking about her trashed apartment.

"You meant to make it better. I know that. But this . . ." She chuffed out a breath.

"Yeah. I get it."

Slowly, he raised his hand and light slid from his fingertips, returning everything to the way it had been when they first walked in, the picture of destruction and unchained aggression.

Oddly, the fact that he'd put it back to chaos offered her more comfort than his attempt to make it all go away. Man, she was one sick puppy.

He turned to look at her, his eyes glittering, and even in this moment of her utter desolation, she was caught by the sheer beauty of him. The hollows of his cheeks. The hint of stubble that shadowed his jaw. The ever-changing colors that flashed in his eyes, more blue now than gray or green, so rich a color.

"I'll help you clean it up, Clea." His voice was quiet, controlled. "But not now. Now we have to get out of here."

She swallowed, her gaze straying to the torn cushions of the couch. Carefully, she set Gram's photo on the table, her hand trembling. She pressed her palms tight against the wall at her, back as the horrific realization chased through her and finally settled with cruel obstinacy.

Her life could never be the same as it had been before Ciarran strode into the Blue Bay Motel and sliced a demon to pieces. He hadn't lied when he told her there was nowhere safe. Hadn't lied last night, or today. She knew that now.

There was nowhere safe in all the world, just like he'd said.

Except by his side.

The certainty of that made her ache to step into the solid shelter of his embrace, made her want to be held in his arms, just for a moment.

"What—" Her voice cracked. She swallowed, tried again. "What happens now?" *What happens to me? What happens to my life?*

She wasn't usually the type to initiate change, preferring the safe and solid reassurance of routine, but if change rolled over her, she *dealt* with it. That's what Gram had taught her to do, what life had taught her to do. She'd thought she could handle anything. Anything. The emptiness of growing up without her parents. The horrific memories of the crash. The sadness of Gram's death, of being so alone. Only now, she wasn't so sure. Now it wasn't the natural course of life, of death, of highs and lows, she had to face. Now it was about making choices, making changes, accepting the impossible.

Now it was about *hybrids* and demons invading her world, threatening her safety. Her life.

It was about magic, and it was about a sorcerer.

Ciarran D'Arbois.

The air crackled, alive with unseen energy, electric heat connecting them. Heart pounding, she held his gaze.

Closer. He leaned closer until their breath mingled, and her heart pounded, and she ached to feel him close the last of the space that separated them, to press his body full against her, to make her feel warm instead of cold to her core.

He inhaled sharply.

"Your two minutes are up." His low voice rumbled through her and he slapped one palm against the wall, pushing himself back. She turned her face away, flustered, forcing her attention to the task at hand. She'd lived here for almost two decades, and now she'd had two minutes to gather up her life.

Nodding, she stepped past him and grabbed her albums and photos, focusing only on her task and not on the destruction that surrounded her.

Resolve flooded her. She wouldn't let the *hybrids* win, wouldn't let them steal all the lovely memories of her home. She had grown up here, just her and Gram, and *those* were the memories she would choose to hold.

"I know you thought this was a really bad idea, but thanks for bringing me. That was . . . um . . . nice," she said, struggling to keep her tone even as she shoved the pictures into a bag.

"Nice," he repeated, a hint of incredulity shading his tone. His eyes narrowed. "It isn't a word that describes me, Clea. I am anything but nice."

And yet, he *was*. Nice. Nice enough to buy out half the store to feed the homeless and buy them blankets and even food for Pickles.

"Don't think it," he said in a dusky murmur. "Don't make me something I'm not."

Reaching out, he went to take the bag from her. She held firm, and their fingers touched, hers caught beneath his. Just like she had that morning in the kitchen, Clea felt a harsh flow of power slam through her. She jerked as though she was hooked up to a live electrical wire, and she cried out in shock as her body twisted tight.

With a snarl, Ciarran wrenched away, his expression one of pain.

Heart hammering, Clea fell back, rubbing her hand, half-expecting her skin to be singed black.

Her gaze shot to his. He watched her, his expression hard, making her think of danger and power, bringing a nervous edge to her movements. She shivered, torn.

Maybe what he said was true. Maybe he really was anything but nice.

Chapter 15

ASA PALEY STOOD IN THE SHADOWS, HIS BACK TURNED to the October wind that blew from the north. His human guise made him subject to human sensation, both a blessing and, at times like this, perhaps a bit of a curse. He studied the squat yellow-brick building that was Clea Masters's home. Such an ugly structure, with its rusting metal balconies and stained brick. He had developed an appreciation for the aesthetic in the decades he had inhabited this dimension, and the building before him offended his superior sensibility.

For this Clea had spurned him, for her life of poverty, for her opportunity to scrabble like a rat in a maze. He had offered her his protection. Not in such a crass and obvious way, but in subtle suggestion and easy banter as he stalked her during her time observing at St. John's Hospital. He had offered a physical relationship, money, clothes, her every desire, subtly weaving his proposition in through their every conversation as they had sat in the noisy cafeteria at St. John's, drinking the noxious brew

she favored. Her rejection confounded him, angered
him, made him all the more determined.

Taking her to his bed would have been almost too perfect. He enjoyed the thought of having her in his thrall,
of using her body for his release, then using her power
as conduit to open the portal and liberate the Solitary.
Now she would pay the price for her rejection. Instead
of a gentle, sweet ride to her demise as he had originally planned, she would find her death both brutal and
bloody.

Such pleasure he would take in sucking her magic
from her core, and then sucking the marrow from her
bones.

Asa glanced at the three *hybrids* that stood to one
side, practically vibrating with eagerness. Their lives
were forfeit, sacrificed to his great plan. They just didn't
know it, yet. He reached out, unsheathing one gleam-
ing nail, honed to the sharpness of a high-quality paring
knife, and ran it along the cheek of the nearest *hybrid,*
leaving a thin line of blood in its wake. A reminder. A
promise.

The man shuddered and tensed but said nothing. Wise
hybrid. To complain was to earn a far worse fate.

"Wait," Asa commanded, his voice barely above a
whisper. "Wait until she is clear of him. You will take
the human female alive. Unharmed. At all costs. Do you
understand?"

They nodded as one, the black spheres of their eyes
turning toward him, then away, their terror palpable, and
he felt a moment's impatience with their weak nature.
He looked forward to the opening of the wall between
dimensions, to the flood of lesser demons that would

pour through unfettered by human keepers, an army of worthy soldiers, his to command. All would be as it should, demons taking their rightful position, humans serving as feed for a superior race. He would be second only to the Solitary. And one day, as his power grew, he would be second to none.

"If you fail, I will not kill you." Asa walked a slow circle around the nearest *hybrid,* the one he had set as the leader of this small group. "I will slice you open, gut you, and eat your intestines one inch at a time. Do you know how many days you can live like that, with the pain and the infection gnawing away at you? Days and days and days. Perhaps weeks. Think of it. Weeks of unbearable suffering. And then perhaps I will heal you. Only to begin it all again."

The *hybrid* made a choking sound. Asa laughed softly, enjoying the sensation of their fear rolling over him. Foolish creatures. They would fail. Three *hybrids* against the sorcerer. The odds were laughable. Ah, but the information he would gain from watching D'Arbois fight. That was invaluable.

"Alive. I want Clea Masters alive. Not a single scratch marring her skin. Not a filament torn from her clothing." Those pleasures he reserved for himself, for after she had unlocked the doorway to the demon realm.

Again.

Just as she had unlocked it two decades past. An unbelievably rare human female born with more than just a spark of magic, she had been his key to the human world. Even as a small child her magic had been strong, strong enough to open a portal. Trapped beyond the wall in the demon realm, he had called her, drawn her, used whatever foul sorcery had been within his scope, pulling human and *hybrid* alike into his perfect plan.

His *hybrid* minions, free to do his bidding in the mortal realm, had made certain that her parents drove to the exact location he needed, on the exact date, with their precious daughter dozing in the backseat. He had made certain that the car had carried the child to the particular place, that her father had lost control exactly as needed. Clea's injuries were so severe that her waning life force let the kernel of magic at her core glide free, and that magic was the key that had slid so fluidly into the lock.

Such effort, such lengthy weeks and months and years it had taken to put all in its place.

But he had had nothing but time. Endless time.

For an eternity he had been trapped in the demon realm. He. Asag. Ancient demon of plague. He had been forced from the Earth by the stinking *Pact,* forced by a pact signed in sorcerer and demon blood to stay on his side of the barrier, to limit his darkness and death to the demon dimension, where there was little enjoyment to be found in his unique skills. He had been trapped there by ancient powers, locked in by the Compact of Sorcerers.

Centuries he had waited for a human child to be born, a child who bore not merely a speck, but a large measure of magic. And she had come. A female child. Clea Masters. She had come, such a surprise, so much more powerful than ever he had imagined possible, justifying his wait, his patience.

That night, the night he had breached the wall, he had cared nothing for her fate. She had been merely an instrument of his success, an inexplicably magical human child whose death would mean naught to him once she had served her purpose. Her purpose had been to open the doorway, to breach the wall, to set him free.

Open it she had, ripping the barrier between dimensions, no small crack, but a great, groaning tear. Her magic had been that powerful. Stunningly powerful.

Yet, one stumbling block had remained. A demon could not walk the world of man without a keeper, and he, Asag, was fettered by the need for a mortal who would summon him. That challenge had been readily overcome. It was so easy to control the mother's thoughts, a dying woman who cared only for her child. Easy to plant the seed of need and desperation with a silent whisper in her mind, to fan her anxiety and convince her to call him forth, to convince her that she called a guardian angel. The mother's dying breath had bid him to enter the human world. Such perfect timing. She had lived long enough to bring him through, but not long enough for his power to link them. She had died as she breathed the last word of the summoning, believing she protected her child.

He had set the stage to perfection, her words and her demise letting him, a demon of immeasurable strength, into the realm of man, invited, yes, but unsaddled by a keeper—a development that had been unexpected but so very welcome. The mother's death on the exact exhalation that completed the summoning invocation had left Asag unfettered by his summoner.

His satisfaction had been immense.

Ah, he could still recall every nuance of sensation as he had stepped into the human dimension, taken human form and guise, the senses he had almost forgotten through the long years of his imprisonment exploding with corporeal delight. The sound of the breeze rustling through the trees had been a nearly forgotten pleasure. The metallic perfume of death, and the sulfur sting of the fire that had consumed the vehicle had filled his nostrils. The weeping of the dying child had been a symphony to his ears. The lovely texture of sharp, sharp bone poking through torn skin as he touched her dead father, and the sticky warmth of fresh blood that spurted from severed artery and vein, a tactile delight.

He remembered the dead woman, Clea's mother, and the precious taste of her as he had squatted low to the ground and bent to run his tongue along her neck, the taste of her terror yet lingering on her cold skin.

Death had fascinated him, and he had dallied, wanting to witness the demise of the child, wishing it could take longer, that the pain and fear could be drawn out for his voyeuristic pleasure.

The delay had been a mistake, to be sure. One that had cost him immeasurably.

The Compact of Sorcerers, ever vigilant in the need to watch the wall between dimensions, had sent a guardian. The one called Ciarran D'Arbois.

Asa licked his lips now as he recalled his attack, fast and brutal, recalled the feel of sorcerer flesh giving way beneath his teeth, the rich taste of blood flowing into his mouth as he tore open D'Arbois' shoulder, his wrist. He had sunk his talons deep into the sorcerer, wrestling him toward the breach. Despite being distracted by the child and weakened by Asag's attack, he had been a worthy opponent, inflicting nearly as much damage as he received.

And the child, Clea, had watched, wide-eyed, terrified, her fear fueling Asag's power.

Bleeding and torn in a dozen places, D'Arbois had almost gone through the portal, almost fallen into the dark, stinking pit of brimstone and damnation. A sorcerer sealed in the demon realm, he would have been torn limb from limb, again and again, destined to suffer unspeakable agonies for all his immortal eternity.

At the last moment, the tide had turned, and instead of D'Arbois being pushed through the breach, it had nearly been Asag who was relegated back through the portal. D'Arbois had struggled, fought, with all he was, and in the end, he had escaped.

But not without paying a forfeit.

Asag had pushed the sorcerer's hand through to the demon realm, enjoyed the struggle, the pained hiss as flesh was torn away by a demon on the far side, one intent on taking D'Arbois' form for its own, using the sorcerer as a bridge. But it was the transition itself, the shift of the hand into the forbidden realm that determined the final outcome, a most unusual set of circumstances and one that allowed a unique result. In his weakened state, D'Arbois had not been strong enough to battle the dark rot, and though he had cast out the demon, the seed of blackness held. It had settled in his hand, the malevolence, the evil, and Asag had believed that it would soon devour the whole.

Such would have been a worthy penance, for the battle had cost Asag, as well. Cost him his strength, his dark sorcery. He had been left almost mortal in a mortal realm. Not Asag any longer, not a great and powerful demon, but Asa, a weakened husk destined to spend decades searching for the treasured morsels of magic buried in human vessels that he required to rebuild him to his former glory.

For that, he owed D'Arbois. For that, it became personal.

But now, he was so close, close to reclaiming his full strength and vigor, close to reclaiming his name—Asag. Close to payback. Against D'Arbois, who had apparently appointed himself the girl's guardian. Against the entire hated Compact.

Betrayal was a savory feast.

One sorcerer had recently chosen to ally with Asa, to betray his own. The irony was truly delicious. The sorcerer had made small forays at first, his intentions so transparent. He had provided nearly worthless tidbits of information in exchange for answers to questions he posed. Asa had seen through the ruse right from the start. A sorcerer who pretended to ally with demons in order to ferret information for their ultimate defeat. Only the sorcerer had sunk deeper and deeper, a slow slide from altruistic intent to true betrayal. The sorcerer had tunneled so deep into the enemy camp that his boundaries, his convictions, had blurred, leaving him hard-pressed to distinguish friend from foe, truth from lie.

Such a delectable paradox.

Now the only thing Asa needed was the conduit. Clea Masters. And to get her, he must battle D'Arbois. How convenient that they had returned here, as he had suspected they would. Humans were so predictable, and despite her core of magic, Clea was human.

Asa glanced at the *hybrids*. They were tonight's sacrifice. A necessity. He needed to judge the sorcerer's strength, needed to watch him fight, study his methods. D'Arbois was strong. For two decades he had held the demon aspect of his own nature at bay, confined by magic-forged alloy, hidden from view in a simple black leather glove, his wrist marked with wards and ancient spells, his forearm guarded by the symbol and breath of the dragon current. As though wards and tattoos would be sufficient to confine his new nature.

But somehow, it *had* been sufficient for twenty years, a state of affairs that was utterly confounding.

Asa knew the sorcerer struggled daily, without a moment's peace or relief.

Yet, D'Arbois' suffering was little enough, for Asa doubted it matched his own. His strength had been sucked back into the demon dimension, his power weakened to such a state that he had barely retained enough to don human guise. Slowly, so slowly, he had taken mortal lives, feeding on any spark of magic he found, a commodity so precious and rare in this human world. It had taken him decades to stoke his power, and all the while he had watched Clea Masters, followed her life, followed the growth of her power.

Ah, how he had suffered, the temptation of her magic seed so great. He had longed to devour her, to take her strength inside himself, to feed on her in a wonderful blood-soaked frenzy. But if he had taken her, the opportunity to use her as conduit would have been lost. He would have doomed himself to an eternity as he was now, yearning for the doorway to open, for the chance to bring forth the Solitary, the great ancient evil that could restore him to his full glory. He could not eat her because he needed her.

It was too perfect that the sorcerer had found her; too perfect that she yet siphoned his magic, just as she had twenty years ago; too perfect that it would be the pilfered magic of Ciarran D'Arbois that would return Asa to his rightful place as Asag, demon of plague, deathmonger of the mortal realm.

Too perfect.

The front door of the apartment opened, and Asa melted into the shadows as he watched the sorcerer step through the door, his body shielding the girl.

Chapter 16

TRANSFERRING THE BAG OF CLEA'S FAMILY PHOTOS to his gloved hand, Ciarran pushed open the glass door with his shoulder and led her out into the night. The light above the front door was broken, flickering on and off at will, and they stepped into relative darkness, the moon and the glow of the distant streetlight only serving to accentuate the shadows.

Clea bumped up against his back, and again he felt a sharp tug, as though his blood were being drawn from him by a suction pull. Only it wasn't his blood that was being sucked dry; it was his power. Her proximity was a danger to him. The surges of magic he had used to clean up the *hybrids'* mess and then to reverse the act had been a foolish waste; but in that instant, her stricken expression had cut him deep, and he had been driven to offer what comfort he could. A noble intent that had weakened him.

The malevolence inside him snarled and hissed, sensing the drain on his strength, desperate to get out, to take him, to steal all he was. Clea tensed, raised her head, her gaze seeking his. She was so attuned to him now that she felt it, felt the demon seed. Each moment saw their link grow stronger, and in the hours they had been together, she had unwittingly chiseled away at the chains that held the darkness in check.

"Ciarran?" She said his name, her tone laced with caution.

"A minute," he rasped, battling against the terrible tide. "I just need a minute."

He paused midstride, the car not ten paces away, feeling suddenly wary. There was a ripple, a shift in the *continuum,* a subtle chime of warning. *Hybrids.*

Gritting his teeth, he called his light magic, feeling the smooth, welcome glide of it, though the power was barely enough to chain the beast.

"Stay close," he commanded, wryly aware of the paradox. The closer she was, the greater her pull, and the more his power slid away from him.

She moved up against his side. Sensing the *hybrids,* he focused on them one by one, locating each in the shadows. There were only three, too few to be of concern, even in his weakened state. Yet there was something else, something that set him on edge. He scanned the perimeter, aware of a stronger current that disturbed him. The odor was faint, the shift in the stream of magic a mere whisper that hovered in the air marking the presence of a full-bred demon, one that had been long in the world of man. One such demon came to mind, one to whom he owed a personal debt.

"Ciarran, I feel . . ." Clea moved closer, shivering, her arm brushing his side, and he felt the lurch of power, unsettled, off-balance, dragged from him into her. If he allowed this siphoning to continue, he would soon be little more than an empty husk.

"I don't feel right," she whispered, looking around, studying the dim outlines of the neighboring buildings, searching for phantoms. Or demons.

He scanned the area, taking note of the low line of scraggly bushes that marked the edge of the property. The bare branches of a lone tree arced above them, casting a lattice pattern of shadows on the dry grass, eerie, shifting forms that swayed and danced in time to the howl of the wind.

Clea rubbed her palms along her upper arms. "There's something out here."

Yeah. Something. No lesser minion, but a powerful demon, flanked by a scattering of *hybrids*.

Ciarran spun a slow circle, testing the flow of magic. He was almost certain of the demon's identity and completely certain of its goal. It wanted her, wanted Clea.

But it would have to come through him to get her.

The thought was almost pleasing, the darkness bubbling inside him, aching for violent release. Gritting his teeth, he shoved at it, trying to bind it to his will.

The *hybrids* came at him, three shadows, moving fast and low, dressed in dark clothing, their attack synchronized. The light from the distant streetlamp bounced off glittering blades, ancient blades. *Christe*. They were armed with daggers steeped in the fires of the demon realm, cooled in the blood of innocents.

Ciarran called his power, casting light and magic, pulling together his drained reserves, and the thing inside him gloried, reveled in his strained resources. Out. It wanted out.

"What *is* that?" Clea inched closer to him, sucked in a sharp breath, and he knew she felt it, sensed the demon parasite that tainted him, slithering through their link. Just what was he supposed to tell her?

The shadow to his right moved, and he lashed at it, his magic falling just short of the mark. *Christe*, he was weakened, his maimed hand on fire, white-hot pain, the monster writhing through him, whispering, wanting. Three *hybrids*. Only three. No match for him. He had to give them a chance. He *always* gave them a chance. He tried to warn them off, to bid them flee as was his wont, but his tongue was thick in his mouth, his blood sluggish.

Forcing out the words of ancient wards and protection, Ciarran built a fortress in his mind, brick by brick, willing the darkness into its cell. He focused on the *continuum,* the dragon current, the harmony of good and evil, willing himself to find the perfect balance within. The effort was not the success he had hoped. The pain flared in his ruined hand, escaping the confines of the alloy glove to sluice through him in great rolling waves. Carefully, his eyes locked on the nearest *hybrid,* he set the bag of Clea's photos on the ground.

"What's wrong? I can feel something wrong."

He could hear her confusion, the growing hint of alarm in her tone.

"Tell me what to do," she said.

"Clea." He paused, noting the change in timbre, the hollow quality to his own voice. "You have to step away. I—" What the hell was he supposed to say? That he was part demon, part stinking hellspawn, and that he was quickly losing the battle to hold that part in chains? That she was pulling the life from him without a clue? "—I don't want you in danger. My magic, you draw too much. From me, into you."

She gasped at his words, but a part of him suspected that his revelation came as no true surprise. She was too smart not to have figured out at least part of the situation by now.

He turned a slow half circle, watching the changing shadows, sensing as they moved closer and closer still. The beast roared inside him, angry, vicious. The *hybrids* would not have her. On this matter he and his demonic parasite agreed.

"You have to stop extracting my power, Clea. Do you understand? I can't—"

"I don't understand." She shook her head, grabbed his arm, and he jerked at the contact as he felt his magic sucked away at an alarming rate. As though sensing that physical contact was the last thing he desired at this moment, she dropped her hand, took a step back.

"Tell me what to do." Her words were fast and high, tinged with fear.

The *hybrids* circled like a pack of starved hyenas.

She looked around frantically, her gaze darting about; then she lunged for a busted length of chain that had once anchored a dented garbage can to the tree, broken now by some unknown vandal, lying discarded on the ground. Pride surged through him as he turned to his task. She had to be shaken, but she was ever valiant, his Clea, standing just behind him, her hands fisted around one end of the thick chain. At least it was a step up from the plastic letter opener.

From the left one *hybrid* charged, armed with a glowing blade, the color of blood, a demon's weapon, one that should have been far beyond a *hybrid*'s modest power.

The razor-sharp edge came down toward Clea, and Ciarran shifted to take the blow in her place. He snarled, pain lancing ruthlessly through him, stark, sharp. Hot blood flowed in rivulets down his arm. His good hand was numb, leaving only his ruined limb for defense.

"Bastard," Clea hissed, swinging the chain hard against the *hybrid*'s shoulder. It yelped and spun at her, blade outstretched.

With a roar, Ciarran felt the icy control he had cultivated for twenty years tear away, decimated by the onslaught of the need to protect Clea at any cost. He flung his gloved hand forward, opening the floodgate, letting his magic flow free. All of it. Darkness smearing the light.

A surge of power ripped from deep within him, dark, threatening. Oozing farther than he had ever let it before, the strength and presence of the demon parasite as it slid through him made his magic far different than anything he had known, so strong it was almost more than he could bear. His gut twisted, and a bottomless burning pain tore at him, flaying his insides. He tried to pull back, tried to check the foul surge that disgorged from him. Dimly, he was aware of Clea's cry of surprise, but he could offer her no comfort.

His weapons had ever been light magic, used under strict control, and only for protection and defense. The power that pumped through him now was nothing he had ever seen, nothing he had ever known. Something he could not control.

This magic was seething strength and absolute destruction, and he had not enough power left to contain it.

A dark twist of thick, vile vapor burst from him like a smothering fog. Engulfed, the *hybrid* jerked, screamed, a sharp, short sound that was cut off as he disintegrated in a splatter of blood and hissing tissue, as though acid had doused him from head to toe. The blade tumbled toward the ground, disappearing before it landed.

Two more *hybrids,* armed with demon weaponry, came at them from right and left. The wound in Ciarran's arm was sizzling, the edges burning with a stark and livid pain. Sweat ran in hot rivulets down his back as he struggled to regain his control. The demon parasite was a sucking miasma, a black haze that colored all he felt, all he was.

"On the ground, Clea." Relief flooded him as she obeyed, dropping to the dry, brown grass.

There was no familiar warmth of shimmering light and razor-honed magic that poured from him now.

One *hybrid* lunged at Ciarran, while the other dove for Clea, closing strong fingers around her ankle. She cried out as it dragged her along the grass, and she kicked at it, then twisted in an attempt to get free. The chain was looped around her fist, and she swung out, the links whistling through the air before slapping sharply against the *hybrid*'s thigh.

Rage such as he had never known coursed through Ciarran, escalating until it was a white-hot ball sizzling inside of him. His ruined hand burned and pulsated as the darkness slithered free to ooze through his veins, an oily, slick glide. He imagined he could feel the dragon tattooed on his arm—a symbol of the *continuum,* the balanced flow of the dragon current—roar in outrage as he gave himself up to the demon swell, embraced it, felt the magnitude of its power. Such terrible power.

Safe. Keep Clea safe. Black blades tore through his skin, through alloy and leather, from the inside outward, slicing the air with a whistling sound, skewering the closer of the two *hybrids.* The creature screamed in agony. With a snarl, Ciarran twisted his hand, twisted the blades, eviscerating the *hybrid* as energy and seething anger flooded him in a violent rush.

Panting, he realized with growing horror that he *liked* it. Liked the intensity. So different than the subtle dance of light magic, new, unfamiliar, a heady force fueled by the very darkness he had battled for two decades.

Disgusted with himself, he gave a sharp yank, pulling free of the dead creature.

The last *hybrid* dragged frantically on Clea's leg as she kicked with sharp, quick movements, landing blow after blow, slowing its pace. With a wet hiss, it loosed its hold and raised its blade, turning full to face Ciarran.

Blood dripping from the wounds on the back of his hand where the sharp tips of his own blades had torn through, Ciarran called the black menace inside him, welcomed it, embraced it. He lunged, sinking the razored talons deep into the chest of the last attacker. With a sharp yank, he dragged the thing closer, looking into the emptiness of its gaze.

The *hybrid* had dared to touch Clea, dared to try and take her, hurt her. With a snarl, Ciarran sliced the great arteries and veins that anchored the creature's pulsing heart and wrenched the mangled organ from its body, blood spurting from the hole in a syrupy rush.

Ciarran froze, shook his head, feeling disoriented, primitive, savage.

Breathing heavily, he stood over Clea, his right arm throbbing with pain, dangling useless by his side. Bloodlust pumped through him, spinning him out of control.

"Oh, God." Clea stared up at him. She was sitting on the ground, shivering, the length of broken chain still clutched in her fist, her arms linked tight across her chest. "Are they gone? Was that the last one?"

He ached to yank her up against him, taste her, claim her.

Her eyes widened. Her lips parted.

Shaking with the force of his emotion, with the effort of dragging the hellspawn inside of him back to its cell, he struggled to rein it all in.

Christe. He had *welcomed* it. *Called* it. Chosen to loose his hold and give the thing a measure of freedom. The realization sickened him.

His gaze shot to Clea. She had to be scared to death. Of the *hybrids.*

Of *him.*

"Yeah, they're gone." Breathing hard, he could barely form the word as the darkness swelled once more, full and rich, making a mockery of any pretensions he had of mastery.

Ciarran's head came up and he searched the shadows. He had neutralized the last *hybrid,* but there had been something else out there, something old and incalculably evil, a full-blooded demon that was still roaming free, a creature that had slipped the bonds of the demon realm and somehow circumvented the rules of magic and the limits of the *Pact*.

Asag. Here. Slinking through the mortal dimension without a keeper. Hunting Clea.

"We need to go."

She nodded, glanced around, then uncurled one hand from across her chest and held it out toward him. Like she wanted him to help her up. Like she wasn't repulsed by him, terrified of him, of what she'd just seen him do. Of what she'd seen released from his soul.

With her arm extended toward him, Clea was still looking up at him.

Waiting. For him.

Willing to let him touch her.

He looked at his gloved hand, at the blood-soaked blades that had somehow become part of him, at the ragged torn flesh that had offered them release. They should not be there. By all rights, every sorcerer developed one perfect weapon. For him, it was the pulse and filaments of light magic. He had never been able to summon a blade. Not in a millennium. Yet here they were, breaking the rules, blades of dark sorcery.

His breath hissed from between his teeth, and he held out his ruined hand to her.

So this was what he had become. He closed his eyes for a moment. No. Not what he had *become*. He had *been* a monster for two decades.

He had just been very adept at pretending he wasn't.

Chapter 17

WINDOWS OPEN, THEY DROVE NORTH, THE WIND howling through the car, wrapping Clea in its frigid embrace. She sensed the savagery of Ciarran's mood and didn't dare ask him to shut the window, or slow down, or even ask where they were going. Fingers curled with white-knuckled strength around the wheel, he drove, staring straight ahead, jaw tight.

He was suffering. That much she could tell. He was . . . different. Intense. Haunted. Closing her eyes, she replayed the terrifying events she had just witnessed and realized there were definite variations from this morning, when he had taken her through a window rather than kill the *hybrids,* and from the night she had watched him take down the demon at the Blue Bay Motel. Those times, it had seemed he would rather fight only if pressed. But tonight, there had been no warnings, no offers of reprieve. Tonight, Ciarran had been . . . primitive, devoid of the icy control that had marked his previous battle.

She glanced at him. He looked as though he might crack. Or combust. It should have frightened her, but oddly, she thought she understood.

Wetting her lips, she thought about the way he'd stood over her, his desire blatant, his gaze hot. Was that part of his battle now?

Skidding off the highway so the back of the car fishtailed wildly for an instant, Ciarran followed a narrow road and finally drew to a stop at the edge of a low cliff that overlooked a ravine. There was no light, no sign of houses or human habitation, just endless night sky. Without looking at her, he rolled up the windows, jammed the heat on full, and practically leaped from the car, pausing only to slam the door behind him.

Clea adjusted the vents, letting the hot air waft across her chilled skin as she stared out the window. Ciarran stood about ten feet away, in the pool of light cast by the headlamps, his back rigid, legs apart, hands fisted at his sides. He was hurting, and she wanted to make it better. Doubly so because, somehow, she was certain that he was hurting at least in part because of her.

With focused intent, she reached out and turned off the ignition. He spun to face her, his chest heaving with each deep breath. With a twist, she shut down the headlights, leaving them both in darkness. Wariness skittered through her, and she hesitated, her fingers pressed tight to the door handle. She could—*should*—stay here. Where it was safe. She should leave him to battle whatever secret pain gnawed at him.

With a ragged breath, she flung the door open and climbed out of the car.

Again, that lightning movement, and he was before

her, so close, the night too dark to offer a clear view
of his features, but she could sense his tension, feel the
thrum of his emotion. A rush of adrenaline shot through
her, making her heart beat wildly and the star-flecked
sky spin. With a murmur, she rested her weight on the
car, cold metal and glass at her back.

He made a low sound, half groan, half curse; then he
reached for her, closing his right hand around her arm,
resting the left one on the roof of the car, and all the
while she could see the glitter of his eyes, sense his blatant, uncompromising hunger.

"Say no," he rasped, his breath fanning her cheek, his
body held wire-tight. "Say no, Clea mine."

As if she wanted to deny him. The scent of him, rich
and male, reached a place deep inside her. She couldn't
breathe, couldn't think, wanting him so badly, the feel
of his mouth on hers, the taste of his kiss. She raised up
on her toes, offering him her mouth, and more, so much
more.

"You don't understand." His voice was harsh, his lips
moving against the skin of her cheek. "You don't know
what lies beneath the light."

The darkness. The terrifying darkness that spun
through him, barely held in check. She knew. She'd felt
it, seen it. And she wanted him despite it. Because of
it. She wanted to soothe him, protect him, stand by him
and help him fight his secret battles. Keep him safe, even
from himself, as he had done for her.

Heart pounding, she reached out, undid one button of
his shirt, then another, until the cloth fell open, revealing the golden skin of his chest, his belly, smooth, taut,

overlying solid muscle and tendon, a purely dazzling arrangement of anatomy that made her mouth go dry.

"Be certain, Clea. There is no going back."

No going back. There had been no going back since she'd first seen him, cloaked in light and danger, standing in the lobby of the Blue Bay Motel. No going back since he'd kissed her that morning, his mouth hot and wet and luscious, the feel of him, the taste of him more than she could ever have imagined in her most fevered fantasies.

She was scared. Not of him, though she sensed that perhaps she ought to be. He was her one constant, her one solid fortification.

He was her one safe place.

She believed that, and she wanted him so badly it hurt. She wanted to help him, to soothe him, to take away his pain. She wanted what he could give her, and she was willing to take risks to have it. Risks. God. That made no sense. She had to take risks to be safe? And yet, it made perfect sense.

Running the pad of his thumb across her lower lip, back and forth, a soft caress, he moved his mouth closer to hers, but still he didn't kiss her. Her breath was lost, gone, trapped somewhere in her chest.

Oh, please. Please. To her utter mortification, she actually whimpered.

Her nipples were hard, pressing against the lace of her bra, and she wanted his hands on her breasts, her buttocks, his mouth on hers. She opened her mouth, licked his thumb, sucked on it, watched the heat flare in his eyes.

Whatever the risk, she wanted him.

"No going back. I know." She did know, felt it on some primal level she couldn't explain, and she sensed he was referring to more than an act of passion.

His mouth curved in a hard masculine smile, and there was nothing kind or gentle about it. The smile was pure male satisfaction as his long body came against her, heavy, blissfully heavy, trapping her between the cold, hard metal at her back, and the muscled heat of him pressed against her front, blocking the wind and the cold. She felt hot, despite the low temperature, wrapped in a sensual haze. The awareness of him was delicious, pouring through her, and the feel of him filtered through her sweater, to her skin, and deeper, to her blood, heating it to boiling.

He tilted his head, kissed her, openmouthed, delicious, and a tight twist of longing coiled deep inside her.

The kiss was not sweet.

Powerful. Extreme. The feeling was anything but sweet.

God. She'd never felt anything like it, this harsh, jarring wave of passion that left her wet, swollen, dragging her right to the edge in a nanosecond.

Opening her mouth to him, she moaned as his tongue pushed into her, the pleasure sharp and fierce as the kiss sank through her, lower, lower, igniting a luscious fire as it went, leaving her feeling like her clothes were too tight, her skin was too tight, like the slow burn of desire that cycled through her was all she had ever craved. She wanted to feel his body, bare skin to bare skin, slick with sweat.

The kiss was deep, rough, tongue and teeth, and his hands, his strong, blunt-fingered hands were on her waist, her back, her shoulders, and she'd never hungered for anything as much as the sensation of him touching her, kissing her. She pulled him closer, arching her back and offering him anything, everything.

She licked him, wet his lips with her tongue, tasted him with her teeth, her body sizzling with a fiendish heat that made her crazy.

Warm and lush and masculine, the scent of him filled her, making her wild, stroking her need to a finely honed edge as he closed his hand around her thigh, dragged her knee up to hook her leg around him, bringing her closer, tighter.

You move, I move. You breathe, I breathe.

A dangerous hunger pounded through him, nipping at the solid walls of his control. Ciarran drew back, staring down at Clea, holding her dark-eyed gaze. Her lids were slumberous, her mouth wet and full. Heat twisted low in his belly, the full rush of arousal. One kiss. One kiss, and she didn't just slide through a crack in his protective barriers; she knocked them down and sent them tumbling like thistle in the wind.

She was exquisite.

Beautiful, brave, brilliant Clea Masters.

His body went still as he let his gaze roam over her features, her dark, silky curls, her succulent mouth.

He wanted to take her slow and sweet, take her hard and dirty right here against the car door. On the hood. On the ground. Any way. Every way.

She drew a shaky breath, and he saw a hint of her pink tongue as she caught the tip between her teeth. Desire kicked him in the gut.

He wanted in. Inside her.

The darkness reared within him, coiling, writhing, the skin of his ruined hand burning inside the glove, as though he'd plunged it into a vat of sizzling oil.

He'd hold it back. Keep her safe. He'd do it. He had to. Because it wanted out, wanted her.

But not as much as *he* wanted her.

Leaning close, he inhaled the scent of her skin, running his nose along the side of her neck.

She hitched in a faint breath, drew back, licked her tongue over her kiss-damp lips. His body roared to life, the punch of desire so strong it twisted him up inside.

Christe.

'Twas madness to take her, with the darkness gnawing at him, demanding release. She'd been subtly draining him all day, of power, of magic, a steady tug on his reserves, and now, in the wake of his fight with the *hybrids,* he was wire-tight, strung to the limit.

He felt too much. Burning lust, and something more, something secret and powerful and fierce. He was nearly undone by it, by the tide of emotion that threatened to tug him under. He didn't want to name it, didn't want to recognize it. Didn't want to have her mean so much to him.

Worse, he didn't have a clue how it had happened.

Lowering his head, he took her mouth. Gently. A subtle caress. Holding himself in check. He could do this, make slow, sweet love to her without lowering his defenses. Hold her at arm's length. He could do it. He had to. Anything else could see his destruction. And hers.

But *not* having her just wasn't an option.

Her gaze was fixed on his lips, her pupils dilated.

Again, he kissed her, smooth, lush, pushing his tongue inside, sucking, biting, rocking his hips toward her.

There were a million reasons he should stop. Now.

And only one reason to continue. Clea. The heat of her. The sweet, sweet, taste. The low, achy moan that told him she was as close to madness as he was. That she wanted him. That she needed him. Needed him to be the one solid thing in her suddenly bizarre, mixed-up world.

The irony of it was that he was neither solid nor safe. He was part demon. Her worst nightmare.

His own worst nightmare.

Her moan was his undoing. He was primed, diamond-hard, blood pounding through him, pooling in his groin with a steady throb.

The pleasure he felt was halfway to pain, flames licking at him and the darkness eroding his control. Just from the taste of her, from the glide of her tongue over his, the press of her lips, the way she was rubbing up against him, like close wasn't enough.

One of her hands was fisted in his shirt, dragging the material half off his shoulder, and the other hand was skimming along the curve of his hip bone, dipping in to the waistband of his jeans.

Dark and threatening, the thing inside him almost slid loose, vibrating with an intensity far greater than any it had shown before, flaying him with sharp talons as he struggled to drag it back. *Christe*. It wanted her, wanted Clea. It wanted to cross the connection, flow into her, take her, and his determination ramped up even higher.

How could she not feel it, not sense the malevolence in his soul? How could she not be afraid?

He caught her wrist, pulling back to study her face, and she laughed, the sound low and throaty. Then she leaned forward and ran her tongue along the ridge of his pectoral, getting a tiny taste of him before she sank her teeth into skin and muscle, hard enough for him to feel it, almost hard enough to hurt.

His cock jumped, and she laughed again, that sexy, husky laugh that beckoned to him.

And the evil inside him uncoiled, eager to slither beyond its cage.

Clea licked him again, loving the taste of his skin. He was holding himself back, bottling his need. She could sense that, sense the harsh edge of his lust. And she wanted that lust, wanted him to lose control, to give himself up to her. To take what he wanted.

Hadn't he told her that? *Sometimes you need to take what you want.*

Well, thanks for the lesson. She was a fast learner, and she wanted him as she had never wanted anything in her whole life.

Tugging his head down to hers, she kissed him, tired of the little game of back-and-forth, tired of him holding back, pulling back, studying her reactions. She wanted him crazy. Wild like he made her wild. He opened his mouth, and she sucked on his tongue, a desperate craving cycling through her. Something fierce and dangerous reared inside him, a little frightening; she could feel it there, lacing the magic that poured from him into her like decadent, rich chocolate, melted and warm.

Only what she sensed was something more. Hungry, dark need, stripped to its most basic core.

"I'm not afraid," she whispered, somehow knowing that he needed to hear it. Except she *was* afraid. Afraid of the bizarre turn her life had taken, the danger that hovered in the air. But not of him. Despite everything she had seen, she definitely wasn't afraid of him.

With a low groan, he moved his body against hers, stoking the flame in the pit of her belly as he pushed his tongue into her mouth and pressed her back against the car. The kiss, the taste of him, moist, deep, tongue and teeth, turned her blood lava-hot, stole her breath.

Catching the hem of her sweater, he dragged it up over her head, tossed it aside, and shoved her jeans down her legs. She toed off her shoes, then her jeans the last bit, and kicked them aside. She didn't feel the cold, and she thought it was somehow tempered by his magic.

Eyes glittering, he stood watching her, and then he smiled, a sexy curve of his lips that made her shiver.

"Take your bra off." His voice was rough with passion, his gaze hot.

Her hands were shaking as she reached up and obeyed, liking the sound of his voice, liking the way he looked at her and the feeling of him watching her, hungry, primal. She couldn't seem to catch her breath, her heart pounding a frantic rhythm. There was something undeniably erotic about standing almost naked under the stars, clad only in black thong underwear, before a man who was still mostly clothed.

Reaching out, he cupped her breast, stroked his thumb along her nipple, pinched it lightly, sending a riot of sensation screaming through her.

His gaze raked her. "*Christe*. Clea. You are so beautiful you defy even a sorcerer's vast imagination."

She was on fire, liquid heat sliding through her veins, and she wanted to feel his skin gliding along her own. A damp throb exploded at the juncture of her thighs, and she was suddenly desperate to have him inside her, hard and thick and deep. She wanted him sheathed inside her, stretching her, filling her; she wanted to unleash his darkest passion.

She took a step forward, her legs like rubber, and pressed herself against him, a shaky laugh tumbling from her lips. Feeling the bulge of his erection, thick and full, straining against the fabric of his jeans, she rubbed her hips slowly back and forth. His hands were on her breasts, kneading, pinching her nipples, twisting gently, then just a little harder. Soft sounds of pleasure drifted from her lips.

He kissed her, openmouthed, luscious, until she could barely think, until she was awash in sensation, pleasure, and the sweet ache of passion. And then he put his mouth on her breast, his tongue circling the sensitive peak.

"Oh, God," she whispered, twining the thick strands of his hair around her fingers, dragging his head closer. "Please. I want . . ."

His lips closed around her, sucking on her, his teeth scraping lightly against the aching flesh, and she cried out, arching her back in ecstasy.

As though he could read her every want, her every desire, he touched her, kissed her, handling her in the exact ways she needed, stroking her until she couldn't stand, couldn't think.

Catching her wrist, he dragged her hand down, helping her ease open his zipper, closing her fingers around the full, heavy length of his erection as it sprang free of the cloth. Oh, smooth, smooth skin and burning heat, the heft of him in her hand, so thick, so hard. He kept his fingers around hers, working their hands together from the crown, down along the shaft and up again, slow firm strokes that made her ache to kneel before him, to suck his erection into her mouth, deep into her throat.

He laughed, a wicked sound that made her shiver, made her ache. "Later," he whispered, as though he could read her mind, and she could feel a change in him, whatever reins he had held tight loosening, freeing just a little.

With a yank, he ripped her underwear off her body and slid his hand between her thighs, pushing two fingers up into the wet, slick heat of her, a smooth movement. She was so ready for him, and his fingers were so unbearably clever, in, then out, then in again, and she cried out, waves of sensation tearing at her, making her rock her pelvis, seeking the heel of his hand where it rubbed her clitoris. The pressure was enough to make her ache, make her moan, but not enough to give release.

God, he was so hot, so hard, so amazingly sexy.

She licked the golden skin of his chest, tasting salt and man, then tilted her head back and met his lips with hers. Savage pleasure spiraled through her, and she could feel the pulse of his magic twined with the dark throb of whatever he held leashed inside himself, desperate to be free, to get out, to get inside her, the intense edge only stoking her already inflamed senses.

"Condom," she muttered.

"I don't catch human diseases." His voice was strained, tight. "And I can't pass any to you."

The connection between them hummed, and she

didn't doubt that he spoke the truth. "I need you inside me."

She felt the pulse of his magic, so hot it almost burned, blending with the sensation of his touch. One more level of pleasure. *I need to be one with you. Joined with you.* The strength of her emotion frightened her, and she pushed it away. Sex. It was only sex.

Only it wasn't. It was a melding, a true joining.

He slid his fingers along the curve of her hips to her waist, his hands closing around her, lifting her, pressing her up against the car door as she wrapped her legs around his waist.

Running her hands over the muscles of his arms, she groaned, loving his strength, the steely firmness of his shoulders, his forearms. God. She couldn't have imagined it. Letting him take her under the stars, up against cold glass and steel, his teeth closing on the sensitive skin of her neck, one big warm hand holding the globe of her buttock while the other guided his erection between her legs. She couldn't have imagined it, but now, she couldn't imagine not having it, not having him.

"Ciarran." His name was a whisper. The feel of him, the head of his cock so broad, so smooth, working into her, slow shallow thrusts, stretching her. He was so big. Hot. Slick. One firm thrust, and he was all the way inside her, the sensation overwhelming. She clung to him, held in the solid strength of his embrace, her body trembling as he hooked his arms under her knees, hiked her just a little higher, giving him better access, deeper access, tipping her pelvis at an angle so right, so perfect, that every stroke shot bolts of pleasure radiating from her core.

She dug her fingers into his hard shoulders, pushing

herself flush against him, wanting him deeper, wanting him frenzied, wanting him pumping into her as consumed by frantic hunger as she was, as driven by need.

"*Christe*. Clea. I can't—" A sharp hiss escaped him, and he pulled her tighter, thrust into her with fast, hard strokes, sending them both into a crazy spiral. He dipped his head, took her nipple in his mouth, sucked on her, a hard, tugging pull.

The power inside her swirled in concert with his, and for the first time, there was no pain to accompany the glowing rhythm, the energy, the magic that was her long-held secret. Her power, led by his, a concert, beautiful, sensual, joining them on every level. She sank her teeth into her lower lip, her head falling back against the roof of the car, her body trembling as she began to convulse in the throes of her climax, her pleasure sizzling along the magical current that connected them.

White light and stark satisfaction. She had never felt anything like it. And still he moved within her, slower now, sheathing himself inside her, withdrawing, prolonging her pleasure as she whispered his name again and again, the throbbing in her body drawn out in an endless road of delight.

He felt her orgasm, the sensation unutterably erotic, the swell of her rapture reaching across their bond, from her, into him. Gritting his teeth, Ciarran held himself in check, battling sensation and utter need, unwilling to drop the last of his barriers, unwilling to chance the demon's release.

"Let go, Ciarran. You won't hurt me." Clea laid her palm against his cheek, her eyes dark and slumberous, as she moved against him, her hips rocking to meet his thrusts, increasing the rhythm once more.

Oddly, he believed her. In their joining was strength, not weakness. He was stronger than the demon within.

With a groan, Ciarran reached down, his fingers sliding over her swollen clitoris, stroking her until she squirmed and moaned, so slick, so beautifully responsive. He moved his hips, slowly at first, the sound of her sighs and whimpers pushing him ever closer to the edge, his body shouting for release.

Panting, she was panting, her body straining against his, and he sensed she was going to come again, unravel around him in a burst of light. His rhythm changed, and she met each thrust, fast, hard strokes until she tensed, her nails raking his skin as she climaxed. The strength of her orgasm and the feel of her muscles clenched tight around him again shoved him over the edge. His cock jerked inside of her as he came in an intense throbbing wave, bodies intertwined, magic intertwined, her pleasure inseparable from his.

He held her for a perfect eternity, or perhaps it was only a moment, the buzz of ebbing pleasure humming through him. As the aftershocks subsided, he let her slide the length of his body until her feet touched the ground, her hands straying lightly along his arms, as though she was yet unwilling to break their physical connection.

In a fury, the thing inside him, the part that was dark, stinking demon, jerked viciously at its chains.

Chapter 18

SILENTLY BLESSING THE HEATED CAR SEATS, CLEA reached out and tilted the vent in the dash. Hot air fanned her skin. The bag she'd taken from the apartment bumped against her leg as they turned a corner. In the bag were two photo albums, the framed pictures of Gram and of her parents, the case that held her precious CDs with the photos she had transferred onto them: her fifth birthday, sitting on a pony while her father stood so proudly beside her, grinning brighter than the sun; Halloween, the year she turned six, her mom smiling for the camera as she painted Clea's face to look like a cat. Memories. Treasures.

That bag held the sum total of everything important that had been in her apartment. She wasn't certain if that made her staggeringly nonacquisitive or exceptionally pathetic.

Her gaze slid to Ciarran. He had killed for her, to protect her. Again.

And he'd made love to her. Mind-blowing, wicked, amazing love.

There had been an instant of pure connection, a wonderful moment of completion, and then as though a metal grate had clanged down between them, he'd pulled back, his demeanor, his expression so controlled. She felt as though the aftermath of their lovemaking had sealed him in a stark, empty room with his own private pain, pushed him away from her rather than drawing him closer. As though everything depended on him keeping up an imaginary wall.

Now he stared straight ahead, steering with his left hand. His jaw tensed each time he used his right hand to change gears, and she knew he had to be in pain. His arm was bleeding where the *hybrid* had slashed him, the edges of the deep gash gaping wide. She thought she could see bone.

"Shouldn't you be healing by now?" she asked, appalled by the extent of his wound, doubly horrified because she had been so caught up in the heat of their passion, she hadn't even thought of it until now.

"My magic is depleted." His tone was harsh.

Depleted. By the battle with the *hybrids*? With a rush of heat, she thought of the way he'd lifted her against the car, pumped into her with strength and power. That definitely could not have been good for his injury. So, no, she didn't think he was depleted only by the battle.

She caught hold of the shoulder seam of her sweater, using her teeth to gnaw enough of a hole that she could tear the sleeve free. Shimmying the cloth down her arm, she pulled it off and deftly wrapped Ciarran's wound.

He glanced down, then returned his attention to the road, saying nothing.

"You need to get to a hospital," she whispered, staring at the blood that was already seeping through the makeshift bandage.

Red, red blood. It had been everywhere. On her hands. The ground. Pouring from her parents' bodies like twin fountains. Pouring from her own body, from her leg, from the gaping hole in her belly. The crash. Images flashed at her with vivid clarity, images she had not known were branded in her mind. God. No wonder she'd buried the memories so deep.

She shuddered, remembering the sight of her abdomen gaping open and her intestines spilling out like thick, fat worms. Blood everywhere. And the smell of sulfur and death. Those memories made no sense. They must be flawed, because she bore no scars, and the injuries she recalled would definitely have left marks.

Actually, the wounds she recalled should have killed her.

"A hospital?" Ciarran shot her a sardonic glance. "St. John's?"

Thrusting aside the horrible images that assailed her, she focused on Ciarran's question. She frowned, thinking of Terry's assertion that two women had died at St. John's, but thinking, too, of something more, something that nagged at the edge of her thoughts. She tapped her fingertips against her thigh, concentrating, the connection evading her.

St. John's.

Something about the hospital . . .

And then it hit her, a thought too absurd to have any possibility of being accurate.

Asa Paley. Suave, handsome Asa, who had pursued her and wooed her when she'd put in some observation time at St. John's. He should have been her dream man. In fact, on occasion she'd had the thought that he was too perfect, his words too pat. For some inexplicable reason he hadn't seemed all that attractive to her. There were times she'd even thought he repelled her, though she couldn't have pinpointed exactly why that was so.

Thinking about it now, she could *swear* she'd seen Dr. Asa Paley tonight, lurking in the shadows outside her building just before the *hybrids* had attacked. And how crazy was that?

"No, don't go to St. John's." She shook her head. "General is closer, maybe ten minutes—"

"I don't need a hospital." His tone didn't encourage discussion.

She glanced at his arm. The cloth she'd tied around it was already soaked, stained red, glistening wetly in the glow of the streetlights that illuminated the car.

"You're not healing," she pointed out. Not the way he'd healed the previous night when the demon cut him, or when they'd jumped through the window this morning. He was different somehow. She could feel it. "What happened back there? What . . . ?"

The question caught, a glutinous mass trapped in her throat. Did she really need to hear the answer? Did she want to?

He wasn't the sorcerer of light she had thought. Not all bright and good.

Oh, he had saved her, but the threat, the unfettered

power and pulsating menace that had crashed from him in waves, the acid mist and the polished blades that had ripped his skin, tearing their way free, those things had seemed more apt for one of those demons than a light sorcerer. She had a definite feeling that something wasn't right.

The look on his face as he battled the *hybrids,* lips peeled back in a feral snarl, had been danger and menace and deadly intent, *without restraint.* Not the way he had been at the Blue Bay Motel, when he'd shown such icy control, so politely inviting the demon to leave, only battling when the creature refused to go.

No. As he had fought the *hybrids* tonight, he had been something else entirely, something she did not recognize. Unfettered. Without checks and balances.

She should have been afraid, but when she looked at him, her bruised and battered champion, she saw only the man who was her lover. Her rescuer.

She wanted to rescue *him,* save him from all his darkest torments. And she was absolutely certain that he had those in spades.

Turning down a narrow alley, Ciarran drove to the very end before killing the headlights and the engine. Sound and light filtered from the main road, and Clea squinted, studying her surroundings. On the right was a wall of dirty red brick, marked by graffiti, with cracked and rotting boards nailed across the windows. On the left was a building of drab gray concrete, with barred windows on the second floor and an industrial door at the top of a short staircase. The balustrade was torn from its mooring, hanging loose like a ragged hangnail.

"Umm . . . I thought you said you were taking me

home. Are you sure we're in the right place?" Clea asked, looking around warily as Ciarran opened the door and stepped from the car. This dirty alley sure didn't fit with the way she had imagined he lived.

"Yeah." Resting one hand on the roof of the car, he ducked his head to look at her, his expression unreadable. "We're in the right place." He shut the door and walked around to her side.

After climbing from the car, she turned to watch as the wind sent a sheet of newspaper tumbling along the ground, end over end, until it came to rest atop a small hill of paper and cardboard that lay in a damp pile against the wall where crumbling concrete met filthy pavement. The refuse melded into a miniature mountain at the side of an overflowing Dumpster that spewed garbage, tainting the air with the stink of rot and decay.

"Nice." Clea laughed, a nervous sound that ricocheted off the walls. He was so close, a damaged angel, with his perfect, perfect face and his warm skin, smooth over steely muscle. The dark stain of his blood oozed from beneath the makeshift bandage she'd made, dripping down his arm. *God*. She hated the sight of his blood because it felt wrong on so many levels. She hated that he'd been hurt and, worse, that he'd been hurt protecting her.

Turning away, she made a sweeping gesture with one hand. "I love what you've done with the place."

"Open your mind, Clea." His breath was warm against the skin of her nape as he stepped close behind her, and she inhaled the scent of him, clean and fresh and so luscious as it wrapped around her, blocking out anything, everything, else. How could he smell so good after what he'd just been through?

"Choose to see that which is unexpected," he said. "See between the molecules and atoms. Color outside the lines, Clea mine."

Clea mine. She swayed, mesmerized by the sound of his voice, smoke and velvet, weaving around her and through her, so seductive. "I don't understand."

"See beyond mortal reality. Some realms overlap, occupying time and space in perfect synchrony. This"—he reached around her to make a smooth gesture with his gloved hand—"*this* is my reality."

She felt it, the glow of his magic, jumping from him into her; then she did see. A door. Unexpected. Lovely.

With a gasp, she stumbled forward, laying her hand on the intricately carved wooden door. It looked ancient. Beautifully preserved. So out of place here in this alley . . .

Spinning, she saw that the alley had faded away.

Now the moon drenched a courtyard with a fountain, painting it in shades of variegated silver, a dazzling luminosity. She saw it. She *saw* it.

Moving as if in a dream, she walked toward the fountain, dipped her hand in the water, felt the cool wetness on her skin. She studied the shimmering rivulets as they streamed from her fingertips. Laughing, she turned to face Ciarran and found him watching her with naked longing.

Touch me. Take me. Make love to me again. She barely held herself back from going to him, from smoothing her fingers along the harsh line of his jaw, tunneling her hands into the strands of his thick hair and dragging his mouth down to hers.

He was so savagely beautiful, it almost hurt to look at him. Tonight, the wizard had been the darkest kind, primitive, even frightening, clothed in the shroud of menace that breached his control. She knew the darkness was there still, just beneath the surface, lurking, surging, trying to get free. She had felt it as they made love, and she felt it now.

Pressing her hands against her thighs, she ran her palms up and down. She swallowed, looked away. Why did she feel that she had somehow been the catalyst, that she was somehow responsible for unleashing the beast and somehow responsible, too, for helping to cage it? It made no sense.

Crazy. She felt crazy. Not like herself at all. She had thought that following her usual routine, feeding her friends at Box Town, would make her feel better, stronger, more like Clea. And it had. Definitely. But at the same time, she felt so *unlike* herself. Strong, too strong, like she could do anything. Jittery and hot, her skin tingling and, deep inside, her power coiling.

Her gaze shot to Ciarran. She'd wanted him so badly. The recollection of it washed through her now, hot enough that it almost had her dropping to her knees. She wanted him again, despite what she'd seen, despite what she'd felt, the terrifying strength and the infinite threat that pulsed deep inside his core. He was not human. And he was not pure light and goodness. He was darkness and power and barely leashed danger. He was not anything safe or tame.

She didn't care. They were linked somehow. She was

bound to him, to the darkness as much as to the light, to what he had become there outside her apartment. Disturbing. Terrifying. Protecting *her*.

Yeah. This was crazy. It was far, far outside her experience, and all she knew was that she wanted to be close to Ciarran, plastered up against him, kneeling over him, running her tongue along the salty warmth of his skin, sucking on him, biting him, feeling him push up, into her, deep inside her. Again. She wanted him again.

"What's happening to me?" she whispered.

"Nothing." His voice was a low rasp.

Only she knew he was lying, or if not exactly lying, not exactly telling the truth. She felt . . . different. She was different.

He crossed the courtyard and opened the ornately carved wooden door, moving carefully, as though he didn't want to get too close, didn't want to touch her, not even the most casual contact. "Come on. Let's go inside."

Following him through the open door, she stumbled to a halt and stared. Stunned, she turned a full circle, tried to take it all in. "Wow."

Marble columns shot to the ceiling, defining an enormous entry hall. She tilted her head back to look up, way up. "You know, from the outside, this building didn't look quite so tall."

He made a low sound of amusement. "Look between the molecules, Clea. See what's really here rather than what you think is here."

If she could see demons and *hybrids,* then it was no big stretch to see marble columns. Nodding, she turned back, peeked out the door they had just passed through.

The alley was there, just beyond the courtyard. She leaned out, craning her neck until she saw the Dumpster pushed up against the wall, the pile of rotting cardboard at its base.

"Nothing has made sense since that demon showed up at the Blue Bay." She pulled the door shut, closing out the night. "So I guess that my whole world has changed, right?"

"Much has changed." The way he said it made her think that it wasn't just much; it was *everything*.

She stepped farther into the hall and looked around. The walls were lined with gorgeous vases, artwork, even weapons. She moved closer to look at a glass case filled with tiny hand-painted bottles. For a moment, she studied them, then realized she had seen an exhibit like this at the museum. Chinese snuff bottles.

"Are these real?"

"That depends on your definition of *real*."

Semantics. She shot him a reproving glance, her gaze lingering on his bloodied arm. "Do they actually exist? In the human world?"

"Yes." Leaning against a column, broad shoulders angled to take his weight, arms crossed over his muscular chest, he studied her.

"I think I need to stitch your arm," she said.

"Not necessary." His tone did not invite discussion.

Turning back, she looked at the bottles and the poster hanging above the case. WORLD EXHIBIT 2004. SPONSORED BY CD PHARMACEUTICALS. She was no expert, but she had a feeling these bottles were priceless.

CD Pharmaceuticals.

She frowned.

CD . . . Ciarran D'Arbois.

"You own CD Pharmaceuticals," she said, whirling toward him.

"Is that an accusation?"

"You donate millions of dollars' worth of medications to third-world countries!"

He exhaled on a breathy sigh. "It's forbidden to heal dying mortals by magic. It isn't forbidden to provide the means for them to heal themselves." He stared at her for a long moment, his expression defensive, as though he expected to be rebuked.

Forbidden? By what law? She didn't understand.

Abruptly, he turned and led the way down a long corridor. She followed, trying not to gawk at the artwork . . . the weapons . . . his gorgeous butt.

Trying not to freak out because every piece she uncovered only made the puzzle more confusing.

"You can use this bedroom." He pushed open a door at the end of the hallway and stepped back to let her precede him. "Bathroom's the door on the right. Closet's the door on the left."

She laughed. "I don't have anything to put in a closet." She stepped into the room and gasped.

The bedroom was *his*, his stamp, his personality apparent even at a glance. Masculine clean lines. Expensive taste, just like his clothes, his bike, his car. An enormous plasma screen filled the far wall, and shelves of DVDs were arranged on either side. What looked like the most expensive, comfortable couch she had ever seen was angled in front of the screen. And the bed. It was bigger than a small country.

"Let me guess . . . six-hundred-thread-count sheets?" she asked.

The corners of his mouth kicked up in the barest hint of a smile. "Egyptian cotton."

"I—" She swallowed, glanced at the bed. He slept there. And he wanted her to sleep there. . . . "I didn't know that you sleep." Okay. Dumb. "I mean, that sorcerers sleep—"

"Sorcerers sleep." He stepped closer, studying her, his gaze intent. "Less than mortals. Once per week is adequate for me."

Clea nodded, her breathing shallow, her pulse kicking up a notch. In her whole life no one had ever looked at her the way Ciarran did, the lights in his eyes like dancing flames, licking at the deepest part of her.

"*I've* always needed less sleep than everyone else," she whispered, her mouth grown dry as something in his assertion struck her as significant. "Three, four hours a night and I'm good to go. That was the reason I managed to work and go to school and take care of Gram. I just had more useful hours than most people."

He was watching her, his expression ruthlessly neutral.

"Why is that, Ciarran?" Her heart rate accelerated as she waited, already knowing the answer, half-afraid he'd confirm it. Half-afraid he wouldn't. "Why don't I need a lot of sleep?"

Lie. That's what he was going to do. She could see it in his eyes, read it in the tightening of his jaw. Only she wasn't going to give him the chance.

She crossed her arms tightly over her chest, dragging her courage about her like a quilt. And then she just asked the question, a little breathless, her voice wavering just a bit.

"I'm like you, aren't I? I am what you are." Oh, God. Was she? Deep inside, was she the same dark, terrifying beast that she had seen him become?

And if so, was she strong enough to wrestle it into submission as he had?

Uncertainty. Wariness. The cold metallic taste of her fear. She swallowed, her thoughts spinning.

He stood there, looking grim, his hard mouth compressed in a tight line. "I don't know. You should be human."

"But I'm not? Since when?" Backing away from him, she felt panic gnaw at the edges of her control. Memories bombarded her, harsh and stark: the dark empty road, the sound of rending metal. She remembered hurtling through the air and the terrible sound of someone screaming. Herself. *She* had been screaming, and then whimpering, her voice fading.

The crash. She was remembering the crash again, clearer now, the smell, the sounds, the feel of dry grass poking her cheek, and the hot trickle of blood. The images were too sharp, too vibrant, like she was watching them through the lens of a camera rather than through the long-buried memories of an eight-year-old child.

She pressed the back of her clenched fist to her mouth, feeling sick, and he watched her, saying nothing, letting her work through to her own conclusions.

"*You* were there that night. The night my parents died." Her throat felt parched, scored raw, and her voice rasped as she spoke.

"I came too late, Clea."

Too late. Too late. For what?

Her gaze dropped to his hand, hazy memories coalescing into certainty. A monster; a *demon*. She remembered that. A horrific struggle. A single, agonized scream. Ciarran's scream.

Nausea churned inside of her.

"I remember the light," she whispered. "A glowing ribbon of light, wrapping me, taking my pain, warming me." Her gaze snapped to his. "Beautiful light. It called to something inside of me. I wanted that light, needed it, and so I took it."

A chill slid through her veins, smooth, cold, leaving her shaking and numb. Oh, God. Let her be wrong. Please. Let her be wrong. "I took it from *you*."

Stepping toward him, she blinked against the sting of tears. He watched her, making no move to stop her, his body tense. She reached out, caught the edge of the leather glove, peeling it away from the skin of his wrist.

There were symbols tattooed in his skin, fanning out from the mouth of the dragon like flames, winding about his wrist in a thick band. They looked like letters of a long-dead language.

She tugged on the glove, trying to see the rest of his hand, and he clamped an iron grip around her forearm, stopping her quest. "Wards and spells," he rasped. "To deflect the darkness."

Her stomach churned, and she tore her gaze away from the inked markings. She remembered the night of the crash, remembered the feel of his magic, the way he'd tried to pull away, the way she'd refused to let go.

"Earlier, in the hallway, you said it's forbidden to

heal dying mortals by magic." She swallowed. "So you weren't going to save me. What did you mean to do? When you touched me that night with your light . . . your power?"

His breath hissed from between his teeth. "Take your pain. I couldn't stand to see you suffer."

"Like you did for the demon-keeper when he was dying." Breathing fast, she tried to understand the thoughts that were hammering at her. "You were going to let me *die*."

He met her gaze, unflinching, and a muscle tensed in his jaw. "I wasn't—I can't heal a mortal who's already passed beyond all capacity to heal. It's forbidden by the *Pact*."

"And the *Pact* is what? Some kind of law?"

"An ancient agreement that binds all sorcerers. Human life must include mortality. Human death. Such is the circle, and we are forbidden to interfere."

Suddenly it was all so clear, everything finally clicking into place. "But I didn't die."

"No."

"Why not?"

He hesitated, then said, "Because you refused your fate."

"Uh-huh. By doing what? How did I refuse? I was a half-dead eight-year-old." Her voice was thin and high, and she felt panic clawing at her.

"You took what I meant to offer as comfort and turned it into your salvation."

"I *took* it? What? What did I take?" She sucked in a breath. Of course. "The power you used to ease my pain." She understood now, with a clear and bright lucidity. She'd *taken* it, stolen his magic that long-ago night, set in motion the events that had led them here, to this moment. She was the catalyst for what had come to pass.

"It's my fault. All of it." Horror congealed in the pit of her stomach, the hard knot sawing at her, a deep and terrible pain. "I *stole* your magic. Stole your power. Weakened you somehow. The night that my parents died, and now, too. Tonight. That's what this is about, isn't it? That's what you meant outside my apartment to-night when you told me to move away from you. That's why your wound isn't healing."

She was breathing heavily, the magnitude of her real-ization staggering.

He'd protected her. Made love to her. Stayed by her side. Made her feel safe. No, not just *feel* safe. He had kept her safe, but at what cost to himself?

"Oh, God." She moaned, stumbled back. "I'm toxic to you, aren't I? Like some kind of poison?"

He took a step toward her. "Clea—"

"Tell me the truth. Please."

His mouth tightened, and she felt the air shimmer around them, dark, threatening. "You're definitely dan-gerous. To me. To my power. To my ability to do my job."

"Your job as all-powerful, world-saving sorcerer," she said.

"Yeah." He smiled, a bitter twist of his lips. "And I can't seem to make myself do the sensible thing and stay the hell away from you."

Closing his hand around her arm, he dragged her up against him, his expression savage; then his mouth was on hers, hot and hard and hungry. She came alive in a heartbeat, electricity ramping through her, every nerve animated, throbbing.

His magic weaved through her, and she felt a flare of panic. She couldn't stop its flow, didn't know how to temper the greedy pull.

With a harsh sound of frustration, he tore away from her, anguish and desperation etching hard lines, bracketing his mouth. For an endless moment, he stared at her, his breathing rough and ragged.

"Get some sleep," he said. And then he turned and left her, left her body hot and screaming for him, her soul aching for his.

Chapter 19

GRITTING HIS TEETH, CIARRAN SHOVED THE NEEDLE through his skin, felt the glide of the thin thread as he sutured the wound that lacerated his arm. It wasn't the first time he'd had to sew himself up. Some battles were more draining than others, taking uncommon amounts of his reserves of power, and on rare occasions throughout the centuries he had been forced to turn to mortal methods to heal wounds. Still, the experience was not a pleasant one. He much preferred the use of magic as healing balm, but he didn't dare diminish his assets any further.

He secured a bandage over the gash and stepped into the shower, a wry smile tugging at his lips as he looked around the unfamiliar surroundings.

Had he ever showered in this bathroom in the years he'd lived in this place? He didn't think so. There had been no reason for him to utilize a guest bedroom in his own home.

Until now.

Tipping his head back, he let the hot water stream over his head, his shoulders, careful to draw only enough magic to maintain a barrier over his freshly sutured wound. A small and necessary use of his power, but one that, in his current depleted state, tugged at him nonetheless. Almost everything he had was focused on containing the demon parasite that writhed and twisted and snarled to get free.

He needed to rest, recover, gather his strength, but he sensed that such luxuries were not to be his. There was an element of urgency that chewed at him, something wrong in the *continuum,* something dangerous to both sorcerer and man. He had every conviction that it had a direct relation to the demon he had sensed tonight and the traitor within the Compact of Sorcerers.

Clea was linked to all of this. She was the conduit, the key to the gate. Her power was mushrooming in an exponential growth pattern, her proximity to him only escalating the rate as she pulled from him despite his best efforts to stop her. She was going to hit a crest that would not only be strong enough to breach the wall, but perhaps strong enough to shred it, to annihilate the barrier that protected all mankind.

Only a sorcerer possessed such strength. But she was *not* a sorcerer. She was human. Or at least, she had been until now.

"Fuck." The word echoed off the tile wall, a stark expression of his frustration. He had no explanations. Clea was a sorcerer now, and he had no understanding of how that could have happened.

Stepping from the shower, he reached for a towel, hesitating but a fraction of a second as he realized the towel rack was on the opposite side to the one in his own bathroom. With a shake of his head, he scrubbed the soft cloth over his damp skin, then wrapped it around his hips as he wondered why he hadn't simply installed Clea here instead of in his own chamber.

His hands stilled as certainty slammed through him. Because he wanted her *there*, in his bed, his linens gliding over her naked skin, the scent of her on his pillow.

The thought made him hard. He closed his eyes, recalled the scent of her skin, the heat of her as he'd thrust deep, the breathy sound of her release. It made him want to walk down the hallway, push open Clea's door, and let himself into her room, into her bed. He wanted her lips on his. And lower. Wanted the damp glide of her mouth and the scrape of her teeth on his cock. Wanted the mindless pleasure.

The image was damned erotic.

And damned disconcerting. He dragged on clean jeans, noting the fact that there were times that even well-washed and comfortable denim was a tad too tight in places.

For twenty years he'd held himself in check, and suddenly he felt as though a floodgate had torn open. Clea. He couldn't get enough of her. He wanted her any way he could get her, wet and slick, taking him inside her and coming in a wild rush, screaming his name, her muscles taut, her body shuddering under his. He wanted her flat on her back, her legs splayed, her hands fisted in the tumbled sheets as he licked her and sucked on her and made her gasp and throb.

Hell. Since the first second he'd seen her wielding her plastic gold letter opener at the Blue Bay Motel, he hadn't been able to put sex out of his mind. Now that he'd had her, tasted her, buried himself so deep and warm and full inside her, the wanting hadn't gotten any better. It had only grown stronger, more intense.

Because it wasn't just sex. Not with her.

He felt as if he *knew* her.

Knew her jigsaw puzzle pieces and secret places and dreams and wants and fears.

And valor. Knew her incredible valor.

She was imprinted with his magic, a bond that could not be broken. Only *she* possessed the power to deny him, to decline him. She could choose. And there, up against the car, with the recent danger of the *hybrids* and the heat of battle still swirling through them, she had chosen him.

Chosen him.

Made love to him.

Despite what she had seen him become. She'd seen the blackest part of him, but she'd held out her hand, accepted him for all he was. And all he was not. *Christe*.

He yanked a T-shirt over his head, wincing at the rush of pain in his injured arm. Shit out of luck for a comb, he raked his fingers through his damp hair, shoving it into some semblance of order, trying to wrestle his thoughts, and his private demon, into similar manageability.

Focusing his energy, he tested the limits of the darkness within. It writhed and twisted, seeping through him like an oil slick oozing outward to pollute clear waters. But it *was* contained. For now.

Ciarran knew his next course of action. He needed to consult the Ancient. Get some answers. If anyone had them, the Ancient did. And he needed to give warning to the others of his kind. Asag, a demon of ancient and vast power, was here, in the dimension of humanity, a blight and an immeasurable danger.

Rage bit at him. There was a sorcerer who knew about Asag, who used that knowledge for some twisted gain, allying with the demon, breaking all laws and rules. The situation had the makings of wholesale mass destruction, and it was Ciarran's duty to stop it.

Closing his eyes, he visualized the Ancient, the oldest of them, the most powerful, the leader of the Compact of Sorcerers. The Ancient had been at the signing of the *Pact*. He had battled the demons for millennia. His knowledge and vast experience could help Ciarran find his way.

Magic moved smoothly through him as he summoned it, weak, a paltry force. He dared channel no more than what he absolutely needed. The majority of his power remained focused on holding the darkness at bay.

The sound of rushing water spun around him, and crashing waves and the roar of a great storm. Then the wind was cool on Ciarran's face, a light breeze, and the scent of beeswax flavored the air. There were new sounds. The soft scrape of a footstep. The low huff of regular, even breathing.

A smile tugged at his lips as he recalled Clea's asking if he surfed waves of magic, her innocent question leaving enough of an impression on his thoughts that he had indeed ridden a wave to his destination.

Opening his eyes, he found himself in a huge, dimly lit chamber, the walls swathed in dark fabric. A single fat candle rested on a low table in the center of the room, casting flickering shadows across the layers of cloth and leaving the corners in darkness.

The Ancient had ever preferred to prowl the shadows and hug the dimness of darkened nooks.

There was a noise behind him, and Ciarran turned, his power already coalescing at his fingertips, his body shifting low, at the ready.

Two men spun into the circle of light cast by the candle, their bodies perfectly balanced, their movements in synchrony, a deadly dance. One man was as tall as Ciarran, though he carried less muscle, his form leaner. His look was that of a warrior, stark and savage, his features angular, his dark brown hair cut in a short, haphazard style clearly meant for convenience rather than good looks. Though in truth, he was by no measure lacking in the latter.

Ciarran recognized him immediately.

Dain Hawkins. Sorcerer of the light-staff. Magus of illusion.

The magus whirled, dropped low, and slashed at the legs of his opponent, the Ancient. A lean form of moderate height, he moved with artful ease. His features were obscured, his every action no more than a shifting shadow. Dain grunted as a solid blow landed against his shoulder with a sharp *thwack*.

Ciarran drew back his magic and watched for a moment, thinking how many times he had trained just so, with the Ancient, with another sorcerer. He still met regularly to spar with Javier and Darqun, and even Baunn on occasion. Fighting demons was not something that could always be done from a safe and antiseptic distance. They needed to keep their skills at their sharpest.

As he watched, unease skittered across his skin, raising his hackles. There was something odd about this match, something *wrong*. Dain was dressed in a black silk shirt and black slacks, his attire hardly appropriate for a sparring match. Which suggested that the combat was unplanned. A suspicious incongruity.

An instant later, the two combatants drew apart, the termination of the match far too abrupt to be its natural conclusion. Ciarran felt as though they ceased for his sake alone and that they had some unfinished business they would return to later.

The Ancient melted from sight, blending into the cloth-draped walls as though he had never been, and Dain paced, walking off his tension, breathing heavily, his aura sparking with his agitation.

"Dain." Ciarran stepped closer to the candle, letting the light show his face. "I didn't expect to see you here."

Dain stopped midstride, his posture stiff as he turned his face slowly toward Ciarran. Light and shadow played across his features, showing the lines of tension about his mouth and the wary cast to his eyes. "Any reason that I shouldn't be here, D'Arbois?"

The words were an unexpected and unwelcome challenge.

An eerie sense of disquiet twisted in Ciarran's gut, perhaps a true wariness, perhaps an artifice of the chained beast. Ciarran frowned as he studied the other sorcerer, a man he had known for centuries. He looked haggard, fatigued, as though some great weighty matter sat heavy upon his shoulders.

Dain's behavior was odd. Unexpected.

The darkness within laughed, a harsh and ugly sound, and a whisper came from between the bars of the beast's cage. *The traitor. Dain is the traitor. You know it. You can sense it. 'Twould be easy, so easy, to kill him. Now. Before he has a chance to do great harm.*

Clenching his gloved hand into a fist, Ciarran took a step back, twisting tight the chain that held the malevolence at bay as he forced a deep breath. The urge to give in, to let loose the demonic part of himself was strong. Stronger than it had ever been.

Christe. What the hell was he turning into?

This was *Dain,* for Christ's sake.

"I'm an ass." With a shake of his head, Dain stepped forward, his mouth curved in a smile that failed to reach his eyes. They were the cold, flat gray of poured concrete. "I meant no offense."

Dain grabbed Ciarran's right shoulder and hauled him into a hard embrace before stepping back to study him, his brow creased in a concerned frown.

"Your demon gnaws at you, my friend. I sense it"—he thumped his chest with a closed fist—"here."

Ciarran snorted. "Yeah. The thing has teeth."

"Strange coincidence, yes?" Dain quirked a brow. "The two of us arriving in the Ancient's anteroom in tandem, a happenstance that seems questionable at best."

Ciarran shrugged. "Coincidence? Is there such a thing?"

"So you figure I planned this? Or was it you?" Scraping his fingers back through the short, shaggy layers of his dark hair, Dain gave a hard laugh. His posture was wire-tight, and a sarcastic edge laced his words.

"Or perhaps it's the Ancient who has his own secret design."

"Secret design? The Ancient?" Ciarran asked, not bothering to conceal his incredulity. His tone grew hard. "What are you doing here, Dain?"

"I came to ask a question and to extract a promise. But the Ancient was in no mood to share. So I got nothing; no answers, no reassurance." Dain rubbed his open palm back and forth against his silk-clad shoulder and grinned. "But I do come away with a bruise."

"A question and a promise." Did the guy even know how to give a direct answer?

Dain's mouth curved in a mocking smile. "And you, Ciarran? What are you doing here?"

"I'm here to find out what the hell is wrong with the *continuum,*" he said bluntly, studying the other sorcerer's reaction, wondering if they were here on the same errand. Maybe Dain felt it, too. "To find out if we have been betrayed, if a traitor taints the Compact of Sorcerers."

"A traitor?" Dain smiled, a thimble's worth of movement, but he showed no surprise. His gray eyes narrowed. "And you suspect me, D'Arbois?"

The darkness stirred inside him, fed by a sharp tug of suspicion. "Should I?"

Any hint of good humor faded, and Dain stared at him, his expression taut, his eyes pinched. When he spoke, his tone was harsh. "Do you know what it means to serve the Ancient day upon day for centuries? To study and hone skills under his tutelage? To spend an eternity in a quest for knowledge?" Dain gave a low grunt of derision. "And ultimately to fall short of his exacting standard?"

There was no mistaking the bitterness and the simmering resentment. Ciarran felt the darkness stir again, stronger, his hand ablaze now with a cold flame, white-hot pain, the demon seed stoked by the other sorcerer's black emotions.

"No one made your choices for you, Dain. The role was filled willingly, as I recall."

"Can one truly be willing if they are not fully cognizant of the repercussions of their choice?" Dain's lips twisted in a sneer, and he leaned a little closer, his gaze dropping to Ciarran's hand. "Would you have made the same choices, had you but known?"

Ciarran clenched his gloved fist, anger swirling up like a dust storm, choking out all else. He had asked himself that question every day for twenty years. "Why waste energy thinking about it? I can't go back and choose a different path."

"No shit. And there is no way to know if the outcome would be any better, is there?" Dain asked, no longer mocking, his gaze intent. "In every war battles are won and lost. Paths determined. Sides chosen."

"What's with you tonight? Why are you trying to mess with my head? We chose our sides an eternity past," Ciarran said softly. They had chosen to protect mankind, to guard the wall, to maintain the separation of the realms. To honor the *Pact*.

"And in such choices are great enmities fueled, hatreds bred. Mistakes entrenched."

Enmity. Hate. Ciarran almost laughed. Dain could have no concept of the depth, the dark cold pit of such emotions. But Ciarran knew. They were the treasured delicacies his demon craved, the food that stoked its strength. "What exactly is your point? You're talking in riddles, Dain."

"I've been told it's an annoying habit." Dain studied him for a moment, then smiled thinly. He moved, his shoulder brushing Ciarran's as he strode past, and a white mist swirled from the ground, bright against the dark contrast of his clothing. The mist twined about his feet, his calves, his thighs, working higher and higher. An illusion, Ciarran knew. Though Dain's single perfect weapon was the staff he wielded with such expertise, illusion was his preferred magic. He was ever the showman, ever the magician.

Dain cast a last, hard glance over his shoulder. "In such choices are mortal enemies made."

Mortal enemies and traitors. Tension ratcheted through Ciarran as he studied his friend's back. The mist thickened, obscuring Dain's form, leaving him a dark wisp in a white cloud.

"Do you practice being an enigma?" Ciarran snarled, though he didn't expect an answer as he watched Dain disappear in the fog.

"A rhetorical question?" The sound of an amused voice made Ciarran turn, and he came face-to-face with the Ancient. He was dressed in clothing that was loose and comfortable, simple garments that had neither style nor determined shape, just layers of soft, dark material hanging on a slim frame. His hair was so light it looked white in the candle's dim glow, tied back and hanging in a single plait to his waist. His face was smooth, unlined, so fair as to be almost feminine. His eyes were a pale blue, rimmed in navy, the effect truly startling.

"Ancient." Ciarran reeled in the surge of temper that Dain had called, and inclined his head, a mark of respect but not subservience. Among the Compact of Sorcerers, the Ancient was the oldest by far, the most experienced, likely the most powerful, though none had ever tested his limits.

The other man gestured to the pillows that littered the floor beside the low table. "Sit, Ciarran. Please," he said, his voice a quiet huff of sound, laced with steel, commanding attention and respect.

Ciarran lowered himself to the pillow, waiting as the Ancient did the same. He studied his mentor, noticing no changes. How many years since they had seen one another? More than a decade.

For a time, after the demon had first settled inside of him, Ciarran had sought the Ancient's counsel, searching for answers and for a way to be free. Until he had come to understand that he could never be free, could never rid himself of the dark torment, the dark enticement that gnawed at the deepest limits of his power. The demon would not be displaced. It was a parasite that dwelled within him, fed from him, truly a part of him, and the best he could hope to do was to wall it off, keep it chained.

He was as much a prisoner of the demon as it was of his will and his alloy glove and his tattooed wards. There was little doubt in Ciarran's mind that someday the captive might well become the captor.

He would fight until he knew he could fight no more. And then he would seek the Ancient to put an end to the demon before it did true harm. Only one way to succeed in that. Inevitable. The time would come, in the near or distant future, when the Ancient would terminate Ciarran. There was no other way that he could see this ending. The Ancient would excise the demon seed, and Ciarran would die.

But not tonight.

Blowing out a slow breath, Ciarran rocked back, forcing his body to relax. "Time has led me full circle, back to the role of protector that I fulfilled two decades past. The girl. Clea Masters. Somehow, she's not human. She has magic. Power."

"Ah." The Ancient studied him, his expression serene, but something flickered in his eyes. "Great power over *you*."

There it was, sliced deep and laid bare. "She draws my magic like I'm a milk shake with a big goddamned straw. How the hell is that possible?"

"Unusual, but not impossible."

Ciarran jumped on that. "It's happened before? A human made sorcerer?"

"She was never human." The Ancient leaned closer, his words coming low and intense. "She is an anomaly, a sorcerer born to two of mortal creation." He shrugged and leaned back. "Somewhere in their ancestry there must be sorcerer blood in both her maternal and paternal trees."

"I have to keep her safe."

"What you have to do is keep her as far from you as can be arranged."

The Ancient's pronouncement sawed at Ciarran's control, made him feel an inexplicable desperation, a raw anguish at the thought of Clea leaving him. He shook his head. "She's the target of *hybrids,* of demons. She can't be left unprotected."

"Yet her proximity leaves *you* unprotected."

Ciarran opened his mouth to protest, but the Ancient met his gaze, and something in his eyes stopped Ciarran cold. "Give her into the care of another, Ciarran. For the good of all."

For the good of all. Except Clea. He couldn't risk it, couldn't trust another to keep her safe. She was *his.* His to protect.

His to love.

Christe. He couldn't have these thoughts, these emotions. Not now. Not with so much at stake. Ruthlessly, he shoved his feelings aside.

"There is a traitor among us," Ciarran said flatly, feeling the bitter taste of the words on his tongue. "Which means I don't trust anyone to guard her."

The news brought no change of expression, and the Ancient watched him calmly, listening as Ciarran summarized his experience with the demon-keeper from the Blue Bay Motel, his meeting with Darqun and Javier, even his odd discomfort with Dain. But Ciarran said nothing of Asag. He could not name a reason for his omission other than shame at having failed to terminate Asag decades past, and again tonight.

Hubris, perhaps.

The Ancient nodded. "And so you would keep the girl with you, by your side, where she poses the greatest threat to your power, your purpose, even your immortality."

"I would keep her safe." Forever. For always. He couldn't stomach the thought of demon claws touching her, demon stink marking her. His blood, his pain, even his life were forfeits he was willing to pay. The irony was not lost on him. *He* had touched her, marked her. And what was he if not part demon? "The demons want her. She's the conduit. She's the key, and she's packing more power than she ever did as a small child."

"She is filled with your magic," the Ancient pointed out. "Enough to tear the wall asunder and let a great outpouring of demons into the realm of man."

"Yeah." Her magic was his, and what the hell was he supposed to do about that?

"Take her to the gate, to the breach that was made years past. Use her power to better seal the void."

The idea was a startling one but not without merit. Use the key to strengthen the lock. "Your suggestion has value," Ciarran mused.

"Better still, give her into the keeping of another to do the deed. Perhaps Javier. Or Dain."

Like a switch opening a gate, the suggestion sent a cold, greasy slither of darkness weaving through him, and Ciarran snarled as he thought of letting Clea go into another's care. The risk was far too great. He narrowed his gaze, his jaw tight. "And if one of them is the traitor?"

"Whom do you suspect, Ciarran?"

"I suspect no one." Ciarran clenched his fist, modulated his tone. "And everyone."

"The demon is strong inside you. I feel it." The Ancient's voice was low, soothing. "Does it tempt you, Ciarran? The darkness? The power?"

Ciarran took a slow breath, the memory of dark magic a succulent lure. He thought of the black blades, the killing mist, such tools and such strength, obtained by loosing the beast just a little. What if the chains were cut, the darkness freed to glide thick and oily through his veins, to feed his magic and feed *on* it, and turn it into something foreign, something far greater than it had ever been?

"I am a light sorcerer," he said. The assertion was fast and forced, and it circumvented the question.

"Yes. With a light sorcerer's limitations. But the demon seed tempts you, cajoles you. Whispers and promises." The Ancient rested his long, tapered fingers on the edge of the table. Perfect serenity. "Are they empty, those promises, or do they hold some measure of truth?"

Ciarran realized he was drumming his own fingers on the smooth surface in a slow, steady rhythm. He disliked this turn of things, disliked the possibilities, the lure, the temptation. And yet he liked it all very much. What was the Ancient implying? That he should embrace the darkness?

"In knowledge is truth. In knowledge is power. Do not spurn that which is foreign simply because you fear it," the Ancient said. Reaching out, he laid his finger on Ciarran's arm, on the sutured wound. There was heat and a sharp twist of pain; then the gash was healed.

"You are wise to suspect no one, and everyone, Ciarran D'Arbois." The Ancient's lips curved in a faint smile, and again, something indecipherable flickered in his gaze. "You are less wise in your lack of acceptance of yourself."

Chapter 20

CLEA WANDERED ALONG THE HALLWAY, FOLLOWING a faint, rhythmic clacking sound. She'd awoken to cool sheets, alone. The recollection of Ciarran's absence that morning set off a cascade of convoluted thoughts and emotions.

They'd had sex under the stars. Crazy, heart-stopping, up-against-the-car-door sex. No, more than just sex; it was something deeper, some emotion that she'd felt sifting through her, and she'd sensed its match in him. There had been no time to talk, to share. He'd brought her here and left her to sleep alone.

She wasn't sure how she felt about that.

Disappointed that he hadn't crawled in next to her. Grateful that he'd given her some space to catch her breath. Freaked out by the fact that she was enthralled by a man who wasn't exactly human and by the bizarre and incredible implication that somehow she was no longer exactly human, either.

What did it mean to be what Ciarran was? To

wield magic and power and filaments of light—she shuddered—and, yes, to wield darkness?

She was afraid, amazed, staggered by the changes wrought in her life. Her emotions were stretched to the point of tearing, and questions were cycling through her thoughts at a crazy rate. They'd been there last night before she'd fallen asleep, and she'd woken up to their wild cacophony this morning. During a long, hot, amazing shower with twenty-odd jets hitting her from varied angles and music videos playing on the plasma screen on the side wall, she'd managed to soothe her body but not her restless mind. The answers she came up with only made her more confused.

When she was done, all clean and dry, wrapped in the biggest, softest bath sheet she'd ever seen, she'd checked the bra and panties she'd washed in the sink the previous night. They were still damp, which had meant going commando. She'd gone rooting through Ciarran's closet in the hopes of finding something to wear. Oh, the guilty pleasure of that. Of running her hands over his Italian silk shirts, of catching a glimpse of the vain part of him that drove him to have endless pairs of expensive jeans and khakis and dress pants and shoes and boots and jackets. . . . Everything in his closet could be on the cover of a men's fashion magazine.

And everything was far too big to be of much use to her.

Then her search-and-rescue mission had yielded something that was wearable, if not exactly a perfect fit: a black cotton T-shirt that she tied at the waist and a pair of sweatpants. If she pulled the drawstring as tight as it could possibly go, the pants managed to do a slow slide down her hips, catching there and sliding no farther. Which was a good thing, given her lack of underwear.

Natural shyness might have kept her holed up in Ciarran's bedroom for eternity, but she was hungry. Starving, actually.

Now, as she continued down the hall, drawn by a steady *clack* that sounded like drumsticks knocked together, her every thought revolved around Ciarran. Where had he slept last night? Had he slept at all?

The bedsheets had smelled like him, clean and a little spicy, the scent of his skin haunting her as she had drifted off to sleep. She'd wanted him. Wanted to go and find him.

But, man, she was his weakness, his Achilles' heel, sucking the life out him. Literally. He'd admitted it. How the heck was she supposed to come to terms with that?

She should leave. Go. Her presence was dangerous to him, and she couldn't bear that. Problem was, the thought of leaving him, of not seeing him, not being near him, made her feel a deep ache, as though she were ramming a blunt blade through her gut.

Steady, rhythmic, the sound of clacking grew louder now, and she followed it to the end of the hallway. The corridor ended in a vast open space with polished wood floors and a high cathedral ceiling. There was no furniture, but there were two men. Huge men. As tall as Ciarran. Muscled. Wielding long, narrow swords in an intricate series of moves.

She glanced down. Beside her on the floor were two neatly aligned pairs of shoes. Very large shoes.

Clea hesitated, something tugging at her memory. Okay, yeah. She had it. In high school, a friend had taken karate. She remembered that the students didn't enter the dojo wearing shoes. So this must be some sort of martial art. It bore no resemblance to any she had ever seen, but, hey, she was definitely no expert.

The clacking ceased abruptly, the two men stopping midlunge and turning to face her. Her breath caught as she stared at them. And they stared at her.

"Clea Masters." The one on the left inclined his head in greeting. He seemed to know her, though she had no recollection of ever having seen him before. And, oh, she would have remembered.

He was gorgeous. *Brown* hardly seemed the right word to describe the color of his hair, so rich and thick, shimmering with countless highlights, hanging in a straight sheet to his square chin. He had the kind of hair that would look perfect no matter what, even first thing in the morning, the kind of hair that couldn't hold a tangle if it tried. Raking a hand through the honey brown strands, he pulled them back from his forehead. His eyes were dark, and as he smiled, a dimple appeared in each cheek. A boyish detail in that ruggedly handsome face, but underneath his charm, she sensed that he was no boy.

As he studied her, his eyes narrowed; then his smile faded, his expression turning to one of bemusement. A slow hiss of air escaped him.

Clea took a step back, suddenly feeling oddly defensive, as though this stranger had looked inside her and somehow found her to be something other than he had expected.

"I am Darqun." He gestured at the second man, who was staring at her like she was a two-headed calf. "And that's Javier."

Javier was equally imposing, his build lean and fit, his hair so dark and shiny it looked black. Blue eyes studied her from beneath straight brows, and his eyelashes were so long and thick she could hardly believe they were real. Still, he looked anything but feminine, the stubble that shaded his jaw and the thin mouth giving him a rough, dangerous look.

"Hi." Okay. That was eloquent. But they were just so . . . overwhelming. She looked back and forth between Darqun and Javier. God. Send them out in public with Ciarran, and they'd create a riot.

Javier continued to study her, his expression quizzical, as though there was something he couldn't quite figure out. She shot him a tentative smile, before shifting her gaze to Darqun. He looked positively forbidding.

"Kumdo." Ciarran's voice, a low rasp close to her ear. The sound made her heart stop, then start pounding again with a solid, thumping rhythm as she turned to look at him.

He was here. Beside her. She could feel the heat of his body and the sizzle of his magic. Something shifted in the shielded center of her heart, behind the wall of competence and reserve she had erected so long ago. Her chest tightened, and she felt like her throat was blocked, her lungs starved of air.

Her pathology classes hadn't covered this, but it was no huge stretch to figure out what was wrong with her. She wasn't just enthralled by Ciarran. Wasn't just attracted to him.

She was falling for him. Falling hard. For his kindness and his generosity, and, yeah, for the steely edge. He was so hard, so tough, a solid wall between her and anything that might come after her. She'd always dreamed of being safe, and when she was with him, she felt safe. She was falling for the way he believed in her, the way he seemed to think she was strong enough to be his match, to take all comers. Like he had faith in her.

God. This couldn't be happening to her. A bolt of terror shot through her. Everyone she loved died. And now, here she was, half in love with a sorcerer, who, if he had a single molecule of intellect, would stay the hell away from her before she stole every last shred of his power.

She threatened everything he was.

She was his poison.

And she wanted him with every shred of her being.

Confusion surged inside her. She'd just been getting her balance, finding her way in life. And now this. A cataclysmic event.

She almost laughed, but only because it beat crying.

"The sport they practice," Ciarran said. "Kumdo. Some call it *kendo*. An ancient Asian form of swordplay. Japanese. Korean." He jutted his chin toward the two men. "They like it for the discipline. The exercise. The synchronicity of movement."

Yes. She could see that. Their movements had been a warrior's dance, every step perfect, every thrust and parry timed and choreographed. A blow to the head, to the body, to the wrist. And each blow stopped by an equally timed block.

They weren't practicing now. Instead, they were just standing there, their swords dangling by their sides.

Darqun was watching her still, and the look in his dark eyes made her shiver.

"It's all right, Clea. These are my . . ." Ciarran hesitated for a second, then continued. "My brothers. My comrades of the Compact of Sorcerers."

At Ciarran's words, Darqun raised a brow, and she wondered if he disapproved of Ciarran's sharing that much information with her. He continued to study her, his expression coldly forbidding and oddly intent, as though he wanted to see inside her, to know her secrets. Moving a step closer to Ciarran, Clea felt the comforting bulk of his arm press against her shoulder and the less comforting sizzle of magic arc and swell between them. With a sigh, she stepped off, cutting the connection.

Darqun made a small gesture, so subtle that she might have missed it if she hadn't already been feeling a little weirded out by his focused stare. As though in response to an attack, power coiled inside her, tight, angry. She gasped, pressed her forearm against her stomach, battling a hot twist of pain on the inside and something else from the outside. An *intrusion*. Like something foreign was trying to get inside her.

Her lids flipped up, and her gaze clashed with Darqun's. He was doing something to her, from way across the room, something she didn't like.

Without thinking, she lashed out, with her heart, with her mind, with the pain and heat that coiled inside her, willing the magic to do as she bid. A hard kick of power flared bright and knocked the sword from Darqun's hand, sending it arcing through the air, end over end, until it smacked against the far wall.

Her heart was pounding, and she felt ill, a sick swirl of nausea writhing in the pit of her stomach.

"He tried to get *inside* me," she whispered. She'd felt it, felt him, Darqun, in her mind.

With a snarl, Ciarran stepped in front of her, his body glowing gold and light, and she jerked back, away from him, away from contact because she knew what harm she could do, knew the threat she posed. He'd protect her, even against a man he considered a brother and even at the risk she would draw his magic.

God, what a mess. She needed to fix it, make it better, only she had no idea how. It wasn't anything like the sort of coping she'd done throughout her life. Nothing like getting a job to pay the bills, or sleeping less to fit everything in, or cooking a meal for the homeless. How did one go about fixing a tormented sorcerer and the resident darkness in his soul?

By leaving so she didn't kill him with good intentions.

"Leash your power, Dar." Ciarran's voice was pitched low, laced with both warning and regret. "I have no desire to leash it for you."

"My apologies. I meant no offense." Darqun looked directly at Clea and shook his head, as though stymied by some particularly difficult conundrum. "I was taken by surprise."

She watched him cautiously, disinclined to accept his apology, and so she said nothing. The way he was looking at her, at Ciarran, the wary amazement in his eyes, wasn't quite right. And there was something else she sensed, something threatening. The whole situation was making her horribly uneasy.

"I had not expected to feel . . ." His sentence trailed away, unfinished, and he transferred his attention to Ciarran once more. "You have taken her to apprentice,

without benefit of the Compact's approval, without sanction of the Ancient?"

"Whoa." Javier backed up a step, clearly appalled.
"You did *what*?"

Oh, man. Whatever they were talking about was not
good. And it was about her. Which made it doubly not
good.

"I have been to see the Ancient," Ciarran said, and
she had the distinct feeling that there was a whole lot he
wasn't saying.

"And he gave you sanction to take her to apprentice?"
Darqun's tone was laced with incredulity.

"I did not *take* her to apprentice. She just *is*." Ciarran
blew out a breath. "She took herself."

"What the hell does that mean?" Darqun snarled.
"She has no wards, no limits, and she's got enough frigging power to give Jav here a good run for his money.
Which makes no sense, because she's *human*. What the
hell is going on here?"

"Leave it alone, Darqun," Ciarran growled.

"I'm learning to control it," Clea said evenly, stepping
between them. "Umm . . . the power, I mean . . . not the
being human . . ."

They were talking over her, around her, as though she
weren't there. She hated that. And she hated the fear gen-
erated by what Darqun was saying. No limits. No wards.
She was not a hundred percent sure what he meant, but
she got the gist, and it made her feel a little like a nuclear
warhead with no safety switch.

Darqun raised a brow and glanced at the sword she'd
knocked from his hand, then back at her, his expression
incredulous. She refused to be cowed. She *was* control-

ling it, or, if not controlling it, at least not losing control
as she had in her kitchen the previous morning when
she'd knocked chairs and coffee cups around, doing little more than making a terrible mess.

No. Not true. She'd done a lot more than that. She'd
sucked Ciarran's power, creating a vortex inside herself. Now all she needed to do was figure out how to get
within ten miles of him without feeding on him, weak-
ening him.

God. What she really needed to do was leave him.

Looking around the room, she realized that everyone
was silent, watching her. She figured they might have
been doing that for a while.

"So, uh, any luck tracking down Asag?" Javier asked,
sounding a bit forced. She glanced up to find his blue
eyes fixed on her.

"Yeah," Ciarran replied, his tone cold. "I had him in
the frigging audience last night while I sparred with a
handful of *hybrids*."

Something about his comment caught Clea's attention, but she couldn't think what it was. She'd seen
no audience, and she couldn't imagine he would have
welcomed one. Though he had made no mention of
any need for secrecy, Clea had the definite impression
that the existence of the Compact of Sorcerers was not
knowledge that should be shared with the general mortal
population.

"You appear unscathed," Darqun said.

Clea turned and studied Ciarran. He was dressed in a
pair of black jeans and a black T-shirt, the short sleeves
baring his arm where he'd been slashed open the previous night. Now there was no cut, no scar, just healthy

skin. A sigh of relief slipped from between her parted lips.

He had healed.

Whatever her proximity had cost him, it was obviously less than she had imagined, and her relief was a sweet river flowing through her.

"Did you see his mortal guise?" Javier asked, drawing Clea's attention.

"Asag?" Ciarran shook his head. "No. I sensed him. Felt his putrid touch in the *continuum*." He paused, as though deciding whether or not he should say more. "He didn't fight."

"What?" Javier raked his fingers through his dark hair, and the strands instantly settled back into perfect symmetry. The mark of an uberexpensive haircut, Clea thought wryly.

"I had the feeling he was there with a purpose, with the intention of observing my interaction with the *hybrids*," Ciarran said.

"And did he see anything of note?" Darqun glanced at Clea, then strolled over to the wall to reclaim the sword her magic had sent flying from his hand.

Her magic. *Hers*. The power she had known she possessed since she was eight years old but had been unable, unwilling, to acknowledge. Now she faced it, claimed it.

Hers.

"He saw me kill *hybrids*." Ciarran shrugged. "Nothing of great interest there."

Blowing out a slow breath, Clea held her silence. He wasn't exactly lying, but he wasn't exactly telling the truth. Yes, he had killed *hybrids*, and she had to assume he had done that before. But the *way* he had done it *was* of great interest.

He'd talked about light magic, and she had a feeling that he was used to using it as his weapon, just as he had the night at the Blue Bay Motel against that minor demon. He was used to cool control and calculated limitation of his power. She had seen that the night he faced the demon.

The unharnessed power of the killing blades and the darkness she had seen last night . . . something told her that they were new and that Darqun and Javier would be most interested in hearing about them. She could feel Ciarran beside her, close but not touching. His tension shimmering just beneath the surface, though he gave away nothing, his true thoughts hidden behind a casual pose.

She figured he didn't want to share the story of his unusual weapons with his friends.

Well, they wouldn't hear about them from her.

Ciarran reached over and looped his arm casually across her shoulder. She felt the sharp tingle of their connection, energy and magic, and a subtle whisper of something else, a warning. Sending him a quick glance, she caught him looking at her, his incandescent eyes shadowed and dark, bidding her to hold her silence.

To keep his secrets.

Chapter 21

"PAGING DR. GRIFFITHS. PAGING DR. STEPHANIE GRIFFITHS."
The noise of the hospital cafeteria melded with the sound of the page.

"We make strange bedfellows, do we not?" Asa Paley studied the sorcerer who sat across from him, his ally. For now.

He had never asked the sorcerer why he betrayed his own, why he betrayed the ideal of centuries. What he did know was that it had started as a ruse. The sorcerer had come with the intent to ferret information, to strengthen his kind, to protect the human realm. Where was the boundary between subterfuge for noble intent and betrayal, however unplanned? Perhaps the sorcerer had known the answer once.

Asa could muster only mild interest. He was certain the immortal had his reasons, and they were of little consequence. Perhaps he would ask before he killed him. The knowledge might serve him well in the future, should he ever need to seek out a sorcerer ally again.

"I would not call us bedfellows." The sorcerer sounded bored, his tone offending Asa in the most basic sense.

"No?" Asa laughed coldly. "What, then?"

"Merely two who have set enmity aside and chosen a similar path for the greater good." The sorcerer's gaze roamed the faces of those near him, studying them with casual interest. "I am of temporary use to you, and you to me. Nothing more, nothing less."

Riddles. The man spoke in riddles. Asa fought the urge to roll his eyes. A fool, this sorcerer, to believe they had set hatred aside, to think they were true allies when in fact he was merely a source of information. How very surprised the traitor would be when Asa turned on *him*.

Bored, Asa glanced about. A woman cried softly at the adjacent table, tears sliding along her cheeks. She sipped on a cold juice, mourning the changes in her aged father as he died a slow death in a room upstairs. Asa let her misery surge into him, cherishing it, relishing it. Human suffering was wonderful, a marvelous treat.

"You sacrificed three of your own," the sorcerer observed.

Asa gave an elegant shrug. "A necessary expense. I needed to ascertain D'Arbois' power and the strength of the demon seed within. The results were shocking. I expected the evidence of inner turmoil and the arrogance inherent to the sorcerer breed. But the weapons that D'Arbois called . . . the blades . . . the cloud of killing mist . . ."

There. His recitation brought out a tiny crack in his companion's composure. Asa raised a brow and continued. "I had thought it was not possible for any sorcerer to channel more than one perfect skill. But D'Arbois did, and the weapons he called were a strange, exotic mix, part light magic, part demonic darkness—"

Asa broke off, turning his head and smiling as he sensed the approach of another doctor. All bluff amiability, he offered his hand in greeting.

"Gavin. Good to see you. How was the conference?"

Gavin flashed him a toothy grin and clapped him on the shoulder. Rage slithered through Asa at such an affront, a mortal daring to defile his person, but he kept his smile in place, his thoughts hidden behind a mask of congenial normalcy.

"Great. Great. My only regret is that Abby couldn't join me." Gavin waggled his eyebrows. "We might have made it into a second honeymoon. The weather was great."

Asa smiled and nodded, until with a last little bit of tedious chatter, Gavin moved off, completely unaware that Asa had a companion. The sorcerer had a penchant for illusion, and at Gavin's approach, he had taken the guise of an empty chair.

"Let us discuss the girl," Asa prodded.

The sorcerer steepled his fingers. "D'Arbois is enamored of her."

A slow curl of rage sifted through Asa, like a pungent, choking cloud of smoke. Clea Masters was *his*. Her magic was his. It infuriated him to think D'Arbois might mate with her, might claim her. She was to have been *his*.

"You gave her to me once before. Sacrifice her again," he breathed, the thought sending a sharp coil of pleasure through him.

Months ago, using the information provided by the

sorcerer, Asa had found Clea doing observation time here at this very hospital. He had seen to it that her grandmother did not respond to treatment. Such an easy matter for him, he who had once been Asag, the demon of plague. Human cancer was a simple demise. Let the cells grow uncontrolled, and they would kill the host. Yet, even buffeted by her heartbreak and loss, Clea had not turned to him as he had expected. She had chosen instead to stand alone and strong, facing her grief with an almost heroic composure.

Dealing with it, she said, because such was the way of life.

He hated her for that. For her strength when he so longed to prey upon her weakness and desperation and fear.

"Give me the information I need," Asa hissed.

The immortal shrugged, toyed with the untouched bottle of water that sat on the table before him. "I told you where to find her, and find her you did. The failures that occurred from that point on are solely your own. What reward do I gain by offering her up a second time?"

Asa could barely maintain the façade of composure, and his body vibrated with anticipated pleasure as he contemplated the sorcerer's demise. He would take his limbs, his blood, his magic, his life, for though the creature was immortal, there were ways and means to see a sorcerer's end, and they were unpleasant. Truly, deliciously unpleasant. Just contemplating the possibilities made him quiver in expectation.

His collaborator would become his prey, cornered, desperate, squirming and wriggling like a skewered worm. The thought sent little pulses of delight coursing through him. It was all he could do to control his expression, betray none of his thoughts.

"Your reward will come with the arrival of the Solitary," he said, leaning across the table and lowering his voice, attempting to betray none of the frustration he was feeling. "I need to know where she is *now*."

He had searched for Clea and failed to find her, losing her trail when he had returned to her apartment building late last night and tried to track her from there. D'Arbois had hidden her away somewhere, and Asa knew he had none to blame but himself. He'd missed his opportunity. Instead of merely playing the watcher as D'Arbois battled the *hybrids*, he should have joined the fray and taken her. Snatched her from the arms of her protector. A lovely twist that would have been.

"Give me Clea Masters," Asa said, returning his attention to the sorcerer. "I must have her. She is the conduit, the key."

"I would prefer that she not be harmed."

Asa blinked. Laughed. A dull flush of anticipation suffused him as he pictured Clea naked beneath his teeth, beneath his talons, flayed and skinned slowly for his pleasure, her screams an opus, her magic sucked into the black vortex of his appetite.

With D'Arbois there to watch.

"And I would prefer harming her." He waited a moment, long enough for the silence to be noticeable; then he offered a compromise. A lie. "Her life is forfeit, but I shall grant you a boon to assuage your conscience. I will see to her quick and painless demise."

Clasping his hands tight around the water bottle, the

sorcerer met his gaze for a long moment, and then nodded. "You will not be able to breach the wards set by D'Arbois. She is well protected, cloaked in his magic. You will have only one chance at her, and to waste your chance on attacking the fortified bastions of his home is foolishness."

Rage flushing his body with a bitter heat, Asa clenched his fists. *Foolishness*. This worthless magician dared speak to him so.

"Better to draw the girl out and take her from the street," the sorcerer continued.

"And you believe he will leave her unprotected long enough for her to follow the scent of the bait to the trap?" Unable to contain his incredulity, Asa laughed.

"Yes." The sorcerer slid a photograph across the table, the *shush* of paper on plastic barely audible in the noisy cafeteria. "You will find these two in Box Town, under the Bathurst Street Bridge. The woman's name is Terry, and the dog is Pickles. If she calls, Clea Masters will answer, and she will open the door."

"And you know this how?" Asa asked in a silky whisper.

The sorcerer met his gaze. "Subtle questions to a colleague, a friend, a coworker. Just enough to glean information without raising suspicion. A simple matter to follow the path of a girl with such a predictable life. Work. School. The occasional social outing." Pulling a small digital camera from his pocket, the sorcerer offered it for inspection. "The photograph was an easy thing to obtain. Amazing, the advances in human technology."

Asa studied his collaborator, watching for signs of treachery: a flickering gaze, a subtle tension about the lips. But there were none. Only the open and honest gaze of a creature about to betray his own kind. An interesting paradox. "And D'Arbois will let her go unprotected because . . . ?"

"I will see to it that he is summoned," the sorcerer said, his mouth twisting in an ugly, mocking smile. "His *honor* will ensure that he turns up."

Chapter 22

CIARRAN PUT A BOWL OF FRUIT AND PEACH YOGURT in front of Clea. She was sitting at the counter in his kitchen, watching him as he prepared breakfast for her. He'd offered cereal, eggs, pancakes, waffles . . . and what had she chosen? Fruit and yogurt. And that after claiming to be starving. He hated to imagine what little she ate on a day she was feeling less than hungry.

Frowning, he flipped the pancakes he was preparing for himself and popped in some cinnamon-raisin bread for toast. Maybe she'd be enticed by the smell.

He studied her. The mussed curls, tumbling to her shoulders in silky disarray. Her dark eyes, watching him, analyzing, evaluating. Smart, sexy Clea.

She'd kept his secrets.

Darqun and Javier had definitely sensed that something was off, unbalanced, but without proof, they had had no reason to insist on staying. Explaining things to them right now was beyond him. The acid mist. The dark blades. Worse, the way that Clea was draining his power, the fact that he ought to get her as far away from him as possible, and the reasons he could not trust her to the care of another.

He could make no explanation without turning it into an accusation, and that he was unwilling to do. Bad enough that he had handled it so poorly with Dain. He had no wish to compound the issue further by making unfounded accusations against Darqun and Javier. At least not until he knew the identity of the traitor. Then, he would be duty-bound, honor-bound, to terminate the problem, despite centuries of friendship. A horrific proposition.

If the traitor was Dain, then Ciarran knew he'd made a hash of it, given him a heads-up when he shouldn't have. His only excuse was that he wasn't thinking straight, and that was no excuse at all.

Less than an hour past, Darqun and Javier had left after a brief conversation, though not without some small measure of reluctance. They had obviously wanted explanations, and he was in no mood to provide them.

Right now, Ciarran could say that he didn't mourn the loss of their company.

Pouring Clea a cup of freshly brewed coffee, he glanced at the bowl he'd given her. "You need to eat more."

She met his gaze, smiled, scooped up some fruit, and let out a low hum of appreciation as she chewed and swallowed. Then her pink tongue came out to lick across the back of the spoon, sending his imagination into overdrive. He froze midmovement, the coffee cup poised above the counter. It was all he could do to stop himself from leaning over, twining his tongue with hers, and licking the taste of peach yogurt from her lips.

Her gaze locked with his, big dark eyes, slumberous enough that he was left with no doubt that her thoughts were running a parallel course to his. And what the hell was he going to do about it? Sacrifice everything just for one more chance to be inside her, one more chance to take them both to heaven?

With meticulous concentration, he set the cup of coffee on the counter, wrestling his lust into submission. He looked up and caught the quizzical look she sent him.

"What?" he asked.

"I guess I didn't picture you cooking." She smiled. "Or brewing coffee. Or cutting up fruit."

"No?" He added a portion of cream to her coffee, glanced at her, recalled the caramel corretto she'd loved so much, and added a little more. "You thought that sorcerers do not eat?"

She took the mug as he slid it across the kitchen counter, then shifted on her stool to reach for the sugar. Ciarran followed the movement of her hand, the graceful stretch of her arm, the shift of the thin cotton T-shirt over the lush swells of her breasts.

Measuring out a teaspoon, she dumped it in and stirred. "I figured you just *conjured* everything . . . you know . . . like you did with the whipped cream on my caramel corretto."

"There was a purpose in that."

"Yeah? What?"

"It got your attention." He couldn't help it. He was staring at her breasts, and she caught him. A shaky little laugh escaped her, and her eyes widened.

"I have a preference to avoid the mundane use of magic," he said, his voice a low rasp. He wanted this conversation to come to an end, wanted his mouth and hers busy with things other than talking. Hot things. Sweet things. Wild, erotic things that would make her hum, and moan, and, yeah, make her scream.

Her smile faded, and she dropped her gaze. "I'm gonna. . . umm . . . go. After breakfast. I'll go."

Icy pain lanced through him. She was intending to leave him. "What are you talking about?"

She raised her eyes, and he saw the desperation and the sadness. "I'm no good for you. I drain you. I know it." Her hand shook as she touched the countertop, flattening her fingers. "I think if I stay, you're going to suffer."

Suffer. *Christe.*

"You are going nowhere." He felt like his chest was full of poured concrete. "I need you safe. I need you here."

She shook her head, her eyes shimmering. "I don't understand what's going on, but I *know* I'm a danger to you just by being in the same room—"

"You go, you die," he snarled, cutting her off, aware of his ebbing restraint. The thought of her leaving, walking out the door, putting herself in harm's way, kindled a dark fury inside him. He took a slow breath, caught the tail of his fleeing control, and hauled it back into place. "I can't let you go."

A jagged little gasp left her lips, and he figured she understood everything. Not just what he'd said, but what he hadn't said. She was so close, he could smell her hair, her skin, and he was alive, electrified by the need to touch her.

Why not? What harm? He shook his head to clear his thoughts, remembering his conversation with Darqun that night at Slinger's. He hadn't known for certain then, hadn't been sure exactly what he might become should the beast slip its chain even a little. Then, he had only suspected what sort of monster he might become.

Now, he *knew*. Just as he knew the taste of Clea's lips, the sounds of her pleasure. He knew with certainty that joining with her tore through his defenses, made him vulnerable to the darkness he had so long held at bay.

The worst of it was the dual temptation.

He had found true ecstasy in Clea's arms, in her body, in the warmth she offered him with a true and caring heart, the first warmth he had known in decades.

She pulled his magic, weakened the cage around the demon parasite he harbored, freed him to taste its dark lure. He had found it far from unpleasant to let loose the demon, to feel it coil through him, blending darkness with his light.

The Ancient had sensed that. *Does it tempt you, Ciarran? The darkness? The power?*

Yes, it tempted him. All the more so because in order to have Clea, he must court his damned demon right along with his woman. Embrace it if he wanted to embrace her.

Making love to her once had not been enough, could never be enough. He was chained to her and freed by her, and he knew he would want no other.

But would she be willing to accept him, accept the light sorcerer with the demon seed growing ever darker, ever stronger, in his soul? What right had he to ask it of her?

She stirred in a second teaspoon of sugar, tasted her coffee, and added a quarter teaspoon more. Her hand shook just a little, testament to the turmoil he'd awakened, the emotion he'd pulled with his refusal to let her go.

"You could just tip the whole bowl in," he suggested, a wry grin tugging at his lips.

Flashing him a tremulous smile, she shook her head. "Yeah, I could. But I won't."

Her smile hit him in the gut like a blow. He wanted to make love to her. There it was, reeling through him, a powerful force. He was so *conscious* of her. The soft exhalation from between her parted lips. Her inhalation and the resulting movement of her breasts. The outline of her nipples.

Breathing deeply, he took in the scent of her, intoxicating, fascinating. He let his gaze wander along the curve of her waist, a naked band of smooth skin between the tied ends of the T-shirt and the waistband of her low-slung sweatpants . . . *his* sweatpants, actually. A self-mocking smile curved his lips. He envied his goddamned clothes, because right now he'd give just about anything to be plastered up against her in their stead.

He took a seat on the stool beside her, ate his breakfast, when what he really wanted to do was taste her, let her melt on his tongue like cotton candy.

The tension was there between them, an unsubtle weight, and all he could think of was the many, many ways he would like to take her, please her.

"I don't think your friends approved of me." She was laughing, the lilt in her voice betraying it. He had the feeling that she didn't care what they thought of her, and he liked that, liked the fact that she was that comfortable in her own skin. He was nowhere near as accepting of himself as she was. Of course, she didn't have a demon eating at her insides.

A grunt was pretty much the best reply he could conjure.

"Is that why you didn't invite them to stay for breakfast?" she asked. "Because you sensed they weren't fond of me?"

Swallowing another mouthful, he thought about his answer and decided on the truth. "I never invite them to stay. It would only put them in the position of declining. They like noise. People. At least, Darqun does. He cannot bear silence. Solitude. Not even for a short time. I think if he could choose, he would never be alone."

"Wow." She didn't look at him. Palms wrapped around the steaming mug, she blew on it, then lifted it to her lips and drank. Her chest rose and fell, too fast, as though she'd jogged a block rather than sitting here beside him. "That's terrible. I think I actually feel sorry for him." Breathless. She sounded breathless.

He looked away, then back, couldn't contain his smile. Because she was here. Beside him. And no matter what honorable intentions she had of protecting him, of saving him, he was not letting her go. "They always eat at the greasy spoon up the road. It's packed on a Sunday morning, with a line out the door. I've eaten there, and I can tell you . . . you should feel sorry for *both* of them."

She was quiet for a moment; then she swiveled on the stool, turning to face him, her expression speculative. "I

think if you could choose, you would always be alone."
It wasn't a question. "You don't like people. Noise."

No. Not anymore. Once, he had liked mortal company,
enjoyed the human realm, but no longer. He needed to
focus, to channel everything he had into the rigid barrier
of his control. "They distract me."

From the demon and his ever-present battle.

The touch of her fingers, featherlight on his cheek,
made him tense, sent a hot swell of desire pulsing
through him, burning a path to his groin.

"Has it been so bad for you?" she whispered, her
voice catching just a little.

Such a vague question, but he knew exactly what
she asked. The darkness. The demon. Two decades of
battling temptation, warring with himself. Despising
himself.

Alone, with only the horror inside him for company.
Until now. Until Clea.

He was connected to her by magic and by the finest gos-
samer webs that enveloped his heart and tied him to her.

Forget the ancient lore and the imprinting of the
magic he shared with her. The truth of it was that given
the choice, he would *choose* her. Clea was everything he
could desire, his just mate.

No. He couldn't face that, couldn't bring himself to
acknowledge the depth of his feelings. He had no idea
what to do with such profound emotion.

Curling his gloved fingers into his palm, he tested
the limits of the cage, and the beast, and his own frayed
control. Quiescent now, the thing was there, a dormant
threat. If he touched her, made love to her, let down the
barriers and restraints once more, what then?

He clenched his fist hard to keep it from shaking; then he gave in, closing his fingers around the metal leg of her stool, dragging it close. Lowering his face, he ran his nose along the side of her cheek. Gentle, he was trying to be gentle, despite the turbulent edge to his desire.

"Go, Clea," he rasped, tried for a smile. "Just don't go far."

"How far? Another room? Another building?"

"If you go, I won't follow. You'll be safe."

"Stay. Go. What is it you want?"

He knew what *she* wanted. He could read it in her expression, feel it in the heat of her body, so close, so tempting.

"You. I want you." Why the hell had he said that?

She pulled back, taking her warmth and her light, and for a moment he thought that she would listen, that she would flee. His heart twisted. *Yes. Leave me. Be safe.*

Hell.

Don't leave me.

"I'm safe right here." Her palms came to rest flat against his cheeks, warm skin, her touch gentle. Her expression gave away her thoughts, and he knew what she wanted from him. Everything. His heart. His soul, what ragged bits were left of it.

Take me for who I am, for what I am. He wanted her to. Needed her to.

Leaning in to press her open mouth to his, she kissed him with a passion that licked at the core of him, an erotic flame, her tongue stroking the length of his in elemental possession.

His lust was a powerful force pounding through him. He would not be gentle, could not be gentle.

"I don't run away," she whispered, her tone fierce, her dark eyes flashing fire. "Whatever it is, I deal with it. It's who I am."

No, she didn't run away, but neither did she stand and let life happen to her, a passive vessel for all that occurred. She took the hand she was dealt, and she made it into something she could live with.

He knew that.

And he loved her for it.

Chapter 23

*O*H, GOD. CLEA'S BREATH CAUGHT AS SHARP YEARN-
ing stretched molten fingers to her core, leaving
her wet and trembling and so ready for him she thought
she'd combust at the first touch. Coming off the stool,
Ciarran loomed over her, and he kissed her.

Deep, luscious kisses, pouring through her, and the
unbearably wonderful pressure of his contoured, solid
body pressed up against her.

He tasted like the maple syrup from the pancakes he'd
been eating. But his kiss was anything but sweet.

Thrilling. Stimulating. He slanted his lips over hers,
his tongue savoring the inside of her mouth, devouring her.

Sensation washed through her, electrified her, made
her wriggle closer, the firm press of his chest and abdomen and thighs flush against her, strong and male. She
was lost in her awareness of him, drunk on it, so enthralled by him that she was breathless, shaky, her limbs
barely able to hold her upright.

Dragging his hand along her waist, he reached under

her T-shirt, palming her breast, running his thumb over her nipple. A slow hiss escaped her, and she arched into his touch. Aching pleasure. The reality of his kiss, his touch sank through her. So much better than last night's dreams.

She reached between them, rubbed the thick rod of his erection through his jeans. Impatient. Her movements a little rough. Clumsy. Spurred by aching passion.

With a groan, he pulled away, his features taut with barely leashed need. She was left throbbing, her lips sensitive and swollen from his kiss, and she ran her tongue over them, tasting him.

"Clea." His breath came harsh and fast. "I cannot know what will happen. What I will become." His gaze burned into hers. "I cannot bear the thought of harming you."

Such words should have terrified her, but she knew only passion and tenderness and the certainty that she was safe in his arms.

He tried to step back, and she held him, her hand fisted in his shirt. His eyes, those stunning multifaceted eyes, narrowed in watchful contemplation, an edge of desperation etching fine lines.

"You don't know what I am." His voice was hoarse, and his gaze slid away from hers.

Such pain in a handful of words. She whispered with all the conviction of her heart, "But I do. I do know."

She willed him to believe her.

She was the one who was dangerous to him, dragging from him that which kept him safe: his power, his magic. Yes, she knew that, and it tore her apart. All she wanted to do was heal him, take care of him, make love to him, and make everything right and good. And how crazy was that? She wanted to protect an all-powerful sorcerer, wanted to take his pain and the darkness in his soul and turn it all to light.

That wasn't the way it would play out, though. She knew that, too, and she accepted it, accepted him for all he was. And for all he was not. She would love him, love him with all her heart and soul and pray that it would be enough.

Light and darkness. There wasn't a doubt in her mind that she knew *exactly* what he was. Sorcerer. Demon. All the secret, complicated parts of him.

He was danger and heat and need.

He was hers.

"I don't care how far into the shadows you fall. You would never hurt me." Silly words. Perhaps even naïve. But she had no doubt that they were true. She felt the certainty throbbing inside her, the potency of her trust.

Ciarran stared at her, his eyes darkening, and he pulled her up against him so sharply she gasped in surprise. He rocked into her, the thick ridge of his penis pressing against her, tantalizing her. With a rough groan he lowered his head and kissed her, endless, drugging, leaving her heart racing and her body liquid. It wasn't until she bumped against the kitchen counter that she realized he'd turned her, moved her so that her back now rested against the solid surface.

Her hands tangled in the thick gold strands of his hair, and she purred her pleasure as he moved his mouth along her jaw to the column of her throat, grazing her skin with his teeth, his tongue. She could feel the steady rhythm of his heart, fast, strong, pounding out the beat of his desire.

"I want you," he murmured, his lips moving against the skin of her throat. "You make me believe in myself, believe that I am yet the light sorcerer and not the minion of darkness. I want you to trust me, when I can't even trust myself. Trust me to be inside you, and you inside me, magic to magic, mine weaving through you, and yours through me—"

He kissed her neck. Bit her lightly, and her desire ratcheted up another notch, infinitely powerful.

Yours through me. There it was. The reality she had sensed. She *was* what he was. Sorcerer. Or, at least, she was some untrained form of it. Probably had been for two decades, only she hadn't had a name for it until now.

Afraid. She ought to be afraid. But she wasn't. She was deeply, darkly thrilled to be . . . like him. A sorcerer.

Whatever it meant to be as he was, she would cope, because it meant she was his *kind.* He was hers, and she was his.

It was all part of the attraction, the unfettered yearning. She knew exactly what he was.

The goodness in him.

The honorable warrior.

The shadowy demon that lurked beneath the surface.

She'd seen the darkest part, and, God help her, she wanted *him,* craved him, welcomed the hidden edge that made him just a little less than perfect.

He'd killed for her, to protect her. And he would again, if he had to. In her whole life, she'd never felt as safe as she did with Ciarran D'Arbois.

Breathing in the scent of him, she licked his skin, warm and clean and a little salty, sank her teeth into the swell of muscle where his shoulder and neck met. Oh, the satisfaction when he gave a deep, masculine growl of pleasure, the sound echoing through her.

"You make me crazy. All I can think about is you." The sound of his voice, low and raspy, stroked her senses.

Fingers tangled in her hair, he tipped her face to his kiss, a luscious wet joining that sank through her to her core, making her writhe against him. She pulled him closer, tighter, until the heavy ridge of his erection pressed into her.

Sucking on her tongue, he rubbed up against her, and she sucked back, the sensation bringing heated images to her mind. She wanted to suck *him,* bite him, pull him deep into her mouth, feel the smooth glide of his thick shaft against her lips and tongue.

She wanted to bring him to the same sharp precipice, the same edge that he brought her.

Drawing back, he stared at her, his eyes glittering. He ran the pad of his thumb over her lips, and one side of his gorgeous mouth curved in a sexy, masculine smile as he pushed his thumb inside to rub the smooth surface of her teeth, then deeper, into the wet center. She swirled her tongue around his thumb, bit him, watched his smile turn tight with need.

He knew exactly what she wanted to do. She could read it in that knowing smile. With a groan, she sucked hard on his thumb, feeling a deep feminine satisfaction as his smile faded and the breath hissed from between his teeth. Using the pressure of her body, she urged him into a slow spin, pushed him back, kissing him, running her hands over his shoulders, his arms, until she turned their positions and he was leaning his back against the counter.

"Wait," she whispered, her breath mingling with his, the sound little more than a sigh. She unbuckled his belt, unzipped his jeans, and, oh, the feel of him, the broad, smooth length of his naked cock, heavy in her hand.

Grabbing the hem of his T-shirt, he hauled it over his head, shrugged it off his shoulders. The sight of him, golden skin taut over layers of firm muscles and the thin line of honey brown hair that arrowed down his belly to his groin made her mouth go dry. She ran her hand along his arm to the leather glove, weaving her fingers with his, her palm flat against butter-soft leather.

The darkness bucked, flickering between them. She felt the syrupy glide of it, tainting his magic, and with her thoughts and her will she pressed it back, an unwelcome intruder. A key. A lock. She joined her resolve to his, caging the beast.

She kissed Ciarran's jaw, his neck, the solid muscle of his chest, his abdomen, and she sank to her knees before him. Fisting his hands in her hair, he guided her, and she worked her lips around the broad head of his penis, dizzy with the feel of him in her mouth, the taste. Smooth. Slick. So hard. Intoxicating.

A guttural moan tore from him. He rocked his hips forward, the sound of his pleasure twining through the silence of the kitchen until it came to rest in the pit of her belly, a languid heat.

Enthralled by the sheer size of him, the power, she sucked him deep, scraped her teeth along his shaft, traced the smooth skin with her tongue. Her fingers curled into the firm globes of his buttocks. The sound of his rough groan and the feel of his big hands cradling her head only sent her higher, beguiled her more.

"*Christe,* Clea." Smoke and velvet, his voice was rough with passion, and beneath her hands the muscles of his buttocks tensed as she kneaded them.

With a growl, he pulled her up. She stood, trembling, her passion honed to a fever pitch, turned on by the fact that she'd turned him on. Feminine mystery and power. He stripped the clothes from her body, pushed aside his own jeans, bending to kiss her shoulder, the side of her breast, the curve of her waist as he disrobed them both. Naked. The sweet, sweet slide of his skin against hers was so unbearably good.

He was so perfect, so utterly sexy.

She felt the shift of magic, shimmering between them, coiling into her, and she knew she was drawing from him. She focused on that. Determined to stop her unwilling theft of his strength, his energy, she imagined a wall, a thick wall that magic could not pass.

"You are adept," he murmured, his tone laced with admiration, and she knew she had succeeded, at least for now.

His mouth hard and passionate, his kiss lusciously sensual, he spun her deeper into a haze of desire. Catching her lower lip between his teeth, he pulled on it, bit her gently, and she moaned, a half-desperate sound that hid nothing from him. She was so hot, so ready for him. She couldn't think, couldn't move. There was only the wanting, the fathomless, aching wanting.

Bending his head, he licked her nipple, took it in his mouth, and sucked hard. She arched her back, offering him more, begging for his touch. The power of her arousal was overwhelming, sharp-edged, and she whimpered as he transferred his attention to her other nipple, his mouth just a little rough, the sensation purely exquisite. She clutched at his shoulders, her whole world turned upside down.

She was held up by his arm, a band of steel around her waist, holding her weight. If she'd had to rely on her own legs, she'd have been nothing more than a puddle at his feet.

He turned her until her back was pressed to the hard ridges of his belly, his hands cupping her breasts, his fingers tweaking her nipples, pinching them. The feel of his leather glove against her skin was indescribably erotic.

Walking her forward from kitchen to den, he tumbled her over the back of the couch, his gloved hand toying with her breasts, while the other slid between her legs, finding her moist core.

Wanting him was a fever pulsing inside her, blazing with a sensual fire.

"Ciarran . . . please . . ."

His fingers pushed up inside her. Incoherent. Bright delight. Her breath caught as he squeezed her nipple, teasing it with his clever fingers. He touched her. She hungered.

He brought his weight down onto her, his front to her back, pinning her beneath him, his breath hot against her cheek, and she sank deeper against the yielding couch back as his fingers withdrew, penetrated, stroking her until she squirmed and arched her buttocks toward him.

Melting into him, she was giddy with it, with the need

to have him fill her. His fingers withdrew, replaced by his cock, hot and solid between her thighs, between the folds of her vulva. Hard. Silky. Perfection.

As he pushed up into her, she murmured, "Yes. God, yes."

A low, erotic laugh rumbled in his chest.

The weight of him and the thrust of his cock were impossibly perfect, and he filled her, deeper, a smooth glide. So thick. So wonderfully thick.

She sighed. Gasped. Her hips followed his in an intense, arousing rhythm, her buttocks arching back to meet each thrust. Reaching underneath the front of her, his hand between her legs, he stroked her clitoris.

Magic swirled around them, through them, her carefully fabricated wall tumbling to ruins, her every thought focused on him, the smell of his skin, the feel of his body as he held her close.

The darkness was there, and she felt it, melding with him and with her, a part of him.

A part of them both.

He opened his mouth against the nape of her neck, his tongue stroking her, his teeth closing on the tender flesh. Marking her.

"My precious Clea," he whispered.

Yes. His.

Reckless yearning spread through her until she thought she could bear no more. Every place he touched felt sublime. Her body moved in pattern to his, taking them higher, closer.

Lost. She was lost in him.

Adrift, and yet anchored all at once.

She was drowning in pleasure, in the hard thrust of

his cock, the slide of his hot skin against her back and buttocks, and the stroke of his fingers between her legs.

Ciarran. Ciarran. Ciarran. His name was a song, running through her mind.

Every nerve, every cell alive, her body tightened around him. A ripple of ecstasy shot through her. She jerked, panted.

"Ciarran!" She dug her fingers into the couch, her body shuddering as the surge of her climax burst upon her. And then she was floating, the echoes of her pleasure lingering in softly pulsing waves.

Ciarran kissed the back of her neck, her shoulder, holding her tight against him as she shuddered her release. The waning current of her orgasm stroked him, making him harder.

She was slick. Wet. So tight he could melt.

He wanted to feel her come for him again.

A tremor shook her as he shifted inside her, and she murmured, turning in his embrace, face-to-face. Her movement dragged him free of her warmth, the disconnection almost painful. She was pinned up against him, chest to chest now, her buttocks pressed against the couch, her body soft and supple, relaxed even.

And he was still hard as stone, his cock throbbing, nudging at her moist sex. Open and yielding as he kissed her, she sealed her mouth to his in a way that made the ache in his groin pulse even stronger.

"God, I love the way you kiss me," she said, her voice husky with passion. She tunneled her fingers through his hair and pulled him back to her, her kiss wonderfully sensual.

Letting her weight fall back, she pulled him with her,

the two of them tangled together, tumbling over the back of the couch to land on the cushions. He rolled her beneath him, pinned one wrist above her head.

Smiling, she lifted her head, let her tongue lick a wet path along his throat. Her nails scraped the curve of his hip bone, her fingers closing around his shaft. With slow, leisurely strokes that made the breath hiss between his lips, she rubbed him, his body winding ever tighter at the sheer uncomplicated bliss of her touch.

He closed his hand around hers, stilling her movements, then guided himself into her once more, sinking into the white-hot pleasure of it. The pulsing of his cock was so tight it was almost in pain, a deep ache, the wanting of her.

Arching her back, she moaned as he thrust deep. He took his time, stoking her passion, building it up until she writhed and surged against him, low sounds of passion torn from her as she met his thrusts.

She was so hot and soft and tight, melting for him. Her legs were wrapped around his waist. Her nails raked his skin. Waves of searing pleasure dragged at him, and he was so goddamned close.

The beast stirred. Darkness. Feeding off his passion. Oozing past his wards. Pouring through him.

Cold panic roared to life inside him.

Christe. He couldn't breathe. *Clea.*

He tried to pull back, pull away, keep her safe.

"Shhh . . . we're good. We're perfect." She stroked her palm along the length of his back, and he felt her send magic into him, tentative, uncertain, untutored.

There, inside him, he felt her power, winding through

him, calming the darkness. She moved against him, her hips swaying, deepening their physical connection.

"We're perfect," she said again. And he believed her.

Her breath warmed his lips, short, ragged pants that told him how very close she was. He thrust into her. Deeper. Harder. Faster. With a high, keening moan, she contracted around him, coming undone, her body taut as she rode her release.

Sheathing himself to the hilt, he brought his body flush with hers, indescribable pleasure gushing through him. He came in a hard rush, pouring into her, no holds, no barriers, his heart pounding, his whole body shaking.

There was nothing but Clea. No darkness. No light. Only the crashing waves of his orgasm, chasing through him, through her.

Finally, he remembered to breathe, collapsed across her, still inside her, his limbs twined with hers. He had only enough focus left to shift his weight so it did not lie full atop her.

Slowly, he ran his fingers through the strands of her curls. Beautiful. She was so beautiful.

"Ciarran." She said his name like she was tasting it, and her lips curved in an amazing smile. Lazy. Satisfied.

Her lashes lifted, a slow drift, and her dark eyes met his. He leaned in, pressed a kiss to her lush mouth.

And felt the tight edge of his panic sneak back to the fore.

Christe.

He knew how to keep her safe from every threat. Every threat except himself.

He'd almost lost it. Almost let the demon slide free.

Chapter 24

*C*LEA SHIFTED THE PILLOWS ON CIARRAN'S BED, plumping them to her satisfaction before flopping back against them. Somehow, the two of them had made it to his bedroom.

Rolling over, she buried her face in the side of his neck, inhaling him, hardly believing what she was feeling. They'd made love in the kitchen. In the hallway, up against a door. In his bed. And just breathing in the scent of him, warm, sensual, made a haze of desire swirl through her. She wanted him again.

He'd fed her peach wine because she'd said she liked it. And strawberries dipped in chocolate.

Spicy Thai noodle salad. Warm spinach dip with salted tortilla chips.

A ripple of his power shimmered between them, and she tried so hard not to draw magic from him. Tormented by the knowledge of what her proximity cost him, she focused on maintaining the barrier, her imagined wall, lest she siphon all he was.

Her efforts were a revelation. *This* was the struggle he maintained. Day after day, year after year, he worked to hold at bay the darkness inside him. She was exhausted after mere hours of trying to control her blooming power, trying to hold back her pull on his magic. She couldn't imagine what such effort cost him in the long run. But she *would* find the strength to keep this up. She *would* keep him safe.

He was amazing. And she was more in tune with him, more connected, than she'd ever been with anyone.

She'd expected to fall in love someday, with a sedate, conservative, safe guy.

Safe.

Yeah.

She was smack-dab in the middle of a war between good and evil, and she'd never felt safer than she did right now, lying beside Ciarran D'Arbois, light sorcerer, demon host.

So much for her expectations of falling in love, how it would happen, who it would be. He was nothing she had ever imagined and so much more than she could have dreamed. The need to heal him was strong, and she wished she had more to offer. If only she could make him see what she saw, make him understand that he need not succumb, need not allow the monster to wrest control.

"Time for deep, dark secrets," she said, trailing her fingers over his lips. God, she'd been half in love with those lips since the night at the Blue Bay Motel, imagining all the amazing things he would do with them. She smiled. Reality had proved so much better than her imagination. "I'll tell you mine; then you tell me yours."

*　　　*　　　*

Yeah. Like he could do that without sending her right over the edge. Ciarran stroked his palm along her saucy curls, loving the silky feel of them against his skin.

"When I was a teenager, I stole a pair of jeans." Her voice was low, serious.

He almost laughed. Stole a pair of jeans. *That* was her secret. "That's . . . uh . . . bad."

She sent him a reproving look, shimmied her naked body against him.

"No. Really. That's dark. Definitely a deep, dark secret," he muttered, reaching for her breast.

"No. Listen." Her voice was steady, intense, and her expression was earnest as she caught his wrist, halting his quest. "This is serious. Important."

It was. Important, to her. He could see that. And so he let her talk, focusing on her words, searching the nuances of her tone for secret meaning.

"I was fifteen," she said. "In high school. York Mills Collegiate. I was a good kid. Got good grades. Quiet. Never made trouble." She paused. "Not even when I wanted to. The temptation might have been there, but conscience usually overruled."

Watching him, sloe-eyed, tousle-haired, she looked so incredibly sexy, the sheet twined around her in a haphazard way, leaving the length of one leg exposed, and her shoulders, the tops of her breasts. He shifted closer, skin to skin.

Her eyes widened, and she wet her lips.

"Behave," she whispered, and tugged the sheet higher.

He laughed, liking the way she felt lying next to him. Liking her.

"Anyway . . ." She cleared her throat lightly, and her gaze dropped to his mouth, slid away. A jet of heat seared him, straight to his groin. Focus. He needed to focus. There was something she needed to tell him, and the fact that she felt the need to share it made him want to hear it.

"All . . . um . . . all the other girls had these great designer jeans. Shirts. Name-brand shoes. We couldn't afford it." She shook her head. "Sometimes, we had a tough choice between making rent or eating. I was working two part-time jobs just to help Gram with the bills."

Ciarran stroked her skin, the comfort of a loving touch. She had suffered, and the fault was his. So caught up in his own regret, his own personal hell, he had spared no thought for the girl his magic had saved, spared no concern for what her life had become after the death of her parents. He had left it to Darqun to ensure that she had a relative to care for her, and once that was proven a certainty, he had absolved himself of any responsibility. His neglect was one more transgression to add to his lengthy inventory.

"So there were these jeans. And just once, I wanted to be cool. To have the latest style. To dress like the girls who hung with the in crowd." She laughed. "Stupid. I know. But it didn't seem stupid then. It seemed like the most important thing in the world."

He focused on her words, instead of his inclination. He wanted to drag the sheet off her body, kiss her breasts, her thighs. Lick his way to the heat of her sex. Taste her. Make her come against his lips.

His cock was already stiff. But she was trying to tell

him something, and it was significant to her. Which made it significant to him.

"Go on," he said.

"So I went downtown to some trendy store—I can't even recall the name—and tried on these jeans. They were perfect. Absolutely perfect. I'd actually seen them on the cover of a teen magazine the day before. And you know what? It was easy to walk out with them. The antitheft tag seemed to slide off just because I wanted it to."

She reached out and touched him, her cool fingers playing lightly across his jaw, his lips. The glow of magic reared inside him and the howl of the darkness.

"It felt strange, to steal those jeans." Her gaze locked with his, then slid away. "Terrifying. But good, in a horrible way, to be doing something so bad."

Yeah. He knew that feeling. Knew the secret, forbidden pleasure he felt when he loosed the chain and let the dark power flow through him to manifest as black blades and killing mist. It *had* felt good to do something so bad.

"I kept that secret for a week, then two, never daring to wear those jeans, mostly because I hated them. Hated the sight of them and what they said about me. And also because I was so afraid that Gram would know the second she saw them. Know that I'd done something awful. So they sat at the bottom of the drawer, and I never took them out. Then one day, I couldn't stand it anymore. I shoved them in a bag and took them back to the store and left them in the dressing room. And then I went home and told Gram everything."

Ciarran stared at her. That was her darkest secret? She'd given in to temptation, stolen a pair of jeans, and then taken them back. He felt a sharp kick of relief. Despite the hardships of her life, this was how she defined darkness. She looked so serious, so intent, so innocent. She had no idea what true darkness was, and he was fiercely glad of it. Grateful.

True evil, like that which dwelt in his soul, had not touched her. He couldn't speak, couldn't say it to her. Glancing down, he realized that his gloved hand was fisted tight around the sheet, and he made a conscious effort to unclench his fingers.

She thought she knew what lurked beneath the surface, thought she saw the whole of it from the brief glimpses she had been allowed.

"Ciarran . . . I—" She paused, shook her head. "Do you know what Gram said? That there is both great goodness and vast evil in all sentient beings and that we can choose our path, not by stifling the evil, but by accepting its existence. Accepting and choosing. Do you understand?"

Accepting. If he stopped the struggle, the fight, if he accepted what he was, then he would be no more. The darkness would breach his wards, take his body, twist him into something foreign and disgusting. Take his soul.

"Do you think I know nothing of hardship and heartache?" she asked gently. "That I can't understand what you face?"

No. He knew that she had suffered, had known grief and poverty and desperation. Hunger. Fear.

His fault.

Words eluded him. He gave her the only answer he could. Rolling her beneath him, he kissed her, letting himself free-fall into desire. She made a sound, perhaps delight, or denial. He knew she wanted answers, but he had none to give.

With a groan, he caught her wrists, dragged her arms to her sides, holding them there while he sank into the kiss, pouring his need into her, reveling in her response. He moved down the front of her body, kissing her breasts, her belly, his tongue tracing the rim of her navel. Lower, he licked the curve of her hip, smiling as she jerked and gasped.

She knew so little of his darkness, and he wished it to remain that way. But the joining of their bodies gave him succor. In her arms, he found his truth. His salvation.

Nudging her thighs apart, he kissed her there, licked her, felt her muscles twitch as she let the pleasure take her. She shuddered, pressed her heels against the mattress, and raised herself into his kiss. Her wrists shook within his grasp, but he held her, gentle bonds as he licked her and sucked on her, everything in him focused on her perfect bliss. His own passion was a wild heat that stabbed him, tightening his balls, his cock, until he throbbed, her desire fueling his.

"Ciarran—" His name was little more than a gasp; then she pressed her sex against his mouth and came unraveled, her thighs drawing tight, her hips arching, her body shuddering.

He held his tongue still against her, letting her ride her orgasm to its completion; then he slid up her body and thrust deep. She was so wet. So hot.

Her legs came up around him, holding him as she matched his rhythm, the steady pulse of his hips, the long, deep thrusts. Tangling his fingers in her hair, he

sank into her, again and again, until at last he found release, his body slick with sweat. She came with him,
her cry of pleasure surging through him, stroking him,
taking him higher as he poured into her, a physical and
emotional bond that was unstoppable. Unbreakable.

Darqun couldn't say he was in fine humor as he
picked up the phone and dialed Ciarran's number. He
was alone, a state he despised, the silence and the walls
closing in on him, his sheets still warm from the mortal
female he'd been forced to send away. Dain had called
to say that the Ancient had summoned the Compact. Everyone. Honor-bound to obey, Darqun could honestly
say that in that moment, he resented the Ancient, perhaps even hated him.

Centuries of silence gnawed at him. Memories.
Nightmares in the waking hours of the day. The nights
were worse.

"Yeah," Ciarran growled, picking up the phone on the
fifth ring. Darqun had the startling realization that he'd
interrupted something. Or perhaps called at the tail end.

Interesting.

It appeared that Ciarran had succumbed to his desires,
sacrificing some modicum of his control.

"You okay?" he asked, though he knew Ciarran could
hear the unspoken question.

"I'm still sorcerer." Ciarran paused. "Mostly."

The darkness had not prevailed.

Definitely very interesting.

"We've been summoned," Darqun said, and he wasn't
surprised when he was greeted by silence. It was rare
that the Compact would meet, rarer still to meet in per-

son rather than hold a conference call. Ah, the wonders of modern technology. Darqun could easily recall a time when they'd sent messages via pigeons.

Telephones were a definite upgrade.

"When?" Ciarran asked.

"Now." Darqun ventured into dangerous territory. "Ciarran, it might well be about the girl." About the fact that she had magic at her core, that she pulled power from Ciarran, and that it seemed he could not stop her.

About the fact that she was no longer human and almost sorcerer. An impossible mix.

About the fact that Ciarran had taken her to apprentice without sanction.

Which begged the question, what now? Darqun couldn't imagine that Ciarran would sacrifice Clea, especially in light of what likely had filled their recent hours. Though *he* suffered from no such emotional compunction, he could not imagine Ciarran sharing his body without sharing his heart.

A dangerous choice for a sorcerer who was part demon, his heart and soul smeared with evil.

Darqun snapped the cell phone shut. To borrow a mortal colloquialism, he had a feeling the shit was about to hit the fan.

Chapter 25

A T LEAST SHE HAD UNDERWEAR. CLEA CHECKED
her appearance in the bathroom mirror. Ciarran's
T-shirt and sweatpants were definitely not the height of
feminine fashion, but she was pleased by the fact that
the underthings she'd washed in the sink had dried.

Turning, she glanced at the bed, the sheets cascad-
ing over the edges of the mattress to pool on the carpet,
the pillows tossed about. A smile tugged at her lips. She
stepped out of the bathroom and crossed to the bed. She
smoothed her hands across the sheet, taking her time as
she arranged the linens and quilt. Pausing to lift a pillow
to her nose, she inhaled.

A bubble of euphoria fizzed to the surface. She could
smell Ciarran, the clean, fresh scent of him, a little spicy,
a lot sexy. She was so in love with him, so far along the
path that she ought to be terrified, or at the very least, a
little uneasy. But all she felt was happy.

Closing her eyes, she inhaled the scent of him that
yet clung to the linen, reveling in the memories of their

bodies joined as one, their souls connecting. In a way, she was actually glad that he'd been called away by a phone call from Darqun. It gave her a chance to catch her breath, to think, to savor her emotions.

She finished her task of making the bed, unable to stop smiling, and then checked her watch. Almost 1:00. Terry would be outside in the alley any minute.

After Ciarran had left, Clea had called her voice mail to pick up messages. A couple of classmates. Her best friend from grade school, Beth. The landlord, looking for the rent. No big surprise there. But it was the message from Terry that caught her attention.

"Clea," she'd said, her voice sounding strained, even a little desperate. "I need to talk to you. Right away. It's about Louise. And your gram. I'm sorting canned goods at the food bank today. You can call me here." She'd left a number, and Clea had reached her easily.

Terry had sounded distraught, anxious to meet in person. Which had left Clea in the position of making some quick decisions. She was smart enough to recognize the danger in leaving Ciarran's protected abode. Didn't she hate it when the girl in the horror flick insisted on heading out into the darkness, despite the creepy noises and scary background music?

TSTL. Too stupid to live. That definitely wasn't going to be her. No way was she trading the safety of Ciarran's home to go meet Terry, no matter how important Terry perceived the meeting to be. Ciarran had explained to her about the wards he'd set, protective barriers that could not be breached by *hybrid* or demon. Sort of a sorcerer's version of a home-security system. He'd said that these wards were stronger than the ones he had set at her apartment because they were permanent.

She was certain that the *hybrids* would be thrilled if they found her walking around alone and unprotected, which was why she wasn't going anywhere. She wasn't going to risk an encounter with a *hybrid*, or worse, a demon. Just the memory of the one that had stalked her that night at the Blue Bay was enough to make her feel sick. She was safe in here but not out there.

With that in mind, she'd given Terry directions how to find her. Terry definitely wasn't a *hybrid*, so no danger there. And even if they somehow figured out the connection between the two women and followed Terry here, the *hybrids* couldn't pass Ciarran's wards. So there was little risk to her solution, she thought as she wandered out of the bedroom and along the hall to the main entrance.

Given the whole alternate-reality thing, Clea knew she couldn't rely on Terry finding Ciarran's place all on her own. His home was cloaked in magic, hidden from view of the mortal realm. But she had a solution. All she needed to do was open the door at precisely 1:00, watch the mouth of the alley, and get Terry's attention. Problem solved.

Even then, she was cautious. She opened the door a crack, peered out. The sky was overcast, gray, heavy clouds hanging over the city like a damp blanket. Turning her head, she checked the entire length of the alley. The sound of traffic carried from the main drag, but there wasn't a soul in sight.

Clea glanced at her watch: 12:59.

Looking out once more, she searched for some sign

of Terry. The muscles of her neck tightened, and she raised her hand, massaging them lightly. Her chest felt stiff, like she couldn't draw breath, and she rolled her shoulders trying to redistribute her tension.

She definitely had a case of the jitters, but she couldn't figure out why.

The mouth of the alley was clear. After a moment, a group of young men shuffled into sight, baggy jeans hanging low on their hips, equally baggy jackets obscuring their bodies. One of them stopped, punched his friend in the shoulder, then they moved on, laughing and jostling each other.

Swallowing, Clea looked back and forth, scanning the alley beyond the courtyard once more. There was nothing amiss. Nothing out of place. The Dumpster sat at the far end, garbage overflowing onto the ground. A gust of wind sent the pile of paper blowing about in a frenzy. The sheets drifted and finally came to rest against the graffiti-marked wall.

Her throat was tight now, the sensation crawling up from her chest. Clea shivered, wondering at her reaction. There was no one there. No one. Not even Terry.

She stepped back, let the door slam shut, and stood in the hallway, wrapping her arms around herself, staring at beautifully carved wood. She was losing it, positively losing it, sensing monsters in every shadow. Common sense told her she was being ridiculous, but some sixth sense seemed to come alive, tingling, prickling along her skin, arguing a different case.

Something felt off. Weird. She felt like the magic that coiled inside her was getting a case of the flu. Strange, but it was the only analogy that seemed to fit. She felt like something was just plain *wrong*.

Was this the dragon current . . . the *continuum* that Ciarran described?

Wrenching the door open, she peered into the alley once more. A ripple of relief danced through her as she saw Pickles running toward her, tearing through the garbage, barking madly.

"Pickles!" She laughed, looked toward the mouth of the alley. There was Terry, raising a hand in greeting, waving.

Clea raised her own hand in reply, stepped into the daylight, and bent to scoop Pickles up in her arms.

Standing just in front of Ciarran's door, the beautiful fountain a hazy outline to her left, the smell of the alley sharp in her nostrils, she realized what she'd done. She turned her head, a sick certainty crashing through her. Terry wasn't waving a greeting. Her movements were too wild, too big. She was—

Clea spun, her heart clutching as a rough hand caught her arm.

"Steady," Asa Paley said, smiling down at her. So polished. So handsome.

Relief was sweet and cool. She laughed, shook her head, confused by his presence.

"What are you doing here?"

His smile grew. His teeth seemed too big, too long. So many teeth.

Asa Paley.

He must have been here all along, hiding . . . Where? Why?

Her stomach dropped, and her arms felt numb. She

was dimly aware of Pickles as he squirmed free of her and leaped to the ground.

Clea swallowed her horror as suddenly everything clicked into place.

Her aversion to Asa as a romantic liaison.

The link between the missing homeless women and St. John's Hospital. Asa Paley worked the ER there.

Ciarran's assertion that he'd had an audience as he fought the *hybrids,* and her crazy notion that she'd seen Asa Paley outside her apartment building before the *hybrids* attacked. Not so crazy.

Not so crazy at all.

The demon, Asag. The one Darqun and Javier had spoken about.

Asa was Asag. And he was here for her.

She was the conduit. The demon had called her that at the Blue Bay Motel. She was the key to the gate, her magic so much stronger now that she had drawn a heavy measure from Ciarran.

"All I needed was for you to open the door, Clea," Asa said. "Just open the door, breach the sorcerer's wards, and let me in. But you've been so accommodating, stepping right out in the open." He laughed, a high sound that made a swell of nausea crawl up her throat. "You've made things so very easy on me."

Too stupid to live. Oh, God.

He curled his fingers tighter around her arm, biting deep. She knew she'd have bruises.

Closing her eyes, Clea focused on the coil of power inside her. She felt the hot, sharp glide of it, the deep pain, the glow, and she focused it on Asa. He jerked her hard against him, knocking the breath out of her in an abbreviated *whoosh*. The tension between them was enormous, his body drawn tight as he took the blow of her magic with a shallow grunt.

"Lovely," he murmured, and leaned close to run his tongue down the side of her face, her neck, leaving a wet trail in its wake. Revulsion rolled across her skin, leaching through her pores to settle deep inside of her.

"You are powerful. Wonderfully powerful," he murmured. "And you are mine to do with as I please."

Clea struggled in his hold, terror and desperation chasing through her as she heard Terry's muffled sobs and looked up to see her held by a *hybrid*, his meaty palm pressed tight over her mouth. Oh, God, poor Terry, an unwitting pawn in a war she knew nothing about.

"Not too deep," Asa instructed. "I prefer that she die slowly."

"No!" Clea screamed, struggling against his hold.

The *hybrid* nodded, and in a single stroke, he slit Terry's throat.

Blood. Red, red blood, dripping down her neck to stain her shirt. Clea moaned, the world beginning to spin. She was aware of Terry crumpling to the ground, aware of Asa's laugh, of his arm across the front of her waist; then the alley turned hazy and indistinct before her, everything blurring at the edges.

Ciarran. His name echoed in her heart.

She felt a cold wind on her face, and with a cry, she was pulled into darkness.

Pure cold rage flowed through Ciarran as he stalked through the empty rooms of his home, searching for her, though he knew she was not there. His wards were breached and Clea gone.

If he had harbored any doubts before, he could have none now. One of his inner circle was the traitor. One of his closest comrades betrayed him. Betrayed the *Pact*. One of them had lured him away, pulled him from her side and sent the demons to take her.

Christe. A ruse. He realized that now. He had been lured away by a summons to meet with the other sorcerers, an endless meeting of disagreement and dysfunction that had solved nothing, created nothing but ill temper. He'd sat there, talking with them, discussing the evil that invaded the *continuum* of magic.

In his absence, she had been taken.

Who was the traitor? Baunn? Javier?

Dain? Could he have been so wrong? Could it be Darqun?

Who?

Now, as he walked from room to room, he could smell the demon's trace. With a snarl, he wrenched open the front door and stepped into the alley, shifting dimensions, bypassing the courtyard altogether. The stink of the creature was stronger out here, brimstone and rotting death. Asag. Ciarran's fury escalated, a living writhing thing.

Clea's friend Terry lay on the ground in a pool of blood. Her dog was at her side, spinning nervous circles, whining piteously.

Casting magic, Ciarran calmed the frightened animal, even as he assessed the damage. Terry was alive.

This woman was important to Clea, a friend, a significant part of her life. She would want her to be saved.

And he wanted to save her. For Clea. For himself. Because he had not yet let the darkness take him. He was still capable of compassion.

Kneeling by Terry's side, he felt for her pulse. There. Thready and weak. Likely, Asag had reveled in the knowledge that Clea would suffer in the awareness of her friend's horrific circumstance and her inability to prevent it or help her. Clea, who longed to fix the world. The terrible responsibility of her friend's fate would torment her.

One more debt for Asag to pay.

Next, Ciarran turned her gently and assessed her wounds. The *hybrid* had been sloppy, cutting only one side of the woman's neck rather than full across her throat. The carotid artery was intact, the jugular vein incised, though the cut was too shallow to kill instantly.

No, not sloppy. More than likely, Asag had *wanted* her to lie here, to know of her impending demise, to be powerless to stop it. He would have reveled in the certainty of her suffering, would have intended her death to be a slow torture.

He would have wanted Clea to suffer that knowledge, as well.

Ciarran wanted to howl with rage and desperation, but he pulled back his emotions, locked them away where they could do the least harm. Clea's life was not yet at risk because Asag was a creature of ritual and rite.

He would wait for the night, of that Ciarran was certain.

Just as he was certain as to where Asag would take her. To the site of the crash that had claimed her parents decades before. Tonight, Asag would try to sacrifice her, a tribute of blood and pain to open the breach, to bring the Solitary from the demon realm, and in doing so return his own full power.

The demon would do nothing to cause her physical harm in the interim. He would want her power intact, untapped, until the exact anniversary of the crash arrived—to the moment, to the second—the anniversary that had brought Asag to the human realm.

Which meant that for the next few hours, Clea was relatively safe.

Ciarran clenched his ruined fist, feeling the thing twisting inside him, rattling the confines of its cage. His fury was cold, controlled, an icy rage that sucked everything into a vortex of hate. The darkness swelled within him, called by the black emotion in his heart, crying for release. He was tempted, so tempted to set it free, to set it on Asag, to enjoy watching it rip him apart.

If it didn't rip *him* apart first. Therein lay the quandary.

Terry moaned, drawing Ciarran's full attention, and Pickles lay down at her side, nudging her with his nose.

The Compact forbade Ciarran from tethering a soul back to the mortal shell it had departed. Terry's soul was yet inside her. He could still save her, with a forfeit of magic and power, a part of himself.

Calling on his light magic, Ciarran healed her, sacrificing his already weakened reserves, drained by the hours he had spent in such close association with Clea.

The demon seed swelled, taking a little more of him, pushing the boundaries, stealing another piece of his soul.

Chapter 26

CLEA TURNED A SLOW CIRCLE, TAKING IN HER SURroundings, careful to step over the thick chain that tethered her ankle to a metal clasp set in a block of concrete. A shudder coursed through her. On the far side of the road was a bent and blackened tree, a dark and forbidding sentry. Naked branches curled like talons. It looked like the setting of a low-budget horror flick.

Only it was real.

The horror was one she had lived through.

Over the past two decades she had seen that tree's silhouette in a thousand nightmares on a thousand different nights. She knew this place. Knew it in her heart and in the bruised depths of her soul.

From this vantage point, at the top of a low rise, she had no doubt about her location, knew exactly where she was. Oh, God. She had never forgotten that tree. Never.

This was the place her parents had died. She had hoped never to see it again.

She shivered, looking to the darkening sky. Dusk had

always been her favorite time of day. The stunning colors of the setting sun, a fiery ball of orange and pink and red, low on the horizon. Wrapping her arms around herself, she stamped her feet as she fought the chill that seeped through her muscles and bones. She stared at the sunset, thinking that if she survived the night, she would never see it in quite the same way again.

Terror mounting with each passing second, she steeled herself against its chilling tide and willed the sun to be still, to sink slowly, to wait for Ciarran.

He would come. She was certain of that, and she had no doubt that Asa, no, Asag—he'd snarled at her, insisted that she call him by that name, muttering about power and plague and death—knew it, too.

Trembling, she rubbed her hands up and down the length of her arms, stamped her feet harder now against the ground. Cold. She was so cold, the wind biting through her T-shirt and an icy tide of fear rising from inside her.

The night was creeping up on her, eating the sky in great gulps.

"He let them die, your sorcerer. Do you remember? He was there." Asag's voice made her turn, and in her haste, she stumbled on the chain, fell to her knees.

He laughed, a foul, wet sound. Moving closer, he reached out, traced the curve of her cheek. Revulsion sluiced through her, and she jerked away.

"Your parents lay side by side"—he made a languid gesture toward the road—"their blood feeding the hard-packed ground. Do you remember that, Clea?"

"Yes." She could smell the fire of that long-ago night,

the acrid scent stinging her nostrils. Burning rubber, and sulfur, and something else, stronger. Brimstone.

"He could have saved them. Your precious sorcerer. It would have taken a single wisp of magic, a single tether to bind their souls back to their bodies. They had not departed. Their souls were fresh, confused, hovering beside their ruined shells. But even that, he could have changed. You have seen what he can do. You have seen the healing strength of his power, his magic."

She had seen it, more than once. He'd healed the burn on her cheek that first night, healed the terrible bloody scrape to his shoulder the next day. And she knew in her soul, though she didn't consciously remember all the details, that he had healed her the night of the accident that had killed her parents.

No, that wasn't quite true. She had healed herself. She had *stolen* his magic. Cost him his hand. Given the darkness a chance to crawl through him and torment him for decades.

If Asag was looking to lay blame, he would not make her dump it on Ciarran's head.

Asag was stroking her hair now, and the taste of bile burned her tongue. She scuttled away, but one of the *hybrids,* the one who had killed Terry—God, she couldn't think of that now—caught her arm. He jerked it roughly as he shoved her back toward Asag. She sprawled on the ground, her cheek scraping along the corner of the concrete block.

The trickle of her blood was warm and wet on her cheek, and Asag stared at it, his eyes narrowing, his breathing growing faster as he ran his tongue over his lower lip. Squatting before her, he touched the tip of one finger to her skin. It came away red and slick.

With a shudder, he brought his finger to his mouth and sucked it clean. "Delicious," he whispered. "Oh, what fun we will have Clea Masters. Once you have opened the wall, I will take my time with you." He fisted his hand in her shirt, yanked her up against his chest, and licked her bloodied cheek with his rasping tongue.

Disgust choked her, a thick sludge high in her throat, and she lashed out at him, focusing the power inside her until a burst of light shot forth. He fell back, landing in an ignominious heap.

All pretense of his humanity faded. Clea gasped, unable to hold back her horror as the demon shed his skin, leaving it in a pile on the ground, emerging as a gray beast, hideous, terrifying. She scurried back as far as the chain would allow, her heels slipping on the grass. He stalked her, slowly, each step matching her frenzied movements.

"You are wonderfully strong," he crooned. "All the better to open a portal." He reached toward her, his hand a hooked claw. The feel of his sharp talon trailing along her scalp, her throat, her collarbone, made her shrink away in revulsion. He pressed hard enough to draw blood. "And your strength will see that you last long under my tender ministrations."

Turning, he strode away and left her there with her thoughts and her horror, her body shaking with cold and terror, her palms damp with sweat.

Clea had no idea how long she huddled on the ground, her knees drawn up before her, her arms wrapped tight around them in an effort to conserve heat. An hour.

Perhaps more. Night was full upon them, and she could see the shadows of the *hybrids* as they gathered.

Two passed close to her.

"I'm surprised he does not wait for an audience. I thought that a call had been set out for demons to come with their keepers, to watch the arrival of the Solitary," one said, his voice low.

The second *hybrid* grunted and gestured toward Clea. "I think he wants her to himself, for his pleasure, more than he wants an audience. You know the demon code. Were there others here, each would be entitled to his share of the prize."

Clea shuddered as they walked away, feeling a twisted sense of gratitude that Asag had decided to be selfish.

Suddenly, she stilled, her breath catching in her throat, and she fought the urge to raise her head and scan the area. He was here. She could sense his magic, feel his presence.

Ciarran.

Tears stung the backs of her lids, and she kept her head down, her posture unchanged, refusing to search the shadows for him lest she betray his presence to the *hybrid* horde. To Asag.

In an instant, the star-flung sky came alive with writhing tendrils of light, bright and sharp, like lightning touching down and dancing away. She heard a scream, saw the shape of a *hybrid* fall to the ground. Then another. And another.

Strength swelled inside her, and with it came a tide of desperation. She was pulling Ciarran's magic from him. Oh, God. Not that. Slamming her eyes shut, she focused on building her imaginary wall, on stopping the flow of energy from him into her. He could not afford to lose any. Not here. Not now.

She was so cold, her strength depleted. The wall failed. Frantic, she tried again, feeling the hard pull of her power sucking his, the hot pain in her belly warning her as it swelled and grew.

He was *letting* this happen, she thought numbly, letting her drain him. He meant to keep her safe, and giving her the strength to defend herself was one way he could guarantee that. But at what cost to himself?

There was a noise to her right, and she opened her eyes, saw a *hybrid* moving fast and low toward her. Breathing in short, gasping gulps, panic clawing at her, she summoned the same energy she had used on Darqun when she cast aside his wooden sword, summoned the light and power inside of her. A jagged pain cleaved her middle, and a dazzling flare of light haloed outward in shimmering rings. The *hybrid* went flying back a dozen feet, landing on the ground with a solid *thwap*.

There was no time to revel in her victory. Asag was beside her, his claws digging into the skin of her arm as he yanked her to her feet. With a horrible laugh, he raked his talons along her front, tearing her T-shirt, baring the skin of her belly; then he raked her again, his claws biting deep. She moaned and twisted, trying to escape his brutal attack.

Ciarran. Where was he? She could hear the sound of flesh thudding on flesh and a broken moan in the distance.

"Blood." Asag chortled, his fetid breath hot on her

face as she struggled and tried to pull away. "Blood for the sacrifice and your magic for the gate."

With a cry, she focused her power, directed it at him, and he laughed, the sound high and maniacal.

"Yes! Use your power, Clea Masters. Your blood and your spark of magic opened the breach once before. That night, it was *you* who opened the portal, *you* who set me free. Tonight, it will be your blood but no mere spark. A *flood* of your magic, stolen from a sorcerer. Oh, the beauty of it! The beauty!"

She jerked and struggled, the pain from her wounds sharp, the flow of magic a hot brand deep inside of her, and she could feel the power flowing into her, knew that Ciarran was nearby, that she drained him. She focused with all she was, willing it to stop.

Too late. Too late. It was like a dam had been destroyed, and the torrent was unstoppable.

The air before her twisted and writhed, and she saw the night sky distort. The portal. She was opening a door between the realms, against her will, with no conscious intent. She was indeed the *conduit,* the channel that carried magic in a liquid flow to the portal, opening it.

She felt as though a vacuum hose had been shoved deep inside her, suctioning off her energy, her life. The sensation was hideous, and no matter how she fought against it, the portal kept up its steady tug, taking that which she had no wish to give. Was this how it was for Ciarran when she drew his power?

"No-o-o-o!" The low moan stuttered from deep in her throat.

Sounds of a battle carried on the night air, swirling around her. The cry of a *hybrid*. A harsh groan of agony.

A horrible slurping sound, then, *"Christe."* The word was laced with pain.

"Ciarran!" she screamed his name, knowing it was too late. They had taken him. She could feel it, feel his desperation through the connection that bound them.

Where were his brothers, the other sorcerers? Why had they not come to his aid? He had met with them, but he had come here alone. Why?

The moon was full above them. She could see the fallen shapes of a dozen *hybrids*. And then she saw Ciarran, his arms held, and with a satisfied laugh, Asag left her side. He drew abreast of Ciarran, looping chains about him, dark chains that flowed and swayed and looked almost . . . alive. A terrible, malevolent presence.

A sob caught in her throat as Ciarran raised his head, and she saw the blood on his face.

They would kill him. Because of her.

"Let him go," she whispered, and then louder. "Let him go. I'll do what you want. I'll help you. Only don't kill him. Let him go." Foolish words. Desperate words. She would never help Asag, never do what he wanted. Oh, but she would say anything, promise anything to save Ciarran.

"You will help me and do as I wish, regardless. Do you not feel the wrenching pull of the portal? Choice has been taken from you." Asag laughed. "I will have my vengeance against the Compact of Sorcerers. Do you understand the choice that faces your sorcerer, pretty Clea? Do you understand the torment?"

Meeting her gaze, Ciarran sent her a ghost of a smile,

perhaps meant to reassure. She wanted to howl at the tragedy of this, the horror of seeing him chained and battered.

She wet her lips. "Don't kill him. Please."

"Kill him?" Asag returned to her side, stroked her, the contact so repellent that she flinched. "You do not know? Can it be . . . oh, that is far too lovely."

Asag leaned close, his dank breath surrounding her in a sulfurous cloud. "Let me tell you of his suffering. When I cast him through the breach, your sorcerer will find himself a guest in the demon realm, and he will find only anguish and pain. An eternity of torment. Do you know what the demons will do to him?" Asag walked around her, trailing his talons along her skin, the sharp points scraping tender flesh. "Ah, so lovely, the marks I leave on you. Livid weals. And if I press"—he increased the pressure, and she felt a jagged pain as he broke the skin—"the results are even lovelier."

Her clothes were damp, drenched in sweat. Cold fear.

"Ciarran," she whispered, her heart breaking. They were going to kill him. It was her fault. She'd done this to him, sucked the life from him, stolen his magic, when all she'd wanted to do was love him.

"I'll bargain with you," she whispered, her throat raw and so tight, she could barely breathe. "I'll open any portal. Grant you anything. You can have whatever you want, only let him go. Please. Let him go."

"No, Clea!" Ciarran jerked at his chains, and she felt the flow of his magic, as though he was trying to transfer the last of his power to her, protect her.

Asag smiled at Ciarran, if the baring of the demon's

razor-sharp teeth could be deemed a smile. "She begs so prettily, and this before she knows the whole of it." Crossing the space that separated them, he sank his talons into Ciarran's chest, leaving a series of bloody runnels as he sliced through skin and flesh.

Yanking frantically on the chain that fettered her leg, Clea called on the magic that Ciarran had shared with her. Her heart hammered as she felt the hot glide of it; then hope stuttered and drowned in crashing desperation. So weak. So much of it already channeled toward the portal, the terrifying dark area of night sky where the stars did not glow, and the air seemed to bend and twist with a petrifying purpose. It was the strange glow and the preternatural stillness that warned her of the completion of the breach between dimensions, the opening of the gate. She recognized those signs, recalled them from the night of the crash.

The night she had first taken Ciarran's magic.

The night Asag had come.

She struck out, gathering what remnants of strength she had, and a bright shaft burst from her to coil around Asag's wrist and slice through gray demon hide with a sizzling hiss. Snarling viciously, the demon gave one final brutal swipe at Ciarran's shoulder, tearing open his skin, and then spun away, back toward her.

"Let him go? I think not. He will pay the price for the entire Compact of Sorcerers, pay with his torment and his blood. Endure the suffering as I was forced to endure." Asag caught a fistful of her hair. Yanking her head back, he shoved his face close to hers. The stink of decay was nearly overpowering.

She was aware of Ciarran's rage, of the sound of clanking chains and the roar of his fury.

Asag's teeth raked her cheek, her throat, and bile rose, burning inside of her, nausea churning so viciously she thought she would be sick.

"Let me tell you of his fate," he whispered against her ear. "*Immortal*. You understand that your sorcerer is immortal?"

He paused, letting the import of his words reach her. "And that is the best part of all. He *cannot* die. He can only *suffer*. Endless torment. Do you see?"

Immortal.

Of course.

Somehow, she had known that. He would live forever. And she would die at the end of a mortal life.

Then let her die here, now, in his place. Her life was finite; his was not. Let him live to fight, to protect mankind.

Asag drew back, studied her face. "I see I have failed to surprise you. I had hoped for a stronger reaction. Ah, but there is more." Laughing, he ran the tip of one gray talon along her lower lip. Clea gagged, jerking against the grip he had on her hair, desperate to be free. "Immortal. A word you cannot conceive. He cannot die. Not ever. Forever. *No matter how heinous a wound he receives.*"

Pausing, Asag drew back and studied her, watching her face. "Actually, there *are* ways to terminate a sorcerer's life, but they'll prefer him alive. And suffering."

She could hear Ciarran fighting and struggling, jerking against the bonds of the dark chains that held him.

"When I send him through the portal, they will be

waiting for him. A thousand demons, with their talons and teeth. They will rip the skin from his body, tear his muscle, break his bones." Asag smiled, a tight drawing of his lips that bared hideous rows of jagged teeth. "A human would die in a glorious blaze of suffering. But not your sorcerer, Clea. Your sorcerer will live through it, know every second of his pain. And then he will live it again. And again."

"Oh, God." The horror of it overwhelmed her.

Crazy thoughts swirled through her mind, snatches of conversation and half-understood words. She swallowed against the heavy knot that tightened her chest. Asag used her magic to tear down the wall, to open the portal.

It was her power that opened the breach.

Perhaps her power could hold it shut.

If there was no door, then Ciarran could not be cast through it.

She focused on that possibility, desperately willing it to be true. Her skin tingled, and again that bright burst of light shimmered forth. With all her frantic intent, she tried to focus it, channel it. Close the portal. Save Ciarran. Save the world.

Sick comprehension crawled through her as the twisted patch of night sky writhed and grew ever larger. *Worse.* Her efforts were only making it worse.

"A good attempt. How sad that it bore no fruit." Asag clapped his distorted hands together, a parody of applause. "And you, my dear, with your freshly gained power. You, too, will survive a long, long while as my personal plaything."

"Clea . . ." Ciarran spoke her name on a breath.

Where was his brotherhood now? she wondered once more. His Compact of Sorcerers? His brothers had not come. He was alone, his magic drawn to the thinnest point.

She felt him opening to her in a last desperate effort to give her enough power to keep herself safe. At his own peril. He would have nothing left for his own defense. She sensed that he kept back only the barest minimum he needed to hold his demon parasite at bay. His sacrifice was in vain, because instead of offering her protection, his power channeled through her and funneled to open the gate.

She knew the instant he reached the same conclusion as she had, the instant he pulled back on the flow of magic. With her heart breaking, she met his gaze, and it was all there for her to see. The love. The desperation.

The absence of hope.

He was bound by demonic chains, weakened by her proximity and her steady draw on his power. In his gaze, she read the truth.

He could not save them.

Chapter 27

CIARRAN DRAGGED IN A BREATH, CHOKED BY THE futility of his situation. He was chained by demonic sorcery, his power depleted, the parasite within writhing and twisting to get free. He had failed. Clea was not safe. The human realm was not safe. What value did a thousand years of guardianship have if he had let it come to this?

Eyes wide with emotions he had no trouble reading—fear, shock, despair—Clea stared at him as she lurched forward, the chain about her ankle playing out, and then dragging her up short. She extended one hand, and he felt yoked by a crushing despondency. He wished he could touch her one last time.

"Know that I love you," he rasped, wanting to give her that, knowing it was little enough.

Asag chortled, enjoying their misery, watching their interaction with rabid fascination.

"Let me kiss him good-bye." Clea grabbed Asag's wrist, a desperate action that made the demon turn and study her with a calculating gaze. "I beg you"—her voice broke—"one last kiss."

Ciarran gritted his teeth, stifling the urge to rage at hearing her beg the demon for anything. He wanted it too badly, that one last kiss, that memory that he would carry with him to the demon realm, the feel of her in his arms, the scent of her skin. Maybe it would be enough to keep him sane through the millennia of torture the demons would inflict.

His fury and black despair fed the thing inside him. The parasite roared, sensing Clea, wanting her; the beast was barely restrained.

Suddenly, he recalled the way she had looked in his bed, her eyes intent as she told him her story. He heard her words as though she spoke them now. *Do you know what Gram said? That there is both great goodness and vast evil in all sentient beings and that we can choose our path, not by stifling the evil, but by accepting its existence. Accepting and choosing. Do you understand?*

Accepting. What would happen if he stopped the struggle, the fight, if he accepted the darkness, let it breach his wards and barriers? It would take his body, his soul, twist him into something warped and foreign.

The darkest sorcery.

But the demon seed had protected her before, would protect her now. In that instant, Ciarran saw his path, the one slender thread of hope.

Darkness to fight the darkness. If he let go, then it would be free. There would be no way to call it to heel. So his life was forfeit, but Clea could be saved.

She had opened her mind and her heart, called to him,

every part of him, the light, the darkness. The hell-and-brimstone demon that was part of his soul.

Part of him.

His proud and valiant Clea *begged* for him. *Christe.*

Asag smiled a sly, dreadful smile, and seeing it, Clea dropped her hold on him and stumbled back a step.

"Oh, I like that . . . the sound of you pleading," the demon purred. "Do you know that if you touch him, you will draw yet more of his magic?" He glanced at the shimmering oval of night sky, at the distorted backdrop of stars, the twisted halo that carried the threat of destruction. "You will be stronger, open the gate more quickly. And your sorcerer will be weaker, more susceptible to the cruelty of the demon realm." Asag stalked her, moving close enough to press his face against her cheek. She shuddered violently but held her place as he inhaled noisily. "Yes. By all means. Kiss him. And then kiss me."

He motioned to the *hybrids,* and they dragged Ciarran closer. The chains twined and shifted, wrenching his wrists so tightly together he could not move them, biting into flesh—a spike of agony.

"I love you," Clea whispered. With a sob, she leaned against him, raised her lips to his. Ciarran could hear Asag laughing and the *hybrids* cackling in unison.

"Clea mine." He tasted the salt of her tears, felt the wild cadence of her pulse. "The glove. Take the glove," he murmured for her ears alone. "Free the beast. It is the only way."

She took a gasping breath. Her gaze snapped to his, wide, terrified. He could feel the hard drumming of her heart, one beat, two. And then she smiled, a tiny quirk of her lips as her hands slid around behind him, and her fingers curled under the edge of his glove, leather and alloy caught in her grasp. With a hard tug, she pulled it halfway free, baring his palm.

An icy smear of darkness oozed free, and Ciarran breathed with the pain, forcing himself to forgo the training of decades, to remain passive, to erect no barriers in the thing's path.

Asag leaped forward, the back of his hand coming hard against Clea's cheek as he knocked her aside. She fell, her momentum pulling the leather and alloy free of Ciarran's fingers. The glove fell to the ground as the prison cracked open, the cage door fully released.

In that instant, he felt the darkness, a thick, oily sludge, so powerful he could taste it, feel it touch every part of him. He threw back his head, called to it, embraced the pain.

With a howl of glee, the demon in Ciarran's soul slid free.

Demonic power surged inside him as he flung Asag's chains from his body. Two decades of battling the darkness in his soul, and now, as it spilled through him, the sensation so heavy, so fulsome, he wondered why he had denied it. The lure of the demon. *Christe.* Such temptation. He wanted to embrace the darkness, to welcome it, to let the energy swell and take him. Cold and pure, the feeling was indescribable.

He had sampled it—a small sip—the night the killing mist and black blades had come upon him as he battled the *hybrids* outside Clea's apartment. Secretly, darkly thrilled, he had delighted in the weapons, in the feeling of invincibility, so much stronger than he had ever known as a light sorcerer.

That night, it had been all he could manage to pull it back, drag the demon to its cage and hold safe the barrier that surrounded it. Tonight, he would not even try.

Looking down, he flexed his fingers, stared at his ruined hand. The skin was a different shade than the rest of his body, a silvery gray, and the look of the thing was uncommonly strange.

Not human. Not sorcerer. Not demon, either.

Something far different.

He studied the tattooed wards that circled his wrist. They were strong, but not strong enough to hold the beast back on their own. The glove was gone, the alloy prison gone, and he knew the barrier could never return. The darkness was free, roaring through his veins, through sinew and muscle, making him powerful. So unbelievably powerful.

Even his dragon tattoo was changed, darker, shimmering with malice, the eyes glowing bright with unconcealed threat. The speed of the transformation shocked him.

He brought his healthy hand to press against the damaged one, two halves of the whole, a strange and peculiar balance.

Asag scrabbled away. Facing a chained and weakened sorcerer was one thing. Facing the strength of a demon quite another.

A *hybrid* lunged for Clea, and Ciarran spun to face him. He offered no warning, no reprieve. Extending his arm, he let the black blades tear through his skin, a sharp pain. They lengthened, spanning the distance to skewer the *hybrid* through the chest. Blood poured from the wounds, rivulets that merged into a glistening stream. The demon part of him celebrated the sight.

"How—?" Asag stumbled back a step, his gaze locked on the discarded chains, his eyes wide with shock. "That isn't possible. No sorcerer could cast off demon-hewn chains. Only a demon—"

"Ciarran!" Clea cried, her gaze fixed on a point behind him.

He turned, already knowing what he saw. He could feel the shimmer of magic, the terrible rift in the *continuum*, the pull of the portal that the demon had summoned.

Asag had used Clea's magic. Ciarran's magic. Light to beckon the darkness.

Ciarran felt his new power swell and throb. He would give Asag darkness. He would feed it to him until he choked on it.

Within the endless terrain of starry sky, the flickering oval had grown to the size of a man in a matter of minutes. Light refracted from the surface of the rift in the dimensional wall, a warped, twisted thing, tearing the fabric of worlds, building a bridge where none should be.

Some dimensions were never meant to know a link.

With a snarl, Ciarran caught one of the *hybrids* as it lunged for him, snapping its spine and tossing it aside like a broken twig. Power. The power was indescribable. Far greater than light or darkness alone. This was a melding of the two, a strange alliance.

His gaze sought Clea. Shivering, she stood next to a concrete block, her leg shackled. The sight of the chain that held her sparked a burgeoning rage, sending it to coil deep in his gut. The darkness slid through him, riding the remnants of his light magic, blending with it, twisting it.

With a sharp slash of his hand, he sent the black blades through the chain that bound her, setting her free. She stumbled, righted herself, and he felt her willing her magic toward him.

Torn. He was torn by the dual urge to take all she offered, use it to subdue the darkness within, to tether it beyond reach, beyond temptation. At the same time, he wanted to give the demon in his soul free rein. Let it shred the *hybrids* in a whirling frenzy of flesh and blood, let it tear Asag's limbs from his body, let it destroy anything that threatened that which he loved.

Clea.

With a snarl, Asag grabbed her, shoving her before him, his lips peeled back, his teeth snapping at her. She struggled in his hold, kicking him, tearing at his thick, gray hide with her nails, magic sparking from her fingertips, leaving the demon's flesh singed and smoking.

Cold fury thrummed like a chant in Ciarran's veins, calling him to vengeance. Sensing a *hybrid* at his back, he released the killing mist, smiling menacingly as he heard the creature's death cry, which was abruptly stilled as the *hybrid* melted into nothing.

One step and another, Ciarran moved forward, stalking Asag, his eyes locked on the demon's, never wavering.

"Set her free," Ciarran said. Asag shifted, and shifted again, keeping Clea's body in front of him, a living shield. "Set her free, and I will kill you. A boon for your cooperation. Make me take her from you, and I promise you no such kindness. I will return you to the demon realm, to the fate you had intended for me. An eternity of torment, Asag. Think on it, but think quickly."

Asag's eyes rolled about in frenzied desperation as his well-laid plans fell to dust around him. The *hybrids* were deserting him, running like rats.

"The Solitary comes," he hissed. "Tonight he comes. Tonight I free him, and tonight I regain my power, my lost power, my ability to unleash plague and suffering upon the mortal races. Death. I can taste it, so delicious."

He paused, his lips pulling back from rows of jagged yellow teeth as he pushed Clea before him. She struggled in his hold.

"Help me," Asag cajoled, his gaze locking wildly on Ciarran. "Become my ally. You are demon now. You are darkness. Embrace it, and let it embrace you. Let it take you." His talons clutched at Clea, tangling in her hair. Words tumbled from his mouth, fast and frenzied. "You can have her. We will use her blood to open the portal, mingle the realms. Just a bit of her blood. A cup. Only a cup. And then you can have her. She is unharmed. See?" Cackling wildly, he shoved her forward again. Her body arched back, her head tethered by his rigid grip on her hair. "Unharmed. I took only a bit of blood. And I want only a bit more."

Ciarran felt the darkness, rearing wild and fierce inside him, tempted, so tempted by Asag's words. He could save Clea. He could have her for eternity. *Yes,* the darkness slithered through him, coiling about his thoughts. So easy to agree. To save both her and himself.

Horror erupted, a geyser of self-loathing. Already, the thing inside him was stealing all that he was, bit by bit, turning aside his morals, his history, making a thousand years of guardianship into nothing, ashes on the wind. How long until he was purely demon?

The parasite in his soul would take him, all of him, if it could.

If he let it.

Did he have a choice?

Glancing about, Ciarran saw the *hybrids* running, their shadowy shapes sliding down the low hill, across the grass, illuminated by the moon as they ran, helter-skelter, fleeing. Not from Asag. From him.

From what he had become.

Clea cried out, struggling to keep her balance, stumbling as again Asag pulled on her hair, yanked her head back. She righted herself, another low cry torn from her lips.

A deep shudder shook Ciarran's frame. Lethal rage rose inside him, a thick smear of darkness, obliterating the light. Looking up, he found Clea watching him, her eyes luminous, her love, her faith in him a shining beacon.

"I love you." Her gaze burned into his. "Remember what my Gram said."

He remembered. 'Twas her story that had shown him the only way to free himself from Asag's demonic chains. *We can choose our path, not by stifling the evil, but by accepting its existence.*

Choice. Free will.

Certainty came to him in a rush. To kill a demon he must *become* a demon, accept that part of himself, fully and without reservation. Only then could he hope to best Asag. He chose the darkness, forfeiting all that he had been, and as he shot a glance at Clea, he knew that in this choice he had found a way to save her, save the world.

He could not summon even a whisper of regret.

The portal was enormous now, the center of it tearing open, a gaping hole, devoid of all light, all form. There it was, the terrible doorway to a dimension of pure evil, a stinking pit of brimstone and malice, open now. Almost large enough to let a demon through.

Fury swelled inside him. Pounding. Rich and vivid. He savored the feeling, tasting it. The demon part of him was strong. So strong.

With concentrated focus, he squelched the last of his resistance. The light sorcerer was no more.

Snarling, Ciarran lunged forward, his blades sinking deep into Asag's flesh. The demon screamed, and Clea dove to the side, her shoulder skidding along the ground as she landed. Ciarran grabbed Asag, spun him in a twisted dance, closer and closer to the breach.

"Go back to your world, back to your cage." Ciarran's breath came in great, heaving gasps, his heart pounding wildly, the darkness pouring through him. Asag was strong, fed by the blood of countless human lives, his power fueled by desperation.

Asag's cry of rage rang in the air as Ciarran shifted them both toward the gaping hole between dimensions. It was mushrooming in size, growing by the second.

Safe. Clea would be safe.

The realm of man would be safe.

All else was of no matter. Ciarran gave his magic free rein, his light a faint glimmer, nearly overwhelmed by his darkness, and he let the killing blades slide deeper, reveling in Asag's cries of frustration and fury.

Muscles screaming, he shoved the struggling demon toward the void, feeling the frigid pull of it, a vortex that sucked all heat, all light. He summoned his demon parasite, called on the rank thing that bled dry his soul, let it creep to the fore and battle with its own kind. Asag snarled and hissed, a rabid beast, trapped.

With a mighty heave, Ciarran sent him spinning through the portal, back to the stinking pit of brimstone and rot he had escaped decades past. Back to the evil that had spawned him.

A terrible cry tore the fabric of the night, and Ciarran struggled to find a remnant of light magic within himself. So little remained. He needed it to close the gate, slam it shut before Asag, or worse, the Solitary, came through. That job was one no amount of dark sorcery could do.

He locked his gaze on Clea, one final desperate glance to last him an eternity. She was struggling to her feet, her face white and drawn as though she sensed his terrible intent, and he felt the sting of regret and lost dreams as he backed toward the portal.

Before he fused the doorway, he was duty-bound to send one last demon to its realm: *himself*.

He knew he must consign himself to hell, must cast himself into the pit, lest the demon he had become take his reason and his mind, lest it twist him into something that would threaten the mortal world. Then he would seal the breach from the opposite side, bury himself alive. There was no option he could see.

With a strangled denial, Clea ran at him. On instinct, he opened his arms, caught her against him, warmth and love and light, and he spun them both away, in fear that they would tumble through together.

"Don't even think it." She locked her arms around his waist, her fingers intertwining at the small of his back, her body flush with his. *"Don't even think it,"* she reiterated fiercely.

He felt her there, inside him, her magic, his magic, such strength, greater even than the darkness. A blending. A fusing.

"Whatever happens, you *cope,* you *deal.*" She was breathing so hard, he could barely understand her words. "Terrible things happen, but you ride them out, and life gets better."

"That is not an option," he rasped, certain of that. He was not what he had once been. He could never go back.

"You're staying right here," she said, her voice forceful. And then she gasped, clutched him tighter as she stared in horror at the portal.

A foot, horned and mottled, enormous in size, protruded from the ever-widening breach.

The Solitary.

The time for talk had passed. Ciarran called the last vestiges of his light magic, opening a pathway between himself and Clea, melding their power as one. She was a conduit of the strongest kind, channeling an enormous amount of energy, cocooning it and funneling their combined strength. Light burst from his fingertips, a bright glow, and he wove the pattern that he had knit again and again for over a thousand years, sealing the breach, closing the gate.

A horrific, inhuman cry seeped through the shriveled hole, rage and pain and fury. Ciarran dove forward, breaking the contact with Clea. He was too late. The night sky snapped shut, shearing off the foot and sending it rolling erratically across the ground in a smoking, sizzling blur. In the portal's place was a smooth band of sparkling stars, as though the breach had never been.

Ciarran stood, panting, heart pounding. He was on the wrong side of the portal. He was still in the world of man. And he was demon.

With a great heave, the dragon current bucked and finally settled, the disruption in the *continuum* gone.

"Ciarran!" The voice was Dain's.

Hands fisted at his sides, Ciarran struggled for control, a deep resentment snapping at him. Where had they been during this battle, his brothers of the Compact? Two decades past, they had come too late to save his hand. Tonight, they had come too late to help him save the goddamned world.

Clea stepped forward, blocking Dain's approach, as though intent on protecting Ciarran. He smiled in grim amusement. All she needed was a plastic gold letter opener.

Traitor. Dain is the traitor. Ciarran felt the reemergence of his earlier reservations and suspicions, heard the whisper of the darkness as it made its accusations.

He tensed, his body centered and ready. *Kill him. Kill the traitor.* He would kill Dain. Make him suffer. Make him pay for what he had almost done to Clea. To the human race.

Dain stood before him, scanning the carnage, his lips drawn in a grim line.

Not right. Ciarran shook his head. Something did not feel right. The conclusions he reached were too easy, too obvious.

It wasn't Dain alone who had failed to arrive as backup. Darqun. Javier. Baunn. None had come. Why?

The darkness hissed and reared, obscuring his thoughts. Frustrated, he tamped it down, a sharp hiss of surprise escaping his lips as he realized he had calmed it, soothed the beast. *Christe*, how had he learned to do that so easily?

As though sensing his turmoil, Clea moved to his side to wrap her arm around his waist, her touch a balm.

He struggled to clear his thoughts. To be sure. And then it came to him, the identity of the traitor, a concept too terrible to bear.

A theory that could only be conjured by the darkness in his soul.

Except the beast was silent now, and there was only the clarity of his own thoughts in his mind.

The traitor.

Images spun before him, of the fight he had witnessed between Dain and the Ancient. Understanding came, swift and brutal.

"The Ancient betrays us." The words were flat, lacking emotion, devoid of doubt.

Dain's burning gaze met Ciarran's, the truth etched there, stark and bare.

"Why?" Bewilderment stifled him, followed by rage, and finally despair. Ciarran was left feeling as though everything he knew, everything he was, had turned to rot.

"Why?" Dain shook his head. "In the beginning, his motive was pure. Information. He believed that he could deceive the demons, lure them into a position of trust, pick bits of knowledge from them and turn them to the common good."

"You knew this?" Ciarran asked, watching the flicker of pain cross Dain's face. "And said nothing?"

"I suspected. And I was blind to the depth of the deception, blind to the dangers until it was far too late. As was the Ancient."

"I get it," Clea interjected. "It's like an undercover cop who goes too deep."

Both sorcerers looked at her.

"Sometimes, when cops go undercover to investigate drugs or organized crime, they end up sinking so deep they lose themselves, forget why they were there in the first place. They play the role so well, they blur the boundary between the character they're playing and the person they really are, until there's no boundary at all." She shrugged, looked back and forth between Dain and Ciarran. "I . . . uh . . . saw it in a movie."

"Your analogy is apt." Dain inclined his head to her. "The Ancient originally believed that the only way truly to defeat the Solitary was to make him believe he had become his ally."

"How long?" Ciarran asked, as suspicion bloomed. Had the Ancient been involved in the crash that killed Clea's parents, in opening the portal and freeing Asag?

Dain steepled his fingers and brought them to his lips. "I'm guessing a century."

A century. One hundred years of trickery and deceit.

"And the day I came upon you fighting the Ancient . . . ?"

"Was the day my reservations finally overcame my trust and loyalty."

Frowning, Clea listened to the exchange, obviously trying to piece together the gist of their conversation.

Ciarran felt something harden inside him as he recalled the Ancient encouraging him to embrace the darkness, to learn from it. The exchange took on an entirely different meaning in retrospect, a twisted meaning. "Where is he now?"

"Gone." Dain's eyes were pinched with tension. "After you left the meeting today, all began to unravel. I confronted the Ancient, hoping he would deny all." With a slow, measured breath, Dain made an obvious effort at control. "He fled. Darqun sought to follow, but we both know he will fail."

"He'll try again," Clea said. "If what you say is true, your Ancient will do this again. He'll try to summon the Solitary"—she shuddered—"again."

Ciarran recoiled, the magnitude of the betrayal striking him. The Ancient had pledged to the Solitary. The ramifications were beyond thought, beyond reason, too terrible to consider, let alone accept.

"No," he said, but even as he spoke the denial, the pain of the treachery gouged at him.

The Ancient was their mentor, their leader, the strongest among them. And he had succumbed to darkness. Ciarran looked about him, at the corpses of the dead *hybrids,* at the place that had almost become the bridge to the world's destruction.

His gaze dropped to his hands, one strong and healthy, the other twisted and gray, visible testament to his own private battle. Good versus evil. He tipped his head back, closed his eyes.

If the Ancient had surrendered, what hope had Ciarran to withstand the lure?

Chapter 28

*T*HE SUN WOULD BE UP IN A FEW SHORT HOURS.
Clea glanced at Ciarran. His jaw was set, his
gaze locked on the road. They'd driven south and made
it to the edge of the city. The glow from the buildings
and signs and streetlights reflected up, bounced off the
clouds. Everything had a hazy, brightish cast that hadn't
been there farther north.

Night was night, but somehow it looked different, de-
pending on where you were standing. Or sitting.

Breathing in the scent of caramel and coffee that per-
meated the car, Clea was grateful that Ciarran had gone
to the drive-through window at the all-night donut shop.
She took a sip, savoring the taste and the warmth and the
fact that she was alive to drink it. The euphoria of that
was indescribable. Yet accompanying this was a harsh
edge of ambiguity, tinged with worry for Ciarran.

She shifted in her seat, grimacing as the movement
caused a shard of pain to radiate from the scratches
Asag had made on her abdomen. Ciarran stiffened, and

she ached to reach out, to touch him. With a sigh, she stifled the urge. The one time she'd laid her fingers on his arm as they roared along the highway, he'd shifted away from her and sent her a haunted look that made her want to weep.

He had been betrayed. The Ancient had deceived them all, violated centuries of trust, and then he had escaped—a torment to all the sorcerers, she imagined. But Ciarran had paid the highest price.

"So what happens now?" she asked, her mood uncertain.

"The remnants of the Compact of Sorcerers will need to meet," he said flatly. "And decide how to go on from here. A new leader must be chosen."

Her heart broke to hear the weariness in his voice and realize that he answered in generalities rather than in personal affirmation. She wanted to know what would happen to *them*.

"A new leader, huh?" She tried to force a light tone, but it came out as more of a croak. "Who?"

Ciarran exhaled harshly. Of course his brave Clea would stab at the heart of the matter. Who, indeed?

The horrific truth was that *he* was now the most powerful sorcerer, perhaps even stronger than the Ancient. But his was the power of darkness. He hardly considered himself a viable leadership candidate. Perhaps Dain . . .

His grip tightened on the steering wheel, and he focused on driving, on guiding the car instead of touching Clea. Because that was what he really wanted to do. Touch her. Weave his fingers with hers, pull her close, feel the beat of her heart. Love her.

Things he might have won the right to as a sorcerer of light.

Things he had no right to claim as a mage of darkness.

Gritting his teeth, he guided the car along the near-empty streets toward the alley that led to his home. The remainder of the drive passed in tense silence.

Ciarran felt a swell of emotion as he watched Clea climb from the car. She was alive. She was safe. How many times would he marvel at that fact before it became real to him?

She gave him a long, measured look before she walked toward the fountain, pausing there to dip her hand in the water. He waited a moment, then followed.

Pressing her lips together, she glanced toward the place where Terry had fallen, her throat slit by the *hybrid*.

"Thank you," she whispered, looking back at him, her eyes luminous. "For Terry's life. I'm so glad that she'll survive."

Did she judge him? he wondered. For saving Terry now, though he had failed to save her parents those many years ago. Could she understand his reasons and the differences in the situations?

"Terry's soul had not departed. Her wounds were not fatal." He fisted his ruined hand. "It is not forbidden."

"Not forbidden, but not sanctioned either, right?" She stared at him for a long moment; then she nodded. "I'm glad you saved her. I feel responsible for what happened to her, even though I know it wasn't my fault. On some level, I blame myself for her getting hurt."

"Clea—"

"No. No reassurances. I don't need them." She walked to the front door and pulled it open. "It's okay. Everything's going to be okay."

She sounded like she believed it.

"You bent the rules for her, though. Right?" She cast him a look over her shoulder, her expression intent.

"I broke no law."

Turning until she rested her back against the open front door, she watched him, waited for him. "Mmmmm. Didn't break the law, but *bent* it. Ever hear of shades of gray? You *chose* to save Terry."

Her gaze burned into his.

Shades of gray.

Choice.

One side of her mouth quirked in a smile.

"It's about what you choose," she said. "Not about what tempts you or twists you . . . but about what you *choose* to do."

Of course.

His heart lurched, hope flooding him with such intensity that he stood rooted to the spot for a breathless moment, struggling to get his emotions under control. In the turmoil, she was his one constant. He needed her, needed her strength, her warmth, her light.

A few long strides, and he was by her side, dragging her up against him, soft, yielding. Unafraid. She'd *seen* him, seen exactly what he was, the worst he could become, and still she turned her face into the crook of his neck and pressed her body to his as their hearts beat in time.

The feel of her . . . warm . . . alive . . . he was nearly overwhelmed by the magnitude of his relief, and as he held her, he started to believe, just a little. It was real. She was real.

And then he felt it. The tentative slide of her magic, mingling with both his darkness and the tiny bit that remained of his light.

Twirling in a slow circle, he spun them into the entry hall, letting the door swing shut behind them. She rained kisses on him, his neck, his collarbone, whatever exposed skin she could reach, her fingers running over him, tentative strokes, as though reassuring herself that he was whole.

The thought made bitter regret sift through him. He was not whole. He was not anything that he had once been. Tensing, he made to pull away, but she held him, her fingers closing about his tattooed wrist.

Inside him, the beast leaped, reaching for her. And she let it, calming it, taking it into her and easing the pressure in Ciarran's heart, in his soul.

She laughed, and for a moment he thought she was overwhelmed, unhinged by all she had witnessed.

"I'm not crazy," she said softly. "You know that no matter what it is, I'll cope. I'll deal with it. But, the thing is, it's you who has to deal with something now. I've learned so much from you. Now it is your turn to learn from me."

He tipped her face toward him, studying her eyes, her laughing, dancing eyes, and again that crashing wave of hope overtook him.

"What do you mean?" he asked.

She ran her fingers over the wounds that Asag had torn in his chest, a sizzle of magic shimmering from her fingertips as she touched him, healed him. He lifted the shredded hem of her T-shirt, the breath leaving him in a sharp hiss as he saw the gouges left by the plague-demon's claws. She suffered, and yet her first care was for him.

Without thought, he summoned his own magic, casting light on the vicious gashes, closing them, taking her pain. And then he realized what he had done, and froze. There was yet light in his darkness. Somehow, he was surprised by that.

"See? You can choose." She laughed softly, the sound tapering to a sigh of understanding. "You just need to learn to deal with it."

"Deal with what?" Besides the darkness that clawed at him. Besides the uncertainty over what exactly he had become.

"For one thing, your preference for solitude. You'll have to get past that," she said. "You can't ever go back."

He knew that, knew he could never go back, never be what he had once believed himself to be. His body, his magic, even his soul had changed. All his beliefs, his certainties, torn asunder.

"What do you mean, get past my preference for solitude?" He shoved down the hope that flared, a bright flame, unable to imagine that she could mean to stay with him after all she had seen.

"Don't you understand? Alone, you could not win." She cupped his cheeks, her body straining toward him, her expression intent. "But together"—she exhaled in a rush—"together, we cannot lose."

The truth of her words touched him, buoyed him. A surge of emotion rose, clogging his throat, blurring his vision. He had wanted to save the world, save her. In the end, it was their bond that had succeeded where all else failed, their shared magic that had sealed the portal.

If he didn't fight the pull, then she did not draw from him. Instead, she filled him and strengthened him and made him more than he was alone.

Together. That was true strength, the power of two.

She was so beautiful, light shining from her soul. Clea. Brave, resilient, undeniably strong. His Clea. His love. By his side for time eternal.

He reached out to stroke her hair, froze, his gaze locked on his ruined hand, encased in nothing more than the leather glove he had taken from the ground where Clea had dropped it. Beneath the edge of the glove, he could see skin. Gray. Like demon hide, only subtly different. Smoother, with a faint glow. He had left behind the alloy sheath, for it was no longer of any value. The darkness could no longer be imprisoned, no longer held at bay. It was too much a part of him now, never again to be confined by a convoluted brew of magic, wards, tattoos, and metal alloy.

Drawing back, he let his gaze roam her face, and suddenly he couldn't breathe, the choking truth of what he was congealing in his throat. There could be no together for them. He was darkness, danger. He was demon.

"Oh, no you don't." She dragged his head down, kissed him hard on the lips. "You're thinking that you're going to do what's best for me, save me, sacrifice your happiness." Her breath hitched in. "Like you were going to sacrifice your life back there," she whispered, shuddered, and continued, louder, stronger. "No. No. And no. You're going to love me—"

"—I do love you." The words exploded out of him, the purest certainty.

"I know." She smiled, kissed him again. "And you're going to let me love you, for whatever time I have left . . ." A shadowy sadness clouded her gaze. "That's the only thing I'm sorry for. The fact that I've got, what . . . maybe sixty more years? While you've got eternity." She paused. "I wish that was different."

He frowned down at her, not understanding; then suddenly, he did. "Clea, you don't have sixty years."

"Less?" she whispered.

"More." Happiness clawed free of the chains he had imposed, the emotion so foreign that for a moment, he didn't recognize it for what it was. She loved him. She had seen the darkest part of him, and she *loved* him. Accepted him.

How could he do less? How could he not accept himself?

He kissed her then, deep and full, letting all the love in his heart pour into her.

"Eternity, Clea. We are together for eternity."

She gasped, her eyes wide, her brow furrowing in confusion as she tried to assimilate his meaning.

"You are sorcerer. As I am immortal, you are immortal," he said. "You have been since you first took my magic as a child, but your physiological growth and development continued until you mastered your power to an apprentice level. Such is the way of our kind." He pressed his palm against the small of her back, drawing her closer. "And we have eternity to figure out the why of it."

For a moment, she couldn't understand him, couldn't believe him; then she realized that he spoke the truth. Sorcerer. Immortal. By his side.

She could love him for eternity.

She could do so many good things. Work toward cures for dozens of human diseases. Utilize the resources of his pharmaceutical company . . .

Love him for eternity.

"OhMyGod . . ."

Relief surged through her, so clear and sharp that it made her legs weak, rubbery, and she sagged in his embrace, supported by his strength. He tightened his arms around her, the warmth of his body surrounding her, and he smiled against her mouth, kissing her.

Silky strands of his hair brushed her cheek as he drew back, and she opened her eyes, studied him. She loved the way he looked at her, the way his lips parted just a little, the sexy light in his iridescent eyes.

She loved everything about him, the emotion so achingly intense, wonderful and terrifying and beautiful.

There was darkness mixed with his light, but it was not so very bad. Not so very bad at all. Because she could trust him to choose well.

He had accepted the demon, acknowledged it and worked with it. But he had not succumbed to the darkness. He had done as Gram had once told her, facing the evil in his own soul and choosing to walk in the light.

Running his hand along her hair, he studied her, his expression growing intense. He dragged her up against him, put his hard mouth on hers, deep, slow, sultry kisses, spinning her in a web of desire, his body tight against her.

She pulled back, letting her hand slide along his shoulder, his arm, her fingers tracing his and then dropping away.

"You know . . . Your shower has twenty heads," she said as she took a step back, and another, her pulse throbbing. With a low laugh, she spun away, looking back over her shoulder to send him a wicked smile. "I can think of great ways to use about nineteen of them."

Naked desire flared in his gaze. "We can angle one showerhead here—" She ran her palm along the top of her shoulder and took a step. "And one here—" She let her fingers slide down until they rested on the swell of her breast. "And one here—" She slid her palm along her hip, reaching back to squeeze the globe of her butt.

With a strangled sound, he took a step forward. God, she loved the way he looked at her.

"How about you?" she asked, moving farther along the hallway. "Got any good ideas?"

For the longest moment, he just stared at her, and she thought he wouldn't reply. Then he smiled, a slow, sexy shift of his lips that made primal heat stab fast and deep to the pit of her belly.

"I've got enough ideas to last forever," he said in a low rasp.

About the Author

EVE SILVER writes paranormal romance, gothic historicals, and speculative fiction. She holds two degrees, had a career in health care for a decade, and now teaches human anatomy. Living with her husband and two sons, along with an energetic Airedale terrier and an enormous rabbit, Eve is already hard at work on her next novel. Contact Eve via her website at www.evesilver.net.

More dangerous and
sensual romance from

Eve Silver!

Please turn this page
for a preview of

DEMON'S HUNGER

Coming soon in mass market.

Chapter 1

HE WAS ALONE, HORNY, AND IN POSSESSION OF A partially scorched demon bone. Perfect.

Only the last of the three problems was new, but it sure wouldn't provide a solution for the previous two.

Dain Hawkins raked his fingers back through the shaggy layers of his dark hair and gave a low, mordant laugh. Moon-spun purple shadows and pale gray light sliced across his denim-clad thigh, then fanned along the row of brick, stucco, and marble vaults of New Orleans's oldest cemetery. St. Louis #1.

He crouched, waiting, hidden by the white Greek-revival tomb at his side—the voodoo queen's tomb. It was covered in small x's drawn there for luck and festooned with the offerings of the faithful: votives, flowers, hoodoo money—coins left to buy favors.

But Dain wasn't here for voodoo magic tonight. As a sorcerer, he didn't need that kind of help.

He was here for *hybrids*, brutish creatures that had been human once. Faced with death, they had chosen to allow demon will to overtake their souls, to become slavish minions of the Solitary, a malevolent demon of immeasurable power that wanted only to cross the wall between dimensions and turn the human realm into his own personal feeding farm.

Dain smiled mirthlessly. Not while he breathed.

The air was crisp with a hint of winter chill. He smelled the faintest trace of brimstone, sensed the ripple of evil that hung over the graveyard, a fetid mist.

Yeah, he'd come to the right place.

He rose, the material of his long, black coat flowing behind him, an undulating shadow. Walking to the end of the row, he turned and moved on through the city of the dead. Some rows were straight, some twisted, and still others led to blind ends in a tangled maze of family tombs: miniature houses for the dead, complete with low iron fences. Many tombs had been restored since the hurricane; others still bore their crumbled corners, decimated by time and storm, jutting out like barren bones.

Bones. Dain's lips twisted. He was here for more than the *hybrids*. He was here because of the blackened bone that sat heavy in the pocket of his long coat, burning through the layers of cloth into his skin like a brand. He hated the feel of it, the revolting aura that was so strong it sucked the breath from his lungs. Demon stink clung to it, and terrible demon power.

Weeks past, Dain's contemporary, Ciarran D'Arbois, had slammed shut a portal between the demon realm and the dimension of man, and in so doing, he had maimed the Solitary. The demon's foot had been severed when the doorway closed, leaving the powerful demon trapped in the pit that had spawned it. Dain had found all that remained in the human realm, a single burned and blackened bone that carried vestiges of horrific, dark magic.

Since that night, he'd kept the thing locked away in a vault in his home, but he'd dared not leave it unattended while he came to New Orleans. Still, he wondered if he was crazy to carry it about.

Choices, choices. No one to trust but himself. That lesson had been hard learned.

The outline of a cross reflected in the smooth surface of a puddle and the round bright shape of the moon. Dain looked up at the top of a nearby vault, at the cross there, and at the statue of the weeping woman on the tomb next to it. His booted feet scattered the reflections as he walked on.

He made no effort to hide his progress. Let them hear him. He was spoiling for a fight, had been for weeks, ever since the night the Solitary had almost crossed over. That night, Dain had learned that the Ancient, the oldest and most powerful of the Compact of Sorcerers, had betrayed them, choosing to ally with the demons. The Ancient had been his mentor, his friend.

Now, his enemy.

Following instinct, Dain navigated the maze of vaults and low iron fences. At length, he came upon a wider space with a lone, black tomb, brick and plaster torn open to reveal a musty, gaping hole. An old, rotting casket had been dragged out into the moonlight, the lid ripped off, and around it crowded a half dozen *hybrids*, casting long, menacing shadows.

Their clothing was stained, mottled, heavy with the metallic scent of fresh blood. Dain could tell they had fed recently. Not on the long-decomposed remains from the casket. No, they had hunted and killed before coming here to the cemetery. *Hybrids* liked their prey live. Their meat bloody.

And human.

It was the only thing that offered even a temporary relief from the endless physical pain of their existence—a small matter that the demons invariably failed to mention when they tempted the dying to become *hybrid.*

With narrowed eyes, Dain studied the group. They had no idea he was here. Normally, they would have sensed the herald of his light magic long before this, but the malevolent power of the charred bone he carried was so great it obscured much. Hell, he was slathered so thick with the demon aura, they probably mistook his presence as just another of their own.

A valuable stealth tool.

Problem was, he was having trouble sensing them as well. The longer he carried the bone on his person, the more inured he became, less attuned to the current of demon magic. A danger, to be sure, but one that could not be avoided. *Hybrids* were robbing graves all over the world without subtlety or discretion, but with what Dain suspected was a definite plan. Until he figured out what the hell was going on, the scorched demon bone wasn't going anywhere without him.

Yeah, him and his bone, inseparable.

Hanging in the shadows, Dain clenched his teeth, battling the urge to call his full power and step into the circle of *hybrids.* While a fight might relieve his tension, it wouldn't get him answers. He'd wait and watch just a little longer. Whatever the *hybrids* were after, it had something to do with the Solitary and with rotted human corpses.

With a high, cackling laugh, one of the *hybrids* yanked something from the open casket before him: a bony forearm and hand, stripped of flesh by years and inevitable decay, held together by fragile remnants of desiccated tissue. Dangling from the moldered fingers was a tattered and rotting cloth pouch.

Frowning, Dain stepped closer. A voodoo gris-gris? A charm bag buried with the dead?

Whatever was in that pouch had demon stink all over it. The damned bone in his pocket heated, the sensation burning through coat and jeans into the skin and muscle of his thigh, bright, hot. Evil called to evil.

The *hybrids* were after that charm bag, which meant so was he.

Dain stepped forward into the moonlight. One of the *hybrids* jerked its head back and spun to face him.

So much for the covert approach.

The thing lunged with a feral cry. In a smooth execution of movement, Dain tucked, rolled, and rose, avoiding the creature that attacked, coming up next to the one that held the gris-gris. He plucked the cloth bag from the *hybrid's* grasp. Red velvet it was, stitched with red thread.

Old. Very old. Bound by spells to protect the contents and stave off decay in the moist heat of New Orleans. Dain felt rank evil ooze from the small bag into the flesh and bone of his hand. The *continuum,* the dragon current—an endless river of energy that flowed between dimensions—shifted and writhed in protest of the unnatural shift in balance.

With a howl, the *hybrid* he'd robbed swiped at him, a rake of clawed fingers. Dain jerked aside, shoved the pouch into his pocket—the one that didn't hold the demon bone—and leaped back so he was at the edge of the open space, a tomb at his back.

The *hybrids* advanced on him in a loose semicircle.

Dain called up a little more of his power, enough to let the *hybrids* sense his magic, let them know for certain that he was a light sorcerer. That was his warning to them, his single offer of reprieve. They could flee, and he would not chase them, or they could attack, and he would cut them down.

They hesitated, confused by the impossible mix of light magic and demon aura that clung to him, darkness oozing from the scorched bone that had become his constant companion.

He conjured a six-foot staff of acacia wood, ancient, deadly, and he waited.

Snarling, the closest *hybrid* fell on him like a rabid dog. Declining to summon more of his magic, Dain fought, preferring for the moment the physical release of punch and thrust and kick, even when they piled on him, six to one.

Claws sank into his chest, raking deep, and a fist to the jaw rocked his head back. He gave as he got, a jab with his staff, and then he tossed it high in the air, twisted a *hybrid's* head from its neck, snapped out his hand to catch his staff on the descent, his fingers slick with black blood.

The *hybrid's* remains bubbled and hissed and, finally, disintegrated in a stinking gray sludge.

Another *hybrid* moved into the place of the first. Dain

let emotion take him, rage and pain at the Ancient's betrayal, the memory of his mentor's treachery still cutting sharp as a finely honed blade. Grief was there, too, and a centuries-old hatred of demons and their ilk, feeding his actions until there was a thick morass of bubbling ooze at his feet.

A single *hybrid* backed away, the only one left standing. It stood shivering, frozen in terror, then fell to its knees before him. Dain stared at it, chest heaving. The charred bone in his pocket heated with a gruesome energy, a forbidden magic, and the *continuum* writhed at the insult.

Temptation wheedled through him, and with it came a foreign and ugly craving for just one more kill.

Kill, kill, kill.

That was new.

What the hell was wrong with him?

The bone, the goddamned demon bone.

Well, it would be disappointed if it thought to lure him to the dark side. Sorcerers were guardians, not indiscriminate murderers.

Pressing a hand to the deep gouges that scored his chest, Dain spat blood. He was breathing heavily, and his pulse pounded a hard beat in his ears.

"Go," he snarled, and the *hybrid* didn't wait for a second invitation. It scrabbled back like a crab, then rolled and stumbled to its feet, weaving as it ran through the graveyard, the sound of its footsteps echoing hollowly.

Standing in the roadway, Vivien Cairn watched the taillights of her mother's rental car grow smaller and smaller in the distance. She took the first easy breath she'd had in days. Why had she imagined that moving entire time zones away would alter her mother's schedule?

Araminta arrived like clockwork, three times a year: one visit on Vivien's birthday, one visit on Halloween (no explanation for that particular date, but Vivien had long ago ceased pondering the strange workings of her mother's mind), and one visit on the anniversary of the day Vivien's father had walked out. She would call a half hour before her arrival on Vivien's doorstep, and then she would simply appear, her straight, dark hair bobbed to her chin, perfectly dyed and trimmed, her thin lips radiating her disapproval, her lush figure and gorgeous face never showing any signs of age.

They never discussed it, but Vivien couldn't imagine her mother surviving in a time before Botox. At least, she assumed it was Botox, because Araminta held on to her youth with amazing tenacity. She looked like Vivien's contemporary rather than her mother.

Rubbing her knuckles lightly along her breastbone, Vivien sighed, half relief, half regret. This visit had ended with the exact sentiment that every such visit had ended with for the past fifteen years.

"Vivien," her mother had said moments past, taking her daughter's hands in a firm grip. Her eyes had been narrow and intent as she tipped her head back a little and studied Vivien under the overhead porch light, her voice ringing with the hollow echo of vast disappointment and despair. "You are your father's daughter in every sense. There is nothing of me in you. *Nothing.*"

Vivien Cairn, BSc, MSc, PhD, Assistant Professor of Anthropology at UTM, University of Toronto at Mississauga, currently on sort-of sabbatical, was the bane of her mother's existence.

"And *why* did you do this to your hair?" Araminta had reached up and flicked the edges of Vivien's spiky new cut.

"I cut it. It's easier this way."

After a paralyzing moment where Vivien had considered moving her mother bodily into the car, Araminta had heaved a horrible sigh, the sort of sigh that meant that nuclear holocaust was about to fall upon unsuspecting humanity. Then, with a perfunctory kiss to Vivien's cheek that Vivien had dutifully stooped to accept, Araminta had turned and left. Thank God.

There was something to be said for routine.

Now, the red taillights winked and disappeared completely as the road was swallowed by the night, and Vivien walked back toward the house.

At the bottom of the stairs, she slowed, glanced about, the winter air cutting through her sweater. Unease crawled through her like a centipede.

Continuing up the stairs, she paused on the porch, wrapped her arms about herself, rubbed her palms up and down. Turning slowly, she scanned the yard, her pulse speeding up just a little.

Something felt *wrong*. Not a particularly detailed reason for the chill that touched her and the uncomfortable wriggling low in her gut, but it was the best she could come up with. Instinct whispered that she was not alone.

For weeks, she'd been feeling off. As though unseen eyes watched her from the shadows. It was crazy. She knew that. There wasn't actually anyone there. She'd even had a friend, Paul Martinez—an officer who'd worked with her on the ostrich farm case—stomp through the trees with her searching for signs of hidden watchers. They'd found nada. Zip. Zilch. But they'd done it in the daylight. Maybe that was the difference.

Not for the first time, Vivien wondered what had possessed her to buy this relic of a house on Sideroad Sixteen, where her nearest neighbor was a tree farmer five miles up the road, and the road itself was an unpaved stretch of dirt with row upon row of tree-farm trees on one side and an endless field of six-foot-high uncut grass on the other.

She'd wanted privacy, and she'd definitely gotten it.

Pulling the front door closed behind her, she turned the dead bolt, locking out the night. She took off her sweater, hung it on a peg, chose a red lollipop from the bowl on the entry-hall table. Popping it in her mouth, she savored the tangy sweetness and continued down to the basement. The overhead lights were bright; her worktable was clean and tidy, with six very old red velvet bags and their contents arranged in clear containers, lined neatly side by side.

Though she knew perfectly well the contents of each and every pouch, she washed her hands, pulled on a pair of surgical gloves, ready to examine things she had looked at innumerable times before. It wasn't a mere urge, it was a *compulsion*. Great. She wasn't just imagining people watching her, she was starting to show signs of OCD. She sighed. What was next? Washing her hands fifty times a day? Checking the stove in triplicate before she believed she'd turned it off?

She reached for the first bag, the one from her father,

one of the three things that she had to even remind her
that she'd ever had a father. He had left her with a thread-
bare red-velvet bag; a single photo of a tall, handsome
man with mahogany brown hair and hazel eyes just like
hers; and a cold and bitter mother who had never gotten
over the fact that he'd walked out on her and their two-
year-old daughter, never to be seen or heard from again.
At least, Vivien assumed that bitterness was the motiva-
tor for her mother's behavior.

The sins of the fathers . . . Araminta had never for-
given the daughter.

Not that her mother didn't love her. She did. In her
own really special, controlling, eternally disappointed
kind of way. And it wasn't that Vivien didn't love her
mother. She did, in a thank-heaven-she-only-visits-
three-times-a-year kind of way.

They got along fine over the phone. E-mail was even
better.

Vivien ran her index finger along the worn velvet.
With its contents of salt, red pepper, colored stones,
and bones, the bag resembled a voodoo gris-gris. But
the bones themselves were far older than the cloth. A
puzzle. There were other things she'd found in the bag:
hair, desiccated skin fragments. Definitely a charm bag
of some sort. And her father had left it for her. The *why*
of that nagged at her more and more of late.

Leaning forward, she studied the bones, let herself
slide into the cool familiarity of anthropologist mode.
Phalanges: finger bones. Very old. Human. Three of
them, all from the same finger. There was a deep slash
across the middle phalanx, as though a blade had hacked
at it.

Each of the bags she had acquired through the years had similar contents. Different-colored stones. Different bones: fragments of a twelfth rib; a second cervical vertebra broken into three pieces; a fragmented fifth lumbar vertebra; three cuneiforms from the right foot, two of which bore slashes from what appeared to be the same instrument that had marked the finger bone. All the bits and parts had come from the same person. A male.

Who? Why? How had his skeletal remains ended up scattered over the globe in little red-velvet sacks?

And why did she keep stumbling across them?

She'd found one in a head shop on Queen Street years ago when she'd first moved to Toronto. It had been in the display window, a small red-velvet bag sewn with red thread. She recalled how she'd stopped dead in her tracks, amazed, determined to buy the thing because it was an exact match for the one she had from her dad. Then she'd unearthed one in a shop in New Orleans—she'd been in town for a four-day conference. One in Paris—again, a conference. The shop owner had insisted that the bag came from an aristocrat, a confidante of Marie Antoinette, a woman who'd clutched the bag as she was guillotined. The story was gruesome. Maybe the shopkeeper had thought it would up the price.

Another from London from a tiny little store that had smelled like old books and rot. That bag had carried the dubious distinction of having been owned by a victim of Jack the Ripper. Supposedly.

The most recent bag had come to her just last week, in the mail, delivered in a plain brown paper package with no distinctive labels and no return address. Its arrival had creeped her out. She couldn't think of anyone who knew she collected these bags, certainly no one who would send one to her anonymously.

Icy fingers skittered over her skin, and she shuddered, set down the bones, rose to turn a slow circle. *Not alone. Not alone.* The certainty was so strong, but there was no one there. The room spun, and Vivien steadied herself against the side of the table. Her eyes stung and she felt an overwhelming fatigue, soul-deep, a frozen ache.

Pressing her fist against her forehead, she took a slow breath. Maybe she needed food. Her mother's visits always decimated her appetite, and she'd barely eaten the past couple of days. She tidied her work area and turned toward the stairs. The small hairs on the back of her neck prickled and rose.

Someone *was* watching her.

She spun. Her gaze shot to the small basement window high on the wall.

Nothing. Just a thin glimpse of star-dusted sky.

She blew out a hard breath as she stalked up the stairs, wanting to wish it all away, wanting to crawl into her bed and pull the quilt up until it made a warm little cave, wanting to sleep until she could wake up and feel like she was herself again without premonitions and suspicions and paranoia that she was being watched.

Pausing in the kitchen doorway, she pondered her meal choices, finally opting for microwaved soup. She took her steaming mug with her to the back door, where she stood leaning her shoulder against the cold glass, blowing on the hot soup and looking out at the back deck.

Winter sunlight streamed over the wood, kissing it with warm highlights. *Sunlight.*

No moon or stars in sight.

Oh, God.

The mug slipped from her nerveless fingers, falling, falling, until it hit the wood floor with a sharp crack, spraying soup in an arc, droplets speckling her jeans and slippers.

Vivien slapped both palms against the glass and stood, shivering, staring at the cloudless blue sky. *Sunlight. Sunlight.*

She looked at her watch—8:30. *In the morning.* She'd lost twelve hours.

Again.

THE DISH

Where authors give you the inside scoop!

♥ ♥ ♥ ♥ ♥ ♥ ♥ ♥ ♥ ♥ ♥ ♥ ♥ ♥ ♥

*Book Group with
Lani Diane Rich, Diana Holquist,
Eve Silver, and Mrs. McGrunt*

Mrs. McGrunt: Welcome to the Liverpool Public Library. We're here to discuss *War and Peace* by Leo Tolstoy . . .

Diana Holquist: Oh, about that. See, I kind of got to reading Lani Diane Rich's new release *Crazy In Love* (available now) and I couldn't put it down.

Eve Silver: No way! Me too! The one about Flynn Daly who inherits a historic inn *and* her dead aunt's ghost. Awesome.

Diana Holquist: And that cute bartender, Jake. That scene where he picks her up at the train station and pretends he's not there for her—the sparks really fly!

Lani Diane Rich: You know, that actually happened to me.

Eve: The cute guy, the sparks, or the train station?

Lani: Okay, none of it. But I wish it did.

Diana: Especially the cute guy . . .

Mrs. McGrunt: *War and Peace*, ladies! Now, on page 797 . . .

Lani: Did anyone read Eve Silver's *Demon's Kiss* (available now)?

Diana: Is that the one with long, confusing Russian names?

Eve: God no. My sexy new release is about Ciarran D'Arbois, a lethal, seductive sorcerer determined to save the world from demons while saving himself from the darkness invading his soul.

Diana: Oh, I loved *Demon's Kiss*! The demons try to use Clea Masters to break down the wall between the human and demon realms.

Lani: And Clea unwittingly threatens everything Ciarran is. She steals his magic—and his heart.

(Deep sigh from all three authors.)

Mrs. McGrunt: Ladies? *War and Peace*?

Lani: Ya know, in Diana's new book *Sexiest Man Alive* (available now), Jasmine has a major war with herself when she finds out that the one man on earth destined to be her "one true love" is the world's hottest movie star. She thinks there's no way she can live that sort of life.

Eve: She sure does find peace in his bed for a while.

Lani: And satisfaction. And bliss.

Diana: And a Ken doll. Er, guess you gotta read the book to understand that part.

Eve: But when the paparazzi catch them and everything falls apart—it was so touching.

Mrs. McGrunt: Touching *and* sexy! Those gypsies sure know how to ride the wild fantastic! That young man on the cover in his teeny towel sizzles. Hoo-ah! You don't even have to open *Sexiest Man Alive* to enjoy it. *Hey, big boy, I'll hold that towel for you* . . .

Lani, Diana, Eve: Mrs. McGrunt!

Mrs. McGrunt: Okay, okay, so I didn't read *War and Peace* either. I was going to, but then I saw Lani's *Crazy in Love.* How hot was that love scene in the cabin, huh? And Eve's *Demon's Kiss* just had me from the start. I'm such a sucker for a dark, tortured hero. And then, I had to re-read that scene in Diana's *Sexiest Man Alive* where they're backstage and . . . well, wowza!

Lani: Let's blow this stuffy library, get a latte, and discuss some hot, sexy, fun romance novels.

Eve: I'm there! And all you readers should join the group by reading these three awesome new releases.

Diana: They're all on the shelves this month. So don't miss a single one.

Mrs. McGrunt: Okay, ladies, let's make a break for it! We can hide behind this enormous *War and Peace* tome. Cover my back. Go! Go! Go!

Happy reading (and discussing)!

Love,

Lani, Eve, and Diana

Lani Diane Rich

Eve Silver

Diana Holquist

www.lanidianerich.com
www.evesilver.net
www.dianaholquist.com

VISIT US ONLINE
@ WWW.HACHETTEBOOKGROUPUSA.COM.

AT THE HACHETTE BOOK GROUP USA WEB SITE YOU'LL FIND:

CHAPTER EXCERPTS FROM SELECTED NEW RELEASES

•

ORIGINAL AUTHOR AND EDITOR ARTICLES

•

AUDIO EXCERPTS

•

BESTSELLER NEWS

•

ELECTRONIC NEWSLETTERS

•

AUTHOR TOUR INFORMATION

•

CONTESTS, QUIZZES, AND POLLS

•

FUN, QUIRKY RECOMMENDATION CENTER

•

PLUS MUCH MORE!

BOOKMARK HACHETTE BOOK GROUP USA
@ WWW.HACHETTEBOOKGROUPUSA.COM.